Bring Me a Dream

"Look, I'm sorry for what I just said. I tend to be a bit of a sore loser. I didn't mean it. And I want you to know that I intend to honor our agreement. You won, so I'll shut the hell up and let you do your job. What do you say?"

Spencer watched Jasmine's face for anger, but she appeared to be cooler now. And, for the first time since she'd set foot in his home, she broke a smile.

Relief rushed through his body.

"Don't worry about it," she said. "The important thing is that you now understand that I'm qualified to handle this job."

"I understand," he said, rubbing his knuckles. "Believe me, I understand."

Her smile grew. "Good. Then let's start over, okay?" She offered him her hand to shake.

He grasped her fingers. "It's a deal."

She held his grip and stepped in close, planting her foot behind his ankle and sweeping back. For the second time that day, Spencer went down hard.

Robyn Amos

BRING ME A DREAM

HarperTorch
An Imprint of HarperCollinsPublishers

This is a work of fiction. Names, characters, places, and incidents are products of the author's imagination or are used fictitiously and are not to be construed as real. Any resemblance to actual events, locales, organizations, or persons, living or dead, is entirely coincidental.

HARPERTORCH
An Imprint of HarperCollins*Publishers*
10 East 53rd Street
New York, New York 10022-5299

Copyright © 2001 by Robyn Amos
Excerpt from *Say You Need Me* copyright © 2002 by Kayla Perrin
ISBN: 0-380-81542-7

First HarperTorch paperback printing: November 2001

HarperCollins ®, HarperTorch™, and ❧ ™ are trademarks of Harper-Collins Publishers Inc.

Printed in the United States of America

Visit HarperTorch on the World Wide Web at www.harpercollins.com

10 9 8 7 6 5 4 3 2 1

Prologue

*J*asmine White slammed her bedroom door and began discarding her clothes like a disgruntled stripper. "I am way too old for pink taffeta."

Her pumps went hurtling toward the closet like black satin torpedoes. "And if another liquored-up eighteen-year-old *ever* calls me Sweet Thing . . ." She inadvertently ripped her panty hose in two.

"Great. Another ten bucks down the tubes." The bitterness in the pit of her stomach erupted into a wild laugh. "And for what? A glorified baby-sitting job?"

The pink rosebud corsage was next, shooting into the wastebasket with NBA precision.

"Some assignment. A second-rate TV anchorman can't admit that his son's too geeky to get a real prom date, so I get stuck with him."

Jasmine jerked at the gown's zipper, feeling a rush of pleasure as one flimsy strap gave way. The dress represented all that was wrong in her world.

Her five-year plan hadn't included bubble-gum-pink taffeta. Classic black sequins were more her style. Exit pimpled teenager; enter handsome foreign dignitary.

Revisiting the senior prom hadn't been in the plan, either. Tonight, she should have been attending a black-tie, political affair.

"I work three blocks from Capitol Hill, but instead of the senators and diplomats, I get their pampered wives and spoiled brats. What's the point of being a bodyguard if most of my clients are barely out of puberty?"

Jasmine wadded up the gown, locked her gaze on the trash bin, and went for three points. The dress unfurled and parachuted to the floor two feet from its target.

She started toward it, ready to exact her revenge, and caught herself mid-stride. Whoa. She had to bring it down a notch. She pressed her hands to her chest, both to calm the rapid thumping of her heart and to prevent the frenzied clenching of her fists. A frustrated heat was spreading up her neck. She was losing it.

Pulling on a fluffy terry cloth robe in her favorite shade of blue, Jasmine sank down on her bed and took a deep breath.

She had to think about her situation rationally.

Before joining Core Group Protection, she'd spent a miserable six months in private practice. Recruiting clients and all the other headaches of self-employment had taken their toll on her. Before that, she'd spent an even more miserable three years as a D.C. cop.

Jasmine had actually been relieved when Nathan Pruitt hired her as a bodyguard for Core. During the interview, he'd talked a good game, telling her he was looking forward to having a female on his staff. Nathan had convinced her that her feminine appearance and lean build were advantages instead of liabilities. She'd believed him, but ever since, she'd been waiting patiently while big clients were passed on to others. After a year and half, Jasmine had yet to see a decent assignment. All the while, Nathan promised that her turn was just around the corner.

She was going to have a serious talk with Nathan in the morning. If he couldn't do better than a high school prom, she was hitting the road. It was as simple as that.

Jasmine flipped on her clock radio, rolling the dial until she came to a station playing one of her favorite slow songs. Climbing into bed, she listened as the deep, after-hours baritone of the radio host spread through the room.

"This is the Sandman, and you're listening to WLPS Washington, ninety-nine point three. It's one forty-five in the A.M., and we've still got a few night owls hanging out with us. We're going to take a few more calls before the Sandman says good night."

Jasmine curled on her side, hugging her pillow. She was ready to fall asleep when the radio conversation caught her attention.

"Hello, Sandman. This is Tanya, and I have a dream for you and Dr. Gina to interpret."

"That's what we're here for, Tanya. Tell us about your dream."

"Well, I've been dreaming about vegetables a lot lately. Cucumbers, carrots, zucchini. My dreams start out normally. I'm either sitting in my office at work or doing something ordinary like the laundry at home when these vegetables start appearing out of the blue. For instance, I reach into my desk drawer for a pencil and pull out a carrot instead. Or I reach for the soap powder and find a giant zucchini in its place. What do you think that means?"

The Sandman jumped in quickly. "Sounds like long and hard are—" he said, cutting himself off with a smile in his voice. "What do you think, Dr. Gina?"

Jasmine snorted into her pillow. "Men try to make everything about sex."

"My guess is that you're dreaming about vegetables because, on some level, you realize you need to eat more nutritiously." The doctor's authoritative tone was undercut by the Sandman's chuckling in the background.

His co-host ignored the interruption. "If

you've been eating a lot of fast food, or you haven't been taking the time to eat proper meals, you may feel guilty, which manifests itself as the vegetables that keep appearing in your dreams. They may be reminders that you need to improve your diet."

"That makes sense," Jasmine said, propping her chin on her pillow, staring at the glowing numbers on the clock radio.

The caller made a skeptical noise.

"What do you think, Tanya?" Sandman asked. "Does that sound about right?"

"Mmm . . . I don't know. I think my diet is fine."

Dr. Gina tried again. "Well, there's never one right or wrong answer when it comes to dreams. I always tell callers that they are the best judges of their dreams. Think about what's been happening in your life. What do *you* think it means, Tanya?"

The caller was silent for a moment. "Actually, there is something . . . but I'm kind of embarrassed to talk about it."

Jasmine rolled her eyes and flopped over on her back. "Then why did you call the station?"

"Relax, Tanya." The Sandman's voice flowed like warm ripples into the microphone. "It's almost two A.M. Chances are your mom's not listening. What's on your mind?"

"Okay, it was my birthday last month, and my boyfriend"—she took a deep breath, letting her words out in a rush—"bought me a sex toy. I was really embarrassed, and I wasn't sure what to do with it, so I stuck it in my sock drawer. My mother is coming into town next weekend, and . . . well, she's really nosy."

"Ah-ha—" the Sandman started, but Dr. Gina cut in.

"That's it, Tanya," she said. "You're so uncomfortable even thinking about this toy that your subconscious is substituting a safe object, like a carrot. It keeps popping up in unexpected places because you're afraid the toy will be discovered."

"Another mystery of the mind solved," the Sandman said. "Here's a word of advice, Tanya. If his little present makes you that uncomfortable, get rid of it. Especially, before Mom comes to visit. Tell your boyfriend that next year you want a gift certificate."

"Okay, thank you, Sandman. Thanks, Dr. Gina." The call was disconnected.

The Sandman was still laughing. "That just goes to show, Gina. You think men try to make everything about sex, but you've got to admit, sometimes a carrot *isn't* just a carrot."

Jasmine felt her body growing heavy as she listened to their banter.

"We're winding down here at ninety-nine point three. We have time for one more call. You're on the air."

"Is this the Sandman?"

Jasmine's eyes popped back open. "What's

with that voice?" She couldn't tell if it belonged to a man or a woman.

"You've got it, bringing sweet dreams and slow jams. What can I do for you?"

The caller's response was distorted and muffled.

"Can you speak up?" the Sandman said. "We can't understand you."

"I said: It's raining. It's pouring. The Sandman is snoring. He went to bed. I severed his head, and he couldn't get up in the morning."

Jasmine sat straight up in bed, staring wide-eyed at the radio as the station cut to dead air.

Spencer Powell awoke with a start. Then he was moving, rolling—right off the edge of the sofa. He hit the floor hard and, disoriented, lay there.

"Good morning, carpet." He lifted his chin out of the plush shag to spit out carpet fibers.

His head felt thick and achy from too little sleep. After a restless night, he'd finally abandoned his bed to watch a video in the living room. Sleep came quickly once he'd begun to relax.

Staggering to his feet with the grace of a drunken hippo, Spencer dashed a hand down his face and slogged forward. Either he'd landed harder than he thought, and his ears were ringing in three-tone melody, or someone was ringing the doorbell.

He tugged the door open, and his blood immediately started pumping faster. "Well, hello." *God bless the Avon lady.*

Sleep deprived or not, Spencer never passed up the opportunity to appreciate a good-looking woman. And the one on his doorstep was nothing short of stunning.

His gaze skimmed the features of her face, flying by her sleek, short hairstyle to the slim pantsuit outlining her figure. His gaze lingered there, flowing over her curves like molasses. He admired the way her navy jacket dipped in dramatically at her waist.

She was tall, just inches shorter than his six feet, and she had the body of an athlete. His eyes moved lower. Definitely a dancer's legs. Her trendy navy slacks clung to her thighs, revealing taut muscles, before flaring slightly over her chunky-heeled shoes.

Whatever she was selling, he was buying, he thought as every male instinct kicked in. A grin, designed to be charming, spread across his face. Taking a step back, he raised his hands above his head. "If you're my psycho stalker, I surrender."

"If I were, you'd be dead already."

The woman didn't smile, which was a shame, because she had a small mouth with juicy lips perfect for smiling—and other things. Instead, she moved forward, forcing Spencer to take another step back to allow her to enter.

"Do you always let strangers in so easily?" she asked.

"No, but—"

"Then you'll have to do better next time." As she passed, she slapped a card into one of his open palms.

"Jasmine White." He read aloud. "Close Protection Specialist." The rude snort he issued was a reflex, the last vestiges of sleep clearing from his head instantly. "*You're* my bodyguard? You've got to be kidding."

He'd spent the early-morning hours, which he usually reserved for sleep, arguing with his station manager, Talibah Arkou, over this very matter. He didn't need a bodyguard.

Hell, before he came to WLPS five years ago, he'd been a shock jock in Philly. There, crank calls and death threats had been proof that he was doing a good job. Back then, they'd been the rantings of the lonely looking for attention, and he'd bet that was all these threats were now. They came with the job. The only difference was that, back in Philly, no one had tried to force a bodyguard on him.

Maybe he *had* lain awake between spurts of sleep after last night's incident on the air, but who could blame him? Wasn't everyone around him freaking out? He'd tried to get Tali to calm down, but she wouldn't listen. She'd insisted that the call, and the three written threats that had come before it, could escalate into something serious. She'd told him there would be a body-guard on his doorstep come daylight and that was that.

Spencer could have thrown his weight around. He pulled phenomenal ratings, despite the fact that he had one of the least-popular time slots. But he had his eye on the morning show. Rumor had it that Johnny Gallow would be retiring soon, and Spencer was first in line for his slot. He didn't want to do anything to jeopardize his chances, which brought him back to the bodyguard.

Oh, well, it was the station's dime. He couldn't change Tali's mind, so he had to go along with it—temporarily. But that didn't give the station the right to turn him into a public joke.

Sure, he'd complained that he didn't want some dull-witted, three-hundred-pound giant dogging his heels, but *this* was ridiculous. Since when did bodyguards come honey-dipped and fully equipped? And she was so slender . . . he'd bet one good breath would knock her flat.

"First of all, the only kind of protection I have any use for is made of latex and fits in my wallet. Second, even if I *did* need someone to watch my back, you look more like a ballerina than a bodyguard."

Jasmine stopped checking out the house to pin him with a sharp glare. Even with barely controlled anger heating her eyes and bunching her lips, she was pretty.

To Spencer, pretty had always seemed a use-
less description, watered down for those who
didn't quite make the cut for beautiful. Yet, right
now, no word seemed more suited to Jasmine's
face than *pretty*.

Her features were small and feminine. She had
a perfect oval face with smooth skin like dark tof-
fee. His gaze started at her soft heart-shaped
mouth, moved past her miniature nose to those
giant Bambi eyes—that were drilling holes in his
forehead.

He watched as she sucked in a breath, clearly
trying to rein in her temper. After staring at him
for a full minute, she nodded.

"Why don't we save ourselves a little time?"
She walked into his living room and pulled an
end table away from the wall. "Your station manager hired me to protect you, and as you've already stated, you don't feel *I'm* qualified to do
the job."

He rubbed his bristled chin, trying to figure
out what she was up to. "That's right."

"Fine. We can settle this rather quickly." Jasmine set his ceramic chess set on the floor and
knelt at one end of the table. She laid her arm out
and flexed her muscle. "Are you up for it?"

Spencer's mouth fell open. "Arm wrestling?"

"That's right. If I win, you shut up and let me
do my job. If you win, I'm out of here. Then we'll
both just have to hope your overzealous fan is all
talk and no action—as I suspect you are." Her

gaze flicked downward before rising to meet his eyes.

Heat crept up Spencer's neck. That was a blatant challenge, not to mention an insult to his masculinity. Starting to move forward, he caught himself.

He wasn't stupid. If this lady had volunteered to arm wrestle, chances were she thought she could take him. Backing off and firing her the regular way was the smart move. But, though Spencer *was* smart, he was still a man. His pride just wouldn't let him back down from a woman. Shoot, he had to defend his Y chromosome.

Still, it didn't hurt to try another approach. "Screw the arm wrestling. How about we just wrestle? You never know, it could be fun."

Jasmine's hard gaze didn't waver. She simply flexed her hand again, daring him to accept her challenge.

Ignoring his common sense, Spencer knelt at the table and laid his arm alongside hers. "This is your last chance to back out with your pride intact," he told her. "I don't want to hurt you."

Jasmine raised a brow. "All men say that. I have yet to meet one who meant it. Enough talk, Sandman. Let's go."

Great. Just what he needed. A woman with an attitude. Right now he probably represented every idiot who'd ever done her wrong. If she had PMS on top of that, he was a dead man.

When she raised her arm to his, Spencer did

wonder if he could hurt her. Her hands were
dainty, with slender fingers and short nails,
which distracted him from the strength cording
her wrist and forearm. The bones of her fingers
seemed so delicate, he feared too much pressure
would snap them.

They locked hands, and Spencer reached up to
trace their joined fingers with his other hand. He
made a show of studying her nails. "By the way,
you could use a manicure."

Jasmine's grip tightened enough to make him
wince. "You may get away with wisecracks on
the air, but keep talking to me like that and you'll
find yourself flat on your back."

"Ooh, sounds kinky. Where do I sign up?"

The back of Spencer's hand went rushing toward the black-lacquered table. It happened so
fast, he almost didn't recover in time. With all
his strength, he forced their hands back into the
center.

It was on. He wasn't about to let her catch him
off guard again. Gripping the edge of the table
with his free hand, Spencer levered more force
against Jasmine. She resisted, keeping their arms
centered. Spencer squinted, channeling all of his
energy into his wrist. Pricks of sweat formed on
his forehead.

He looked up, expecting to see his struggle
mirrored on Jasmine's face. Instead, he saw bore-
dom. Catching his eye, she smiled sweetly and
winked at him. Gazing down at her left hand,

she flicked the edge of one nail with her thumb. "You're right. I do need a manicure."

She was toying with him! She hadn't even broken a sweat. His stomach lurched. Jasmine held his arm locked in an upright position not because they were equally matched but simply because she could.

Dammit, why hadn't he spent more time in the gym? Fortunately, he'd never had to. He'd been able to maintain his leanly muscled physique on the wind of a high metabolism, a few pickup basketball games, and an undisciplined diet that didn't include beef. She was making him look like a fool.

Anger shot through him, fueling him with adrenaline. He used the sudden rush of energy to force her arm down several inches.

Now *she* gripped the table, working to press his arm back up. Spencer matched her strength, and now he saw her struggling not to lose ground again. Her wide eyes were narrowed in determination and her lips were pressed into a single dark line. He could even see a slight sheen forming above her brow. That was better.

Jasmine leaned forward, nailing him with those shining black eyes. She was dead set on winning.

But now, so was he. He felt his arm beginning to burn, and he knew he couldn't last much longer. Thankfully, he wasn't above fighting dirty.

"You're giving me a great view." He arched his brow, staring down into the vee created by the open collar of her blue satin shirt. As he'd hoped, his remark caught her off guard, allowing him to gain the advantage again.

But it didn't last. Jasmine did lean forward more, and while Spencer got a peek at the lacy, ice-blue edge of her bra, she took the advantage back.

Spencer tried to lever more shoulder into his grip, but he was still losing ground. His sharp tongue was his strongest weapon. Outrageous comments pulled high ratings; maybe now they could pull his fat out of the fire.

"Thanks for the peek. Maybe once we're through here, you'll give me a taste, too?"

He was going down. His hand was dangerously close to the table. Spencer had nothing to lose. "I know I said you looked more like a ballerina than a bodyguard, but I've changed my mind."

He forced her hand up a few inches. "That body's not made for dancing, it's made for fu—"

Slam. His knuckles cracked against the table so hard, he knew they would bruise. "Whoa."

Jasmine untangled her hand from his and pushed away from the table.

Spencer sat there for a moment, trying to register what had just happened. "You win," he said belatedly, shaking out his hand.

She didn't answer. With her back to him, she

paced in front of the window. Whew, she looked mad.

"Look, I'm sorry for what I just said. I tend to be a bit of a sore loser. I didn't mean it." *Unless you want me to mean it.*

No response.

"And I want you to know that I intend to honor our agreement. You won, so I'll shut the hell up and let you do your job. What do you say?"

She turned around, back in control. Spencer watched her face for anger, but she appeared to be cooler now. And, for the first time since she'd set foot in his home, she broke a smile. Her sweet expression was nearly angelic.

Relief rushed through his body.

"Don't worry about it," she said. "You don't know how many times I've been through this. The important thing is that you now understand that I'm qualified to handle this job."

"I understand," he said, rubbing his knuckles. "Believe me, I understand."

Her smile grew. "Good. Then let's start over, okay?" She offered him her hand to shake.

He grasped her fingers. "It's a deal."

She held his grip and stepped in close, planting her foot behind his ankle and sweeping back. For the second time that day, Spencer went down hard.

He lay there, staring up at her smug face. "What the hell is wrong with you?"

"Right now? Nothing."

"Will your agency send out a bodyguard to protect me from you?" Spencer rolled over and came to his feet, backing away from Jasmine. "Or is the policy to beat up clients yourself so that no one else will bother?"

Jasmine folded her arms. "No. What took place between us today had nothing to do with company policy."

Spencer rubbed his back. "I should hope not."

"According to company policy, I am to report any instances of sexual harassment immediately. But before I go through all the legal channels, I prefer to try to handle things my *own* way."

Spencer sobered instantly. He hadn't exactly been Mr. Congeniality so far, and while he'd love to blame it all on sleep deprivation, he knew his male ego was probably more at fault. What guy wouldn't be a little sensitive about having a gorgeous female guarding his body?

Actually, now that he thought about it, the idea wasn't without advantages. Nevertheless, bucking protocol was his specialty, and he'd never been good at keeping his mouth shut.

The station was run primarily by women. It would be impossible to explain his behavior without sounding like an immature idiot. His promotion was a hard sell already. They weren't in any hurry to move an on-air personality pulling good ratings in a bad time slot to a show that ranked high regardless. Once they heard Jasmine's side of things, they'd skin him alive.

"I was hired by your station manager," Jasmine continued. "But you have the right to ask me to leave. Though I guarantee that if I get fired from this job before I've had the chance to prove myself, your station will be facing the biggest sexual discrimination suit of all time."

Geez, this wasn't the first time his smart mouth had gotten him into trouble with the station. No matter how much he didn't want her there, he was going to have to put up with her for the sake of his job. Tali had probably gotten a huge kick out of hiring a female bodyguard for him. No doubt she would take it as a personal affront to her kind if he sent Jasmine away just because she didn't pee standing up.

"That won't be necessary," Spencer said. "I think we have an understanding."

"Perfect. Then let's get down to work."

You're blowing this, you idiot. You're blowing it. Jasmine cursed herself from one end of Spencer's luxury bachelor pad to the other.

As he followed her on the security walk-through, she automatically recommended upgrades to his alarm system, but half her mind was locked on her grossly unprofessional behavior.

Holding her temper had always been a struggle, but it hadn't become an issue until her brief stint as a D.C. cop. She'd worked overtime to prove she could keep up with those idiots. Even when she'd *surpassed* the others in performance, Jasmine never saw an end to the off-color jokes or sexual innuendos at her expense.

Finally, one smart-ass rookie went too far. Trying to substantiate Jasmine's claim that she was more man than he was, Feldmeyer made the mistake of grabbing her crotch. Without blinking, Jasmine pulled her gun on him and threatened to blow a hole in his pride and joy.

For that stunt, the police chief sentenced her to ten sessions of temper management counseling or one week's suspension. Feldmeyer got off with a minor reprimand.

Though Jasmine went to all ten counseling sessions, she never returned to the force. In her three years of dedicated service, she hadn't been able to fit in—despite the fact that there were several well-respected women on the squad. Instead of collecting commendations, Jasmine received more than her fair share of warning lectures. Maybe the chief had been right. Maybe she did have problems with authority.

Had she really dumped Spencer Powell—her first high-profile client—on his rear? If Nathan found out, she'd be out on hers. Attitude or not, even *she* knew some lines were not to be crossed. Getting physical with a client broke every rule in the book.

She was thankful that Spencer seemed to be as

anxious to get past the incident as she was. Despite all her big words about sexual harassment and discrimination suits, there was no doubt that she had more to lose than he did.

During the walk-through, Jasmine tried to reestablish her credibility as a bodyguard. If they couldn't reach a certain level of trust, it would be impossible to keep Spencer safe. And if she couldn't do that, then there was more at stake than just her pride. She'd drop off the case before she would allow a client to get half-assed protection.

When they returned to the living room, Jasmine sat across from Spencer on the sofa. "Let me know as soon as you've gotten those additions made to your security system. They're important because your station is hiring only part-time protection for you."

Spencer, who'd been brief with her up to this point, said, "Thank God. I don't think I'm up for full-time." He slipped a hand into the arch of his back.

Jasmine's face heated. She should apologize. No matter how much the words stuck in her throat, she had to put herself back on civil terms with her client. If he saw her as the enemy, he wouldn't trust her when it counted.

She opened her mouth, but Spencer beat her to it.

"Look, forget I said that. Can we just pretend that the last hour or so never happened? I think we both could use a fresh start. What do you say?"

Spencer's words should have been reassuring to Jasmine. Instead, they pissed her off.

She'd bet he thought that little speech made him the bigger person. He probably thought he was sexy, looking at her with that heavy-lidded gaze.

Jasmine studied him with narrowed eyes. He thought he was so cute with those short, brown curls and that pretty-boy smile. Well, she wasn't falling for it.

His lean, basketball player's build did nothing for her. And his deep, I-want-to-strip-you-naked, radio voice was wasted on her. It certainly didn't thrill her spine every time he opened his mouth. In fact, she hadn't even noticed it.

Jasmine paused. *Damn, girl, you have issues.*

Every time she thought she'd made a breakthrough, she started to regress. Why was she letting Spencer Powell get to her like this?

When Councilman Marquette's wife insisted that her beautician restyle Jasmine's hair, she'd managed to decline gracefully. And she hadn't even lost her cool when some kid threw up on her handbag at the prom last night. But let some sexy-as-sin radio host get a little too mouthy and she turned into Xena, Warrior Princess.

She had to get it together. Fast. Jasmine referred to her mental list: *Temper Management Technique No. 4: When a situation begins to get out of hand, rely on your skills to bring things back under control.* The best way to handle this assignment was to be curt and professional from here on out.

She returned Spencer's smile. "I want to apologize for my behavior earlier. It was inappropriate and unprofessional. I would appreciate a fresh start, too."

Spencer nodded, accepting her apology. He knew better than to offer to shake on it this time.

"My ability to protect you is dependent on your full cooperation. You may need to modify your lifestyle a little bit to keep a low profile."

"Modify my lifestyle? What does that mean?" His brow made a wicked arch. "Are you moving in?"

"You wish." As soon as the words were out of her mouth, Jasmine regretted them. *Cool and professional, dummy!*

This assignment might be harder than she'd thought.

"I mean that's not going to be necessary. As I stated earlier, since your station is hiring only one part-time guard, it's imperative that you take responsibility for your safety when I'm not around."

"Damn, I guess that means I have to give up skydiving."

Ignore him. Keep talking. "At this time we have no reason to believe that your alleged stalker has access to your home. Therefore, I'll escort you to work and then home each day, and I'll be present during any public appearances. Tomorrow, I'll teach you some defensive driving techniques—"

"Cool . . . burning rubber? Driving on two wheels? Jumping open drawbridges?"

"And until the threat against you has been fully assessed, I recommend that you stay out of the public eye as much as possible. Try to keep your personal errands to a minimum."

"What are you saying, that I'm chained to my house?" Spencer's voice rose an octave.

"No, but you really shouldn't tempt fate. Change your normal routine as much as possible. If you usually shop for groceries at the corner market every Saturday at noon, try a different store at another time of day. Vary your schedule."

"Why the hell am I turning my life upside down for some nut who has nothing better to do than make crank calls? Isn't that the reason they hired *you*?"

"Spencer, ninety percent of my job is threat avoidance. Everyone thinks close protection is about looking big and tough and busting heads. My job is to keep you safe, which means avoiding the confrontation. If we manage to come up against the confrontation, then I'm equipped to handle that, too. But my most important task is to make you a hard target."

"No problem there. All you have to do is walk into a room."

Jasmine gnashed her teeth. *Down girl. Cool and professional.*

"Whoa," Spencer said, warding her off with his hands. "Before you slug me, I take it back." He chuckled. "But you've got to cut me some slack here. I work the ten-P.M.-to-two-A.M. shift. My livelihood depends on my ability to come up with zingers. If you're going to stick around, you're going to have to learn not to take it personally."

Jasmine sucked in a calming breath. She could do this. It would be the greatest test of her self-discipline yet, but it would be worth it.

"As I was saying, target hardening means building up enough layers of defense to make you less vulnerable to a potential threat. We should go over your schedule for the next several weeks and see where we can make some modifications."

He saluted her. "You're the boss. I'll be good, I promise."

For the next twenty minutes Spencer rattled off his schedule. He had a number of club shows and special events planned for the coming month, including a live broadcast from Ocean City in a few weeks and a singles event at a D.C. bar that evening.

Jasmine took notes, pausing to tap her pen against her notepad. "It's definitely too late to do anything about your appearance tonight, but I need to talk to your station manager about pulling you off some of these other high-profile events."

"Are you kidding? The success of my show is largely dependent on the live shows I do locally. Making me disappear into the woodwork will ruin my career."

"Extended hospital stays and funerals have also been known to ruin careers. Think about it. This may seem unnecessary to you, but you don't get a second chance at living. If you blow it, it's over. I've seen too many situations go bad because somebody refused to take his safety seriously."

"Have you ever lost a client?"

"No. But I used to be a D.C. cop. The simple truth is that if someone threatens you with bodily harm, chances are, at some point, that person is going to try to make good on that threat. But even if it never happens, you're better off staying a step ahead."

Spencer sank back into silence.

"I know you think it's ridiculous to have a female in charge of your safety, but there are several advantages. For instance, it will be a lot easier for *me* to blend into your daily routine. During your live shows, I can be introduced as a personal assistant. In other situations, I can be a relative, friend, or—"

"Date, girlfriend, lover?" Spencer asked.

Her jaw tightened. "If you think it's appropriate."

"Hmm, this could be interesting after all."

"I'm not concerned with how you introduce me. The important point for you to remember is that I won't tolerate any advances or improper—"

"Say no more, sister. I value the family jewels far too much to get them anywhere near your steel-toe shoes. I have no desire to be pas-de-bourréed right back on my ass."

Again with the ballerina references. Jasmine hadn't had a lick of dance training, but she was sure she could pirouette him upside the—

Cool and professional. She wasn't going to lose her temper again if it killed her. She just needed to bump up the authoritative mode a notch. Once Spencer realized that she wasn't going to lose control again, keeping him in line would be a breeze.

Jasmine looked over at Spencer, who smiled back, looking for all the world like a choirboy gone bad.

Who was she kidding? Even under the best of circumstances, keeping Spencer Powell in line would be like trying to cage the wind.

It was a good thing she liked a challenge.

2

"**S**omebody shoot me." Spencer ducked onto the covered patio of the Lonely Hearts Bar & Grill, hoping the fresh air would calm him. He was visible through the glass doors, so Jasmine wouldn't have to come looking for him. Maybe he could have a moment of peace.

Irvin Jackson, manager of the bar, stood against the brick building with his thick lips bunched around the end of a cigar. "Shoot you? Sorry, man, I left my AK in my *other* pants."

"Hey, Irvin." Spencer walked over to the wooden railing and looked out over the city. Even a little late-spring rain couldn't keep people off the busy D.C. streets. Cars and buildings blurred before his eyes.

All Spencer could see was red.

Irvin stubbed out his cigar and came over to stand beside him. "So who's the new girl?"

"Jasmine?" The ballerina bone crusher? Princess of Pain?

Spencer narrowed his eyes, calling up the prepared cover story Tali had fed him over the phone. "The station has decided that I need a personal assistant. Today's her first day."

"Kind of bossy, isn't she?" Irvin grinned, running a hand along his balding head. He'd grown the rest of his hair to shoulder length and had it pulled into a silver-threaded braid at the nape of his neck.

"Oh, you noticed? What was your first clue? When she made the crew move the deejay setup from the front of the dance floor to the back, against the wall? Or was it when she demanded that your staff disarm the back door alarm so I could enter and exit through the kitchen?"

Spencer knew these were security precautions, but WLPS had been hosting events at this bar for years. His set was only an hour and a half. There were several other people from the station doing sets tonight, and they were going to have to adjust to a lot of changes because Jasmine was taking her job too far.

Why couldn't she just hold her clipboard and look pretty? If she wanted to cling to his side a little and follow him around, fine. But turning the entire place upside down was just her way of trying to look important. Spencer couldn't imagine that there could be a threat here. A lot of the guests were regulars he knew by name. No one would try anything in front of a crowd.

Irvin rubbed the goatee on his chin. "I noticed she made a bit of a fuss."

"More than a bit. When she started giving me instructions on where I should stand and how close I could get to the crowd, I had to make a break for it."

"But you know how it is with the new kids. They feel they gotta make a lot of changes to show they're doing the job. She'll calm down after a while."

"Not soon enough for me," Spencer said, holding his thumb and index finger an inch apart. "I'm this close to firing her."

Irvin chuckled. "Man, give the girl a break. Sounds like she's really looking after you. She asked Tyrone to wait on you personally, so you wouldn't have to walk back and forth through the crowd for your complimentary drinks. She's treating you like a king. You better sit back and enjoy it. Especially since she's so damn fine with that pretty brown skin and those big eyes. Shoot, I'm thinking about getting me a personal assistant."

"Yeah, she's good-looking."

Now *that* he could relate to. Spencer had never had trouble with women, especially not the attractive ones. Jasmine, with her tough girl routine and her smart mouth, was a different story.

But she was still a woman. Maybe if he kept that in mind, she wouldn't be so hard to deal with.

He turned to look through the glass and saw her looking over at them, holding her clipboard to her chest.

"Great. She looks like she's getting ready to come out here." He nodded to Irvin. "It's too late for me, man. Save yourself."

Irvin folded his arms and leaned back on the railing, crossing his ankles. "Oh, no, I don't want to miss this."

"Don't say I didn't warn you." Spencer darted another glance in her direction. "She's tougher than she looks."

"I usually see those little interns from the station fawning all over you. It's about time they hired a woman who isn't afraid to take you in hand."

"Traitor."

Under different circumstances, Jasmine White would definitely be his type. He liked them tall and slim, with all the right curves. And she had his favorite thing—a sweet little derriere any sister would envy.

Too bad she spoiled the entire image with that perpetual scowl. She was marching toward him like a woman on a mission, no doubt ready to bark more orders and instructions. He'd bet she was no different in bed—ordering her men around like new recruits in boot camp—or *booty* camp.

Drop those pants, Private!

Ma'am, yes, ma'am!

Great. Nice going, Spencer scolded himself. He had to shove his hands deep into the pockets of his khakis to hide his body's reaction to the image of Drill Sargent Jasmine in the bedroom. He'd sign up for active duty in a heartbeat.

Jasmine pushed the glass door open and strode up to the two men. "Spencer, the bar opens at five o'clock today. That only gives us twenty minutes to go over these last few details."

"I've done this a hundred times, Jasmine. I know my job." Spencer let his back rest against the wooden railing, crossing his feet at the ankles. "Besides, we don't go live until six, and my spot doesn't start until ten anyway. We have plenty of time."

She gave him an overly friendly smile. "Well, circumstances have changed, and if you're not prepared, the consequences could be severe."

He looked at Irvin and rolled his eyes. "I think I can handle it."

Her eyes flashed. "If you could, I wouldn't be here."

She was so close. Close enough for him to reach out and wrap his fingers around that long, elegant neck and squeeze—

Spencer had just opened his mouth to make a nasty retort when Irvin interrupted with a healthy belly laugh. "You two are a trip."

Her head snapped up as though she were seeing Irvin for the first time.

"Excuse me," Spencer said. "Jasmine White meet Irvin Jackson, the manager of the Lonely Hearts Bar and Grill."

While the two shook hands and exchanged pleasantries, Spencer tried to bring himself back into control. He stared at Jasmine's profile. Apparently, she did have a friendly side, because she conversed with Irvin without a trace of the venom he'd been treated to all day.

Clearly, he was taking her role as his bodyguard too seriously. Maybe it was time for him to have some fun with it.

A wicked grin crossed his lips. An old trick to disarm stressful situations came to mind. It was better suited to public speaking, but that didn't mean it couldn't work for him now.

If he pictured Jasmine in her underwear, maybe it would soften his reaction to her attitude. If nothing else, he'd get a cheap thrill.

Spencer let his eyes glide down her body, erasing the slim-fitting navy suit and replacing it with a soft blue merry widow that matched the lacy bra he'd glimpsed earlier. He pictured it barely cupping her full breasts, lifting the swells until they seemed ready to burst free with the slightest movement. The corset would cinch in around her impossibly tiny waist, and the garters—

"Why are you looking at me like that?"

Spencer blinked away his dreamy expression. "What?"

He looked around, finally noticing that Irvin had excused himself and left the balcony, leaving him alone with a suspicious Jasmine.

She started to say something, then closed her mouth, pursing her lips. Instead she held out her clipboard. "Immediately after your set, I'll escort you through the kitchen exit to my car, which is parked right outside."

Spencer frowned down at the floor plan she held out. "And then what?"

"And then I'll drive you home."

He'd never felt more like a pansy in all his life. "What if I don't want to go home?" He knew it was childish, but he felt a bit like a kid at the moment.

She ignored him, pointing at her blasted floor plan again. "Now, I've had the mike placed over here, so as long as you move around in this vicinity . . ."

Spencer tuned her out. No amount of G-strings or garter belts could warm him toward her as long as she had that "Jasmine, the emasculator," routine going.

That left Spencer no other choice. If she wanted to be his bodyguard, fine. There wasn't much he could do about it, but that didn't mean he had to make it easy for her.

*   *   *

If she got Spencer Powell home alive, she was going to kill him, Jasmine promised herself as she followed him into the Sin City nightclub.

He'd disregarded just about every instruction she'd given him since his ten o'clock set had begun at the bar. He hadn't stayed onstage. Instead, he'd blatantly walked into the crowd to flirt with women in the audience. Then, to make matters worse, he'd disappeared several times, claiming he'd been in the bathroom.

She'd cautioned him to let her know, so she could wait outside the door. Instead, he blew her off with a casual, "Honey, when the urge hits, you've got to go with the flow. No time for spectators."

She'd nearly strangled him then and there. Worse yet, after his set was over at eleven-thirty, he'd invited two other guys from the station out for a night on the town. Jasmine had protested, but Spencer had forced her into it by telling her, in front of the other men, that if it was past her bedtime she was free to go home.

The other men thought she was Spencer's new personal assistant and, of course, wouldn't be obligated to hang out with the guys. So she'd had to do a one-eighty and keep her mouth closed as she drove Spencer and his buddies for forty minutes to an after-hours club in Baltimore.

It was going to be much more difficult to watch out for Spencer in a crowded nightclub, and he knew it. Obviously, he'd decided to make this as inconvenient for her as possible, but she was up to the challenge.

The four of them paid the ten-dollar-each cover charge—which she fully intended to bill back to WLPS—and filed into the main room.

"Looks like we missed the show," Spencer said.

"What show?" asked Juan, half of the Duan and Juan duo, which hosted WLPS's six-to-ten slot.

"The strip show," his twin brother answered. "Some nights they have strippers before they open the floor for dancing. The women get male dancers in this room, and the men get female dancers in the back room."

"Looks like some of them are still here," Juan said.

"Yep, a lot of them stick around after the show, hoping to make some extra money," Spencer said, raising his brows suggestively.

"That's sick." Jasmine hadn't meant to speak up, but the words were out of her mouth before she realized it.

Spencer put an arm around her. "Don't worry, we won't let anyone push up on you. Think of the three of us as . . . your bodyguards." He chuckled in her ear.

Jasmine brushed his arm off her shoulder, ignoring the lingering sensation of his fingers massaging her upper arm. "That won't be necessary."

"On the other hand, if you want to meet someone, we won't cramp your style." Spencer couldn't control his laughter.

She chose to ignore him. "Why don't we find a table?"

She followed them through the club to another room where there were tables and reggae music playing for a handful of people.

They sat down and a waitress came right over to take their drink orders. "Nothing for me," Jasmine said.

The waitress shifted her weight with impatience. "Two-drink minimum."

Jasmine rolled her eyes. "Then bring me two Cokes."

The guys ordered beer and tried to decide which male strippers were gay. Jasmine was busy getting a mental layout of the club. As they'd walked through, she'd taken note of all the exits. It was clear that Spencer didn't intend to cooperate with her protective measures, but she refused to let that keep her from her job.

They were in a good position while they sat at the table, but if Spencer decided to move onto the dance floor, things could get tricky. That part of the club was packed to twice its normal capacity because of the strippers.

Jasmine had never seen so many overdone hairdos in one room. The women of Baltimore had a style all their own—high hair, braids, gel-slicked cones, and hard curls ranging in shades from coppery blond to raspberry black. She also couldn't miss their colorful acrylic nails and bulky jewelry.

The men weren't any better—many of them sporting processed waves, bright shirts with busy prints, and supertight muscle-tees.

Jasmine hoped the guys would finish their drinks and decide to move on, but she knew it wasn't likely that they had driven forty minutes for a few overpriced beverages. She tuned out the guy talk and watched the crowd. Periodically, a stripper would slither over to the table and try to entice one of the guys onto the floor.

Duan was the first to succumb, and his brother wasn't far behind him. Jasmine knew Spencer would be next, and she intended to keep her eye on him. Unfortunately, she had one tiny little problem. Those two sodas she'd gulped down had gone straight to her bladder.

Sneaking away to the bathroom wouldn't have been a big deal at the radio station or even at the bar earlier, but this was the worst possible time for Jasmine to let Spencer out of her sight. She'd just have to hold it.

Feeling warm in the steamy club, Jasmine took off her jacket and folded it over the back of her chair.

The waitress came back to the table. "Can I get you anything else?"

Spencer nodded. "Yeah, I'll have a Coke this

time." He looked over at Jasmine. "Anything else?"

"Nothing for me." If one more carbonated bubble came anywhere near her, she'd explode. Crossing her legs, Jasmine shifted in her seat. Maybe if she took her mind off it, she'd feel better.

"So, do you come here often?" Great, that sounded like a cheesy pickup line.

"Every now and then. Q-one-oh-two is our sister station, and they broadcast live in here every Saturday night. D.J. Quick is my frat brother. We started out on the swim team together at Penn State."

"Really?" It was easy to picture him as a swimmer. He had the perfect build. It was even easier to picture him in a snug pair of Speedos.

"Yeah, he and I still hang out. Last summer we went white-water rafting for the first time. It was incredible. All that water rushing at you, full force. *Whoosh, whoosh, whoosh.* Waves crashing on the rocks."

"Omigod," Jasmine moaned. She was fighting a losing battle.

"Oh, it wasn't as dangerous as it sounds," Spencer reassured her. "We had a professional rafter to guide us. There wasn't any chance of us going over any waterfalls or getting caught up in the rapids."

Jasmine squirmed in her seat.

"Are you okay?" Spencer leaned forward, peering at her face. "Does it bother you *that* much?"

She couldn't take anymore. Jasmine sprang to her feet. "I have to go to the ladies' room," she announced more loudly than she'd intended.

A grin formed on Spencer's lips. "What if someone tries to kidnap me while you're gone?"

"If you do what I tell you, that won't happen. I'll only be gone for a second. Promise me that you'll stay right here until I get back."

"No problem."

Jasmine didn't have time to react to the insincerity of his tone. She turned on her heel and bolted for the bathroom.

Unfortunately, her trip wasn't going to be as quick as she'd hoped. Jasmine was barely able to slip inside the door because of the line of women crowded inside the room.

She boldly pushed to the front of the line. "This is an emergency. Does anyone mind if I go next?"

Several eyes glared at her. A large woman stuffed into a red tank top and ridiculously tight jeans put a meaty hand on Jasmine's shoulder and pushed her back. "Honey, we all got emergencies. You can wait your turn just like everyone else."

Jasmine considered arguing, but she knew if she exerted too much energy, she'd have an unfortunate accident three feet from the nearest toilet.

Biting her lip for self-control, she made her way back to the end of the line. By now, three more women had forced their way in and the line had curved around to the hand dryer by the sink.

It seemed like an eternity before she was finally able to relieve herself. Not sparing any time to check her hair, she dashed back out to the bar.

Just as she'd suspected, Spencer was no longer sitting at their table. Turning around, Jasmine headed for the main dance floor to find him.

She'd never hear the end of it if an incident had occurred while she was in the ladies' room.

It took her only a minute to find him buried in the center of the dance floor with some skanky tramp pressed against him. The woman was gyrating to the hard-hitting tempo for all she was worth.

Jasmine started across the dance floor, then stopped. What was she going to do when she got out there? Drag him back by his ear like an irate mother on the playground? She turned around, scanning the room for a potential dance partner. She spotted a likely candidate in a purple velour sweat suit, bobbing his head on the sidelines.

She marched up to him. "Want to dance?"

He looked her up and down, then his face split

into a wide grin. The strobe light glinted off his shiny gold tooth.

They'd only taken two steps onto the dance floor when Goldy stepped into her personal space and began humping her leg. Jasmine then had the complex task of backing him off her while at the same time luring him farther out onto the floor, closer to Spencer.

Finally, she managed to maneuver him right next to Spencer, and then Goldy was again sucked to her leg like a magnet. She had no choice but to resort to guerrilla tactics.

"Watch out, brother-man," she warned. "Or you might get hurt."

Then Jasmine went into performance mode. She started kicking up her legs in time to the quick house beat—a surefire technique for evading the "leg-humpers." It also worked on the "booty-grinders" and the "hip-huggers."

She smiled as her body naturally picked up the steps other dancers were using around her. Jasmine was no ballerina, but she knew how to club dance.

Spencer hid his yawn behind his hand. Ordinarily, two A.M. was still the prime of the night, but between his restless night and the forty-five-minute nap he'd caught on his living room sofa that morning, he'd probably gotten a total of two hours' rest. It was catching up to him.

The woman before him wriggled in her tight

dress, and he was too tired to react. His body automatically moved in time to the music, but his steps were halfhearted.

He'd only agreed to the dance for Jasmine's benefit. For a while, he'd thought he was getting to her, but he had yet to see much of a reaction. Mostly, she would just nail him with one of her just-wait-till-I-get-you-out-of-here looks. He'd expected more of a blowup, but she seemed to be keeping her cool.

After this morning's confrontation, he'd pegged her for a hothead. Once she began mucking with the layout for his show, he'd figured if he ticked her off enough she'd have a few more outrageous displays of temper and he'd have a solid excuse to boot her out of his life.

Now, glancing sideways at Jasmine while she danced, he saw that she showed no signs of being either tired from the long hours or angry about his blatant defiance. In fact, she seemed to be having a better time than he was.

The music turned to a more mellow, sinuous beat, and the purple sweat suit she was dancing with took immediate advantage of the mood change. He slipped in close, wrapped his arms around her back, and began to rock in the cradle of her thighs.

Spencer grinned, waiting to see if she chose kneeing over punching. Personally, he voted for a good knee in the groin. That would teach him.

But Jasmine did neither. Instead, after glancing up to catch Spencer's eye, she raised her arms above her head and matched her partner's moves.

What the hell was she doing? Spencer felt his neck heat up. She was supposed to be working for him, not getting busy on the dance floor. What if someone snuck up behind him and knocked him out while Jasmine was doing the hootchie cootchie dance with Barney the purple dinosaur over there?

His dance partner was oblivious, slithering in front of him, trying to balance herself on her three-inch platform shoes. Spencer touched her arm to get her attention, then pointed across the room, indicating that he was leaving the dance floor. She nodded, following Spencer through the crowd.

Once they reached the sidelines, he leaned down to whisper in her ear. "I think I'm going to head out."

The girl tugged the hem of her tight red dress down a couple of inches. "I'm leaving, too. Walk me to my car?" She tilted her head, looking up through her lashes.

Spencer had seen that look before. Obviously, once they got outside, the girl was hoping he'd follow her home. He wasn't in the mood. It would be easier to ask one of the bouncers to escort her to her car.

On the other hand, what if he did want to see a

lady home one night? What would Jasmine do? Watch? Even if he didn't want to pick up this particular woman, he had to defend his right to do so.

"Uh, sure. Just let me find my friends. Wait right here."

Back at the bar, Spencer found Duan and Juan having drinks with D.J. Quick and a couple of the strippers. He said a few words to his old buddy, then let them know that he was heading home. Duan and Juan decided to stay behind and hang out with D.J. Quick.

As he made his way back to the main room, someone called his name, then grabbed his arm. It was Jasmine.

"Oh, are you back on the clock now? Don't stop having a good time on my account."

"I was just blending in."

Spencer's temper climbed another notch. "Is that right? Well, I'm about to walk a lovely lady to her car. I don't want to have to explain you, so make sure you *blend* in."

She nodded without further comment, but he could see the spark in her eyes. Nevertheless, during the two-block walk, Jasmine managed to follow them without looking obvious.

Unfortunately, he now regretted not letting her walk with them. She would have been a welcome diversion. The girl, who introduced herself as Vanessa, talked nonstop all the way to the car.

"I just love house music, don't you? This was my first time in Sin City and I loved it. Where are you from?"

"Potomac, Maryland," Spencer said.

"Really? I live in D.C. We're practically neighbors."

Spencer was relieved when they reached Vanessa's car, parallel-parked in the middle of the block. Jasmine continued walking past them, then paused on the corner, studying her watch and looking up the street as though she were waiting for a ride.

Vanessa wasn't in any hurry. She seemed to want to stand there and engage him in conversation. While she prattled on, Spencer kept an eye on Jasmine. They were in a pretty bad part of town, and Jasmine was standing out in the open.

"Well, it's getting pretty late." He started edging back toward the curb.

"Don't you want my phone number?"

He didn't, but he couldn't hurt her feelings. He held up his hands. "I don't have a pen."

"You don't need one," Vanessa said, pulling a business card out of her low neckline.

He looked at the white cardstock. It showed the silhouette of a woman rolling nylons up her leg. "What do you do?"

She smiled at him. "I'm an exotic dancer. I came out to the club to support a couple of friends who were working tonight."

"I see," he muttered, watching as two guys

came up behind Jasmine. One of them was the purple sweat suit she'd been dancing with inside the club.

The guy was obviously drunk. "Hey, cutie! Why'd you leave before I could get your number?"

He couldn't hear Jasmine's reply. She talked to the guy quietly while his buddy smoked a cigarette a few feet away.

"C'mon, brown sugar, you and me were getting busy on that dance floor," he said loudly.

Again, her reply was too low for Spencer to hear, but he saw her place a hand on the man's chest to force him back.

"Call me?" Vanessa asked.

"Sure. Have a safe drive home." He opened her car door, all but stuffed her inside, and slammed it after her.

As Vanessa sped away from the curb, Spencer saw that Jasmine was now holding the guy off with both hands. He rushed over. "Jasmine, is this guy bothering you?"

"Thanks, Spencer, but I don't need any help."

"Yeah, she don't need no help!"

Spencer addressed the drunk directly. "Looks to me like she does."

"Why don't you just stay out of it?" The drunk spun around, stepping into Spencer's face. Slowed by the alcohol, he cocked back his fist.

Out of the corner of his eye, Spencer saw Jasmine lurch forward, ready to grab the guy. But,

Spencer, only too pleased to show her that he could take care of this himself, was already driving his fist into the man's jaw.

As the guy sank to his knees, Spencer turned to Jasmine, feeling smug. Unfortunately, he'd been so busy with the first guy that he almost missed the second guy, who had launched a running attack at his back.

He had just enough time to crouch, preparing to absorb the blow, but Jasmine was already in motion. She caught the guy around the waist, then immediately wrenched his arm behind his back.

"Look at that. See what happens when you don't play nice?" She tightened her grip and the man grunted. "Now, if you don't pick up your friend and get out of here right now, I just might have to break your arm."

The man moaned in pain as she released him. He rushed over, snatched his friend by the purple collar, and the two of them scrambled off.

Jasmine rolled her eyes and grabbed Spencer firmly by the arm, leading him up the street. "Try not to get into any more trouble between here and the car, okay?"

"I'm not saying you should have let him hit you. But the guy was so drunk, I doubt he would have landed the blow," Jasmine said on the drive home. "All you had to do was move out of the way and let the idiot fall on his face. At least then the second dude wouldn't have tried to jump you."

Spencer slouched down in the seat, staring out the window. "I didn't start this. You did. Maybe *I* should be watching *your* back?"

"That's ridiculous. I had the situation under control. Things wouldn't have gotten out of hand if you'd stayed out of it like I asked."

"Hey, I held my own, which you never acknowledged. Why do you have to be such a ball buster all the time? Do you have this problem with your other male clients?"

"Truthfully, for the past year and half, since I've been with Core Group, most of my clients were either female or kids under the age of twenty-one."

"Sounds like that's your problem. Let me give you some advice." He waited for her to glance over at him. "Men have big egos, and they like to feel *they* are the protectors. You can't expect a guy to accept a situation like this unless you're going to respect that."

Jasmine considered what Spencer had just said. She'd been so anxious to prove herself that she hadn't really thought about whether she was undermining his male ego.

After several minutes of silence, she finally said, "You know, Spencer, we don't have to be enemies. I'm only here to help you. I apologize if I've gone about it in the wrong way, but that doesn't mean that this situation can't work. If we continue to talk openly like this, I think we'll be able to reach an understanding. Are you willing to give it an honest try this time?"

No response.

"Spencer?" Jasmine took her eyes off the road long enough to glance at the passenger seat.

Spencer was sound asleep.

As soon as Jasmine's head hit the pillow, the phone rang. Or so it seemed. The five hours that had passed in between were merely a blip in time.

She grabbed the phone off the nightstand and pushed it to her ear, flopping backward onto her pillow. "Hello," she rasped. Ugh, it felt like she had a cotton plantation on her tongue.

"Good morning, Jasmine. This is Nathan."

She propped herself on one arm, blinking rapidly, hoping to clear away the burning ache in her eyes. "Nathan! What can I do for you?"

"I want to know how the Powell assignment is going."

Jasmine rolled her eyes. She should have known Nathan would call and check up on her.

She glanced at the clock. "Nathan, it's only nine A.M. Can't this wait until a decent hour?"

The older man's voice rumbled with barely contained frustration. "Yesterday was your first day with a client like Powell. I just want to make sure you can handle it. Now, how did it go?" he barked.

"Oh, it was great. Just great." Jasmine rubbed her eyes with the heel of her hand, easing into an upright position. It was easier to stretch the truth while sitting up. "Of course, he needs a little more time to adjust to the situation, but we're working through that."

"Why? Does he have a problem with the fact that you're a woman?"

Jasmine's jaw clenched. "He has a problem with the fact that he needs extra protection. You know that's to be expected."

"Okay. We did put this thing together quickly."

Jasmine had marched into Nathan's office yesterday morning and had really let him have it. She'd listed all her virtues and then demanded that she be given a better assignment. In the middle of her tirade, the station manager for WLPS had called and requested a bodyguard. She still couldn't believe that Nathan had picked up the phone to call in someone *else* right in front of her.

She'd raised another big stink, demanding that the Powell assignment be handed over to her then and there, or not only would she walk, she'd send an editorial to the *Washington Post* disclosing Core's sexist business practices.

Nathan had grudgingly given her the job, but he'd made it clear that this was her only shot. He didn't like being pressured, and if she blew this case, she would be fired. No questions asked.

That's why it was so critical that she not screw things up with Spencer—that was, any more than she already had. If Nathan found out how her first day with Spencer had actually gone, she wouldn't even get the chance to explain herself.

"Did you run into any trouble yesterday?"

She gazed up at the ceiling, grateful he couldn't see her guilty expression. "Nothing that I couldn't handle."

Nathan refused to let her off that easily. "Anything I should know about?"

"Why?" She gripped the phone with a tight fist. "Did he call and complain?"

"Not yet."

"Then give me a little room to do my job," she said. "I've only had one day with him. You know it takes longer than that to build a rapport with a client. Or do you think just because—"

"Save it, Jasmine. Your pride isn't the issue here. You just make sure you let me know if you find yourself in a pinch. I won't fire you for admitting you're in over your head."

Jasmine took a deep breath and tried to pull herself together. Up until now, Nathan had been a fairly decent boss. He hadn't become difficult until she'd strong-armed her way into this assignment. Apparently, her previous work hadn't been enough to prove herself in his eyes. It didn't matter; she'd been in this position before. This time, she wasn't going to quit.

With a resigned sigh, she gave him a slightly abbreviated version of the previous day's events. "There were a few times when he resisted my suggestions, but that was only because he's not convinced that he's in danger."

"And why is that?"

Jasmine held her head. All his barking was giving her a headache. "Well, probably because all the threats came directly to the station. I've looked at the notes and I heard the call when it aired. They're impersonal. He has no reason to believe this lunatic is after anything but attention. Thankfully, there haven't been any intrusions on his home or personal life."

"I'm sure you've made him aware that could change any time." Nathan's tone was curt.

"Of course, but you know how these celebrity types can be. They don't want to change their lives to avoid hypothetical danger. They expect the inconvenience of having a bodyguard to be enough. I had a long talk with him about that."

"So, what's the plan for today?"

"It should be a pretty low-key day. Sunday is his day off, and he doesn't have any special appearances planned. He had a late night, so I'm waiting till noon to go over and do some driving exercises with him."

"Fine. Keep me posted."

Jasmine hung up the phone and tried to go back to sleep, but it was no use. It still burned her up when men in positions of authority treated her differently than her male counterparts. Would she ever be given a fair shot?

There were times when allowing men to underestimate her abilities worked to her advantage. Her feminine appearance distracted them from her strength and skill. They never knew what hit them. Arm wrestling Spencer yesterday was case and point. He never would have taken her up on the offer if she'd been a man and built like Schwartzenegger.

Jasmine slid out of bed. She wasn't going to let Nathan's lack of faith discourage her. She just needed to tread carefully. Glancing at the clock, she realized it was only nine-fifteen. She had plenty of time for a workout.

Dressed in a pair of shorts and a T-shirt, Jasmine went outside for a jog. As she was running, yesterday's events began scrolling through her mind. Especially the last part of her conversation with Spencer before he'd fallen asleep.

With four older brothers, Jasmine had learned early to keep up her guard. Even though they'd grown up in a rough D.C. neighborhood, her football player-sized brothers made sure she never had to worry when she stepped outside their front door.

Instead, Jasmine's battles took place *inside* the home. If she wanted to eat, she had to move quickly. If she wanted to be heard, she had to speak up. And if she wanted her way, she had to come out swinging.

She'd found that the same tactics applied when it came to working in a man's world. Although she didn't win many popularity contests, when trouble hit, everyone wanted to be on *her* team.

Obviously, she'd been trying too hard with Spencer. Add her salty attitude to yesterday's "cool and professional" fiasco, and it was no wonder that she'd only succeeded in alienating the man. Proving she was a qualified bodyguard didn't mean she had to pulverize his ego.

Today, she would try another temper-management method: *No. 6: Anger reversal—making friends of enemies.* If Spencer could see her as a friend—or, at the very least, less of an enemy—she could make this assignment work.

She couldn't afford to blow it this time.

This case required more than just professionalism, it required finesse. This time, she'd win Spencer over.

Any minute now, she was going to let him have it, Spencer thought, spreading a layer of mustard on wheat bread. His gaze slid across the kitchen to where Jasmine was reading the Sunday paper while he constructed his favorite turkey sky-scraper sandwich.

Ever since Jasmine had arrived twenty min-utes ago, Spencer had been giving her the same deference and distance he'd give an overdue vol-cano. She'd had time to store up her anger over his rebellion last night, and now she was proba-bly just looking for the least-violent way to ex-press it.

He could handle it, Spencer told himself, as long as she didn't drop him on his ass again. But she sure was taking her sweet time about it. The least she could do was get it over with. What was she trying to prove by walking through his front door smiling brightly? He'd learned to fear that smile.

Ah, now he saw through her game. She was trying to make him sweat, thinking he'd stay off balance wondering when she'd unleash her wrath.

Well, it wasn't going to work. If she could play it cool, so could he. Spencer layered an inch of smoked turkey over his provolone cheese, top-ping it with toasted bread. "Are you sure you don't want one of these? I swear you've never had anything like it."

"I know that's right." Jasmine's gaze fastened on his four-inch-high tower of lunch meat. "Too bad I ate before I came over." She snapped her fingers in mock disappointment.

Spencer chuckled, sawing through the sandwich with a large knife. Well, at least he was sufficiently armed. He might as well get the worst over with.

"Isn't there something you want to talk to me about?"

Jasmine looked up from the paper again. "What do you mean?"

His grip tightened on the knife. "You know, last night?"

She nodded, closing the paper. Spencer waited while she smoothed the creases, folded it in half, then in half again, before setting it away from her on the table. "I was going to wait until after we finished some driving exercises this afternoon, but since you mentioned it . . ."

Jasmine stood, crossing the kitchen to stop before him.

Spencer gestured with the knife. "I'm warning you, I'm armed."

She laughed loudly. "Don't be silly. I apologized once, but clearly that wasn't enough. Yesterday was an aberration. It won't happen again."

He frowned. "I don't get it."

She leaned against the counter, smiling up at him.

Spencer grabbed half his sandwich and took a cautious step back.

"It's my fault that we started off on the wrong foot. Why don't we just forget about yesterday. I don't think it went the way either of us planned."

Spencer squinted, trying to see through her guise. He took a large bite out of the sandwich. "Who are you?" he asked with his mouth full.

"What do you mean?"

"I mean, what happened to the feisty, aggressive, *honest* woman I met yesterday? Where did you get this sunshiny, phoney, can't-we-all-just-get-along crap?" His teeth broke through several layers of bread, turkey, and cheese, causing him to dribble mustard on his chin.

"It's not crap." She handed him a napkin. "All I'm saying is that we've started a pattern of negative energy that may eventually impede our ability to work together if we don't take this opportunity to turn things around."

He wiped his face, staring at Jasmine in bewilderment. "What? Are you supposed to be Dr. Joyce Brothers now? Even Dr. Gina doesn't pull that psychobabble junk on me."

Jasmine sucked in a deep breath. Spencer could see that it was becoming a bit of a strain for her to maintain her sweetness-and-light facade.

"Come on, I'm not buying this new and improved routine. You're a hothead, and we both know you're just dying to go off on me right now."

"That's not true. Yesterday, you caught me at a bad time. I wasn't able to—"

"A bad time? Was it that time of the month?

Are you blaming your Bruce Lee episode on PMS?" Spencer smiled as Jasmine chewed savagely on her lower lip. She was about to crack. He'd much rather see that sexy fire exploding behind her eyes instead of this fake serenity.

"I'm not talking about PMS. What? Do you think every time a woman—" Jasmine caught herself before her tirade got off the ground.

"Yes. You were saying?"

"You're deliberately trying to provoke me," she said stiffly.

Spencer stuffed the remainder of his sandwich into his mouth, pausing to lick mustard from his thumb. "Yep."

She blew her breath out hard. "Why?"

He washed the sandwich down with a long swig of milk. "Because I'd rather see the real you. If you're the type to scream at the top of your lungs and throw a genuine, prizewinning, knock-down-drag-out, temper tantrum, then lay it on me. Hell, I probably deserve it."

"Yes. I'm sure you do, but if you're aware of that fact, then there's no need for me to lose control. I think we've already started communicating more effectively—"

"There you go again. What are you afraid of? If it's being fired, don't worry about that. As a matter of fact, you'd score more points for keeping it real."

"What's the matter with you? Do you get off on conflict?"

He grinned, nodding as he appraised her technique. "Not bad. But I'm sure you can do better."

"Better? What are you talking about?"

"Well, I'd say at this point you've achieved partial reality. Care to go for the other fifty percent?"

"Who the hell do you think you are?"

"That's it. Gimme more," he egged her on, motioning with his hands.

"Stop that!"

"Let it loose, baby."

"Look, first of all, I am not your baby. Second of all, stop behaving like an immature little boy."

She closed in on him, waving her finger. "I'm a woman . . . yes. I'm in charge of your safety . . . so what? Get over it already."

She took another step forward and leaned in. "If you ever stop coddling your poor little ego and start to pay attention to what's going on around you, you might realize that your life is in danger." When Jasmine finished, she stood a hair's breadth from Spencer's face.

He simply stared back, giving her a devilish grin.

She immediately backed off. "Look what you made me do."

"Beautiful." Slouching against the kitchen counter, he nodded. "Now, don't you feel better? I know I do. Waiting for you to blow up was like waiting for my dad to come home from work and give me a whooping."

"Are you satisfied now? I suppose you can't wait to tell your boss that I keep blowing up at you."

Spencer laughed. "Tali wouldn't have any sympathy for me. She already knows I'm a pain in the ass."

Jasmine sat back down at the table with a heavy sigh.

He pulled out a chair, turned it backward, and sat facing her. "Let's be honest. I can't quit making smart remarks any more than you can stifle your attitude. These things are just a part of our personalities. Maybe if we can accept that about each other, we can make this crazy situation work."

She tapped her fingers on the table, appearing to mull over his statement. Finally, she looked up, giving him a twisted smile. A smile he could tell was genuine.

"I hate to admit it, but that's the first thing I've ever heard you say that makes any sense."

"Gee, thanks."

"Oh, I didn't mean it the way it came out."

"Forget it. No more pretenses, okay? Besides—" He looked down at his watch. "I'm due to say something offensive to you in about two point five more minutes."

They laughed together, letting the moment fade into an amicable silence. Finally, Jasmine stood. "So, are you ready?"

"Ready for what?"

"Your driving lesson."

Spencer stood, too. "Yeah, girl, teach *me* a lesson, but do you want to drive? Or would you rather *ride*?" His tone was blatantly suggestive.

Jasmine paused, staring at him.

"Whew!" He glanced down at his watch. "What did I tell you? Right on schedule."

She released an exasperated laugh. "All right, show-off. Save it for the road," she said, punching him in the arm as she headed for the door.

"Hey, that hurt," Spencer lied, rubbing his arm. "And you, She-ra, can save the brute force for my stalker. I'm not paying you to waste all your best moves on me."

Jasmine looked over her shoulder. "A, *you're* not paying me, and B . . . those weren't my best moves." She winked before she turned away.

Spencer quickened his pace, following her outside. "Holding out on me, eh?"

She took out her keys and climbed into the driver's seat of her blue Honda Accord. "Keep it up, Sandman, and you'll get yours."

He laughed wickedly, getting in beside Jasmine. "You promise?"

Suddenly, having Jasmine guard his body didn't seem like such a bad idea after all.

Jasmine put the car in gear and backed out of Spencer's driveway. She would never admit it out loud, but releasing some of the tension she'd been building up had made her feel better. Holding her temper was a lot of work.

It was good to know that Spencer wasn't intimidated by her, but it was also a bit unsettling to have someone accept—and even encourage—the more tempestuous side of her personality.

"How come we're not taking my car?" he asked.

"That goes back to what I told you about keeping a low profile."

"Okay, but it's not like I drive a fancy red sports car."

She darted a glance at him. "Spencer, you drive a gold Lexus with vanity tags that say SANDMAN. Plus, you have a big old WLPS sticker on the bumper. It doesn't take a genius to figure out which car belongs to you."

He chuckled. "I see your point."

"Whenever I'm on duty, I'll drive. Core Group has a pool of nondescript company cars for me to choose from. Do you have access to another car you can drive on those *rare* occasions when you have to get around on your own?"

Spencer didn't answer right away, and Jasmine waited for some smart remark or protest.

"I'll have to think about it. Maybe I can trade cars with my sister for a while," he finally said.

Jasmine threw a glance in his direction. "I don't know if that's a good idea. We don't want to spare you at your sister's expense."

"She lives in Philly, where we grew up. She'd probably be thrilled to trade my Lexus for that clunker she drives."

Jasmine chewed her bottom lip thoughtfully. So he had a sister. She couldn't help wondering what a female version of Spencer would be like.

She parked the car in the empty lot of an elementary school, turned off the ignition, and shifted to face Spencer. "Before we start driving, I just want to go over some basic safety measures."

"Fire away," he said, pushing the seat back and making himself comfortable.

He looked ready for a nap. She wasn't going to let him get away with sleeping through her speech. Keeping a careful eye on Spencer to make sure he didn't doze off, Jasmine reviewed parking lot safety. To her surprise, he appeared to listen attentively.

"Whenever you get into a car, whether you're the driver or the passenger, you should memorize the location of the locks and door handles. You want to be able to find them without looking."

Spencer scowled. "What for?"

"If you find yourself under attack, especially if it's dark, you don't want to waste time fumbling to get out of the car."

He shrugged. She could tell by the expression on his face that he didn't get what she was saying.

She looked out the window, trying to decide

how best to explain it. "Okay, let me give you an example of something that happened to me. I grew up in southeast D.C., and during the time I was in high school there was an epidemic of car-jackings."

"Yeah, we had something similar going on in Philly back then."

"One of the popular methods was to drop a brick through the windshield from an overpass, forcing the driver to stop the car. Since they usually wanted the cars for parts, the kids didn't care about the damage."

He nodded, drumming his fingers on the dashboard.

"Well, one evening my friend's mother was giving me a ride home. Before we realized what was happening, a couple of kids threw something at the windshield. It didn't shatter, but it did crack in a spiderwebbed pattern that made it impossible for Mrs. Whitman to see. She must have realized what was going on, because she shouted, 'Get out of the car,' and bolted. But I couldn't get out."

"What?" He shifted to face her. She had his full attention now.

"I was so scared my hands were shaking, and I couldn't figure out how to get out of the car. You know how it is when you're in a strange car and you reach for the window lever instead of the door latch. Or you don't realize that the car has automated door locks that release with the ignition, and you end up locking yourself back in?"

"Yeah, I've done that."

"Well, it was something like that. In my panic, the more I fumbled with the door, the more confused I became. Mrs. Whitman had to run around to my side of the car and let me out."

He shook his head in disbelief. "What happened?"

"As soon as we got out of the car, the carjackers drove off with it. We had to run across the street to the gas station to call the police."

"Did they ever find her car?"

"Actually, they did, but it wasn't in the condition she'd hoped to find it in."

He nodded. "I'll bet."

"The point I'm trying to make, and not just about driving, is that anything can happen. You have to decide how you're going to handle yourself before you find yourself in danger. If you panic, you can't think straight, and that's how you get yourself into more trouble."

Spencer sighed. "That makes a lot of sense." He paused for a moment, staring out the window. "Some of the things you're talking about I'd like to E-mail to my sister, especially the part about keeping an emergency kit in the car and the things that go in it."

"I can help you do that, but these tips aren't just for a woman driving alone at night. A lot of men take it for granted that just because they can change a flat tire it's safe to get out anywhere and do so. Don't leave yourself open to muggers and thugs. All they need is opportunity."

Spencer looked up at her and smiled. "So did they teach all this when you were a cop? Or did you have to go to some special bodyguard school?"

Jasmine shrugged. "I learned a lot of things when I was a cop. After I left the force, I went into private practice as a bodyguard for a while. I took a few training courses, just to make sure I knew what I was doing."

He gave her a long appraising look, but this time Jasmine didn't find it offensive. "How did someone like you get into this line of work? I'm not trying to be sexist, but you could have been anything. You're certainly smart enough to do whatever you want . . . and you're so beautiful—"

Jasmine blinked in surprise. Was Spencer Powell blushing? She couldn't be certain, but she thought she'd just received her first genuine compliment from him.

Strangely flattered by both his sincerity and his words, Jasmine tried to hide her own embarrassment by looking away. "How did I get into this? That's a good question," she said with a nervous laugh.

"Was it a family thing?"

Her head whipped around to face him in surprise. "What do you mean?"

"A lot of people become cops because their fathers were on the force or something."

"Oh." Jasmine's laugh was hollow. "No, my father was a dentist . . . and a drug addict . . . and an ex-con. But, mostly, he was thin air. I was eight the last time any of us saw him." Jasmine froze, feeling her cheeks heat up again. She'd meant to stop with "dentist." She'd been lying about her father and covering up his past for as long as she could remember. Why had she picked that moment to confess the truth about her dad?

Not wanting to see pity in Spencer's eyes, Jasmine rushed to continue. Despite everything, her home had been far from broken. "Actually, my four older brothers inspired me to go into law enforcement."

"You have *four* older brothers? Was that like some sort of ghetto Partridge family?"

"Something like that. Growing up, they didn't allow me to use my gender as an excuse for anything. Ironically, they're very protective of me now, but back then they treated me just like they treated each other, roughhousing, swearing, fighting. No kid gloves for me. I was forced to act just like one of them. It made me stronger."

He shook his head, his confusion showing on his face. "So you became a cop because . . ."

"Even though my brothers treated me like an equal, I wasn't one. There were still things I couldn't do, places I couldn't go, and situations that made me feel helpless. I resented that defenseless feeling. I became a cop because I wanted other people to feel a little less helpless."

Spencer raised his brows at her. "That's deep."

Embarrassed, Jasmine added. "The other reason is that I wanted to kick some ass."

Spencer laughed. "Well, I can personally vouch for that one. You've turned ass kicking into an art form."

She turned to look at him and felt her heart pound faster. His eyes were filled with genuine warmth. And something else. Something she hadn't been sure she'd ever see in his eyes. Respect.

They sat there for a moment, eyes locked.

Finally, Jasmine snapped out of her trance and reached for the door handle. "Enough chatting. It's your turn to take the wheel. I'm going to take you through a couple of drills that will get you out of a tight spot in a hurry."

Spencer practiced the exercises Jasmine showed him in the parking lot, and then she had him drive around the neighborhood, mapping out alternate travel routes.

For the past hour and a half, Spencer had been fairly well behaved. Jasmine should have known that wasn't going to last.

They had just driven into a rural area when Spencer announced, "This car sucks. Why don't they give you something with a little more juice?"

Jasmine was busy enjoying the late-spring breeze and huge green fields with grazing horses that surrounded them. "No, Spencer," she said with impatience. "The idea is to be discreet. We don't *want* to call attention to our clients by driving around in fancy sports cars."

Spencer revved the engine. "I think it's time to see what this baby can do."

"What are you—" Jasmine lost her breath as he hit the gas hard. They shot down the street, quickly gaining momentum.

"Spencer! Stop this instant!"

Without missing a beat, Spencer stomped on the brake pedal, bringing the car to a screeching halt. As Jasmine was heaved forward, she could smell the burning tires. If it weren't for her seat belt, she was certain she would have been picking glass out of her forehead.

"Are you crazy? What the hell is the matter with you? Get out! I'm driving back."

He grinned at her, managing an angelic look. "Oh, is the lesson over? Then, home it is." He hit the gas again, the car lurched forward, and he took a sharp right.

"What are you doing? This is a one-way street."

"I'm taking a shortcut. You seemed anxious to get back."

Jasmine had just enough time to grip the door handle for support as Spencer brought the car up to ninety-five on the single-lane road.

"Slow down!"

He sped up. "I just need to make it to the next turn and we'll be off this one-way street."

At that moment a van came around the bend, heading straight for them.

"Spencer, look out!"

Both the van and their Honda came to a dead halt just inches apart.

Jasmine gripped her chest. "Look what you did. Now we're stuck. There's no room for that van to get around us, and there's a car behind him."

Spencer still wasn't rattled. He put the car in reverse and started moving backward.

"What's wrong with you? You can't back all the way up this street."

He laughed. "Sure I can. I drive backwards even better than I drive forward. Before he let me go for my license, my dad made me master driving around our court in reverse."

To prove his point, Spencer sped to the intersection backward, then proceeded to turn the corner and back all the way up to the main road, where he finally turned around.

"See," he said, sending her a smug look.

Jasmine just rolled her eyes. "I'm not impressed. You're a *backward*-thinking cretin with an ass-*backward* attitude. It's no surprise you like driving backward as well."

Finally, he pulled into his driveway. Jasmine followed Spencer into his house. "There's no way I'm getting in a car with you behind the wheel ever again."

He went to the refrigerator and winked from over his shoulder. "Why not? I'm an excellent driver, and that's not the only thing I'm very good at."

Jasmine took the soda he offered her, trying to ignore his last remark. Just when she was starting to think he might be a decent human being . . .

Somehow, agreeing to accept the less-attractive aspects of their personalities had lifted a giant burden from their relationship. For a minute, she'd been sure they would start to get along.

Spencer looked at her from across the kitchen counter. "Hey, don't look at me like that. Look on the bright side. We got through that experience without killing each other."

"Not that you didn't *try* to kill us both."

"Why would I try to kill you? We're partners."

Jasmine quirked her brow. "Oh, so we're partners now, are we?"

"Sure. We both want to keep me alive. That makes us a kind of a team, don't you think?"

She thought for a moment. After the stunt he'd just pulled in the car, she wasn't sure how interested she was in keeping him alive after all. Then she remembered Nathan. The only thing her boss had been right about was that her pride was not the issue here. She still had to try to get along with Spencer.

"A team? That's not a bad way to look at it.

Contrary to your first impression of me, we *are* both on the same side."

Jasmine smiled at the idea of her and Spencer as a team. Under different circumstances, she probably would have taken an immediate liking to him. Despite his rebellious nature, at times he could be quite charming.

"You should do that more often," Spencer said.

"Do what?" When had he moved in so close?

"Smile. It's a killer."

"Um, thanks." Jasmine became flustered as a sudden rush of heat spread through her. The last thing she needed was to feel attraction. Her job would be difficult enough without that little distraction.

Despite her self-reproach, Jasmine couldn't stifle the wistfulness suddenly welling inside her. How long had it been since she'd been with a man?

A year and a half.

The reality of it slammed into her. The time had passed like seconds, and for the most part, she hadn't missed the sex. Sure, there were times when she'd felt the absence of male companionship— when she attended weddings alone or turned down invitations to formal events because she didn't have an escort.

Still, those times had been rare over the past several months. She'd been content to focus on her career, remodel her town house, and spend quality time with her nieces and nephews. Her last boyfriend had been such an emotional and sexual disappointment that she hadn't been in any hurry to enter a new relationship.

She'd even begun to marvel at the emphasis the world placed on sex. Her long abstinence hadn't been intentional, but her life had been perfectly satisfying without it.

Or so she'd thought.

Spencer's nearness made Jasmine question that satisfaction.

What was she thinking? She didn't even *like* this man. Just as she was starting to move back, Spencer stepped in closer. "That look must mean you feel it, too."

Then his lips were on hers.

4

*S*pencer held Jasmine close, savoring the softness of her lips and the sweet floral scent of her perfume. She pressed her mouth against his in return for just a moment before he felt her hands pushing at his chest.

He released her and stepped back. Jasmine brought her fingers to her lips, staring at her feet in silence. Slowly she raised her eyes to meet his. "Spencer . . ."

"You're not going to slap me, are you?" He laughed, trying to lighten the mood. He hadn't planned on kissing Jasmine, but he'd gotten caught up in the moment. Regardless of the consequences, he didn't regret it.

Jasmine's eyes took on a strange look. "No . . ."

"But? I can tell there's a but coming." He took a step back and leaned against the counter to wait for it. He should have expected this. For a few minutes, he'd forgotten who he was dealing with.

"*But* . . . you know that kiss wasn't a good idea."

"Why not? It's what we both wanted. Don't bother trying to deny it. You kissed me back."

She fiddled with the gold stud in her ear. He'd never seen her this frazzled before.

"You caught me off guard."

"Proving that your reaction was real."

She gave him a pleading look. "My only focus has to be my job. It's inappropriate for me to engage in this type of behavior with you."

"We haven't behaved *appropriately* together yet. Why start now?" He tried to charm her with his smile. He expected her to put up a fight, but he planned to fight back. Despite her words, there were a lot of sparks flying between them.

"I know you understand what I'm trying to say. Please don't make this any more awkward than it has to be."

Spencer stood rigidly, staring at Jasmine. Why was she affecting him this way? It was clear they had nothing in common. In his head, he knew getting involved with her was a mistake, but for some reason he really didn't want to hear it.

He folded his arms across his chest, feeling tension locking up his muscles. Spencer knew he was acting like a sulky child who'd just been told he couldn't have his toy of choice. If he stood there any longer, he would make an even bigger ass of himself than he already had.

Heat suffused his face. "Fine. Suit yourself."

He could feel Jasmine's eyes on his back as he made his hasty retreat. She called for him to come back, but he pretended not to hear her.

Spencer locked his bedroom door just in case she decided to follow him. She'd already demanded free run of the house for security purposes. His privacy was quickly becoming scarce.

Pacing the floor, Spencer tried to get a grip on reality. Just because she made his temperature rise didn't mean he had to get all mushy and throw himself at her. She probably thought he was some sex-starved idiot.

That had always been his problem. Women mistook him for a player, but he had never gotten the act down pat. He could talk a good game, but when it came down to it, Spencer couldn't help wearing his heart on his sleeve.

Fortunately—or unfortunately—the slick image he worked so hard to maintain kept women from taking him too seriously. And, more often than not, *he* was the one to get his heart broken.

If he wasn't careful, he'd be walking down that same road with Jasmine. It was difficult not to find her attractive. She was so sharp and sassy. Not only did she challenge him, she wasn't impressed by his fast talk.

And she had a vulnerable side, too. He'd finally seen her with her guard down when she'd mentioned her father that afternoon. Obviously, she hadn't meant to reveal that much of her personal life to him—but the more he got to know her the more he liked her.

He had to nip this problem in the bud. Time for damage control. What he needed was a date. Dinner with a beautiful woman would put things back into perspective.

Where was his electronic organizer? He had to decide which lucky lady to call.

As Spencer hunted for his Palm Pilot, he caught sight of something white peeking out from under his bedspread. He bent to pick it up, and a smile of amusement stretched his lips. It was Vanessa's business card. It must have fallen out of his pants pocket when he undressed last night.

When he'd taken the card from her, he'd fully intended to throw it out. He wasn't really into strippers. No mystery there. Plus, he wasn't really good at sharing when it came to women. His taste in stripteases leaned toward private shows.

Spencer walked over to the wastebasket and dropped the card in. "Sorry, Vanessa."

He started to walk away, but instead found himself bending to fish the card back out. He needed a distraction and Vanessa would definitely be that.

On the other hand, if he did call Vanessa, he'd never hear the end of Jasmine's smart mouth.

He started to drop the card back into the trash when a wicked thought entered his mind. He could picture the look on Jasmine's face when she saw Vanessa. It would be worth a lifetime of smart remarks. Spencer picked up his phone and began to dial.

Jasmine paced Spencer's kitchen, tracing the outline of her lips with her index finger. That kiss—she couldn't stop thinking about it.

Why did her first high-profile client have to be such a good kisser?

Worse yet, Spencer had acted as though she'd genuinely hurt his feelings—but that didn't make any sense. Bruised his ego, maybe. That she could believe.

Spencer Powell could have any woman he wanted. She'd heard that he'd even been named one of *Ebony* magazine's "100 Most Eligible Bachelors." So why should he care that the two of them couldn't mix business with pleasure? Ego or no ego, there wasn't any logical reason for him to be offended by the truth.

In fact, she'd said far worse to him her first day on the job. Sure, they'd started to bond while they were in the car. But it hadn't taken him long to ruin the moment with his reckless driving.

One thing was for certain. She and Spencer definitely had chemistry. The question was, did they have the *right* chemistry? Experience had taught her that mixing the wrong particles resulted in explosions.

She didn't have time to clean up any more disasters like her last one.

Whether he liked it or not, Spencer would just have to accept that she was one woman he couldn't have. He'd get over it.

Jasmine glanced down at her watch. He'd been in his bedroom for quite some time now. She'd better check on him.

She went upstairs and knocked on his door. "Spencer? Is everything okay?"

"Fine," he shouted back. "I'm on the telephone."

"Okay. I'll be in the kitchen if you need me."

Jasmine returned to the kitchen and pulled a stool up to the counter. Normally, this would be a good time to read a book or a magazine, but she had way too much energy surging through her to sit still.

In the past few months, she'd discovered that there was one thing that never failed to soothe her frazzled nerves. But could she do it here? Spencer might be offended if he walked in on her. She didn't think she'd feel comfortable doing it in someone else's home.

Her fingers drummed on the counter as she tried to make a decision. Knowing Spencer, he'd probably enjoy it. It might even serve as a sort of peace offering.

With her mind made up, Jasmine began opening cabinets. She'd learned in her counseling sessions that baking was an ideal outlet when she was on edge. Mixing batter and beating eggs released her built-up aggression.

Jasmine was in luck. She found a box of blueberry muffin mix in Spencer's pantry. She preferred to bake from scratch, but beggars couldn't be choosers.

She had to hand it to Spencer; he had a well-kept kitchen. She'd pegged him as a typical bachelor with only a few of the main staples on hand, but he had all the major kitchen accessories and a fully stocked fridge. In no time, she'd prepared the batter, poured it into the muffin pan, and placed it in the oven.

Jasmine was just pulling the pan out of the oven when Spencer wandered into the kitchen.

"What's that smell?"

She felt the heat of embarrassment creep up her neck. Jasmine was sure it was bad etiquette for her to take over his kitchen and commandeer his food without permission.

"I baked some muffins. I apologize for not asking you first, but I needed something to keep myself occupied."

Spencer leaned over the golden brown blueberry muffin domes and inhaled deeply. "Feel free to bake in my kitchen any time you want. These look delicious."

She walked over to the table and sat down. "They need a few minutes to cool, but after that, help yourself."

"Don't mind if I do," he said, taking a plate out of one of the cabinets. Then he moved over to the refrigerator and poured himself a glass of milk. "By the way, I have plans this evening."

"Really? What's on the agenda?" She envisioned another wild night on the town with the guys.

He looked over and locked eyes with her. "I have a date."

Her mouth became dry, reminding Jasmine to raise her hanging jaw. So much for hurting his feelings. Clearly, he didn't have any. It certainly hadn't taken him long to move on to the next woman. Or maybe he'd had this date planned all along and had kissed her anyway.

Typical male, scumbag, pig! He could date whomever he wanted to, but his safety was still *her* responsibility.

The words stuck in her throat, but she tried to recover quickly. "Who will you be going out with?"

His grin broadened. "Remember Vanessa from the club last night?"

The image of a voluptuous woman stuffed into a skintight dress, wild hair, and red talons flashed in her mind. It figured that he went for that type. "I'm not sure that's a wise choice."

"Why not? Are you jealous?"

Her eyes widened. Is that what he was up to? Was he still trying to play games with her? "I have nothing to be jealous about. My job is to protect you. I wish I didn't have to keep reminding you of that. How much do you know about this Vanessa person? How did you meet her? Did she approach you, or did you approach her?"

"She approached me, but—"

"See, there's no way to be sure this isn't a setup."

"That's a bit extreme, don't you think?"

"No. We don't know who or what we're dealing with."

"Well, I refuse to put my life on hold, so you're just going to have to earn your money."

He brought his muffin over to the table and sat next to her. "How does this work? I assume you're going to follow us in a separate car and sit and watch us from another table in the restaurant?"

Jasmine smiled to herself. She bet he would like that. It gave her great pleasure to burst his bubble. "I'm afraid since I'm the only guard on duty, I need to maintain a closer proximity to protect you. We'll ride in the *same* car and I'll sit at *your* table. Deal with it."

She stood and started rinsing off the dishes she'd used to bake the muffins.

"Are you kidding me? How am I supposed to explain you to Vanessa?"

It was her turn to grin wickedly. "That's your problem."

Spencer swore under his breath.

She looked down at her blue jeans. "I suppose I'm going to need to change my clothes. Where are you taking us?"

He named an expensive restaurant. "But I don't know if I can change the reservation from two to three."

"Then you'd better get on the phone right now. I'd hate for you to have to take Vanessa to McDonald's."

On the way to pick up Vanessa that evening, Spencer began to realize that this date might not have been such a good idea after all.

Jasmine sat in the passenger seat, cheerfully humming to the song on the radio. She'd shown up wearing a black dress. Nothing spectacular—except that it ended about four inches above her knees, giving him an uninterrupted view of her long shapely legs in black nylons.

He couldn't wait to get on the road. The sooner he saw Vanessa—decked out in something delightfully trashy—the sooner he'd forget about Jasmine's killer stems.

But once they'd gotten out the door, he'd practically had to wrestle Jasmine for the car keys. He'd refused to travel in her boring little blue sedan, and she'd refused to let him get behind the wheel of his car. It was bad enough that she had to ride in the same vehicle, but he wasn't about to have her chauffeuring him around like he was some kind of low-rent playboy.

She'd finally consented to let him drive, but he still had no idea how to explain this bizarre scenario to Vanessa.

Now, as he exited onto Cabin John Parkway, he was tempted to turn the car around and forget the whole thing. He stole another glance at Jasmine. She looked perfectly content. That would change after he picked up Vanessa.

He punched the gas pedal and turned up the radio. He had to make the best of the situation.

"Slow it down, Spencer."

He stomped harder on the gas.

Jasmine gripped the door handle. "Look, I'm not going through this again. You promised to behave yourself. What are you trying to prove?"

He eased down on the brake a bit, turning to look at her. "I'll confess if you do."

He barely had time to note her stunned expression before the flashing blue and red lights in his rearview mirror distracted him.

"Great. Just great," Jasmine said, slapping her thigh. "I knew I shouldn't have let you drive."

"Damn it." Spencer pulled over to the side of the road.

He rolled down the window, and an officer leaned in. "Do you know why I pulled you over?"

"Speeding?" He passed his license and registration through the window. "Would you believe my wife is having a baby?"

The officer's gaze moved past Spencer to the passenger seat. "White? Is that you?"

Startled, Spencer turned to Jasmine. Pursing her lips, she nodded. "Hey, Rabinowitz."

"Isn't that something? Are you married to this joker?"

Spencer had forgotten that she was an ex-cop. Great, maybe this could work to his advantage. "Yes, she is, Officer."

"What! Don't you believe it, Rabinowitz. This man is a danger to society. Arrest him."

Spencer raised his arms heavenward. He should have known that she'd give him away.

Rabinowitz propped his arms on the open window. "Too bad. The fellows down at the precinct would have loved to hear that you'd finally settled down, White."

"Throw the book at him, Rabinowitz. The way I see it, you've got him on exceeding the speed limit, reckless endangerment, and if you count that whopper he tried to tell you, obstructing justice."

A nerve started throbbing in Spencer's forehead. "For God's sake, will you shut up!"

The officer grinned at Jasmine. "Since he's such a good friend of yours, I'll let him off with a warning. Just slow down for me, okay?" Rabinowitz handed back Spencer's license and registration. "Hey, White. You still working as a security guard?"

"Close protection specialist," she bit out.

"Yeah, yeah. Good luck with that." He punched Spencer in the arm. "And good luck to you, buddy. She's a handful."

Spencer pulled back onto the parkway, laughing heartily.

"All you men stick together, don't you?"

"Hey, get over it. At least I got out of the speeding ticket. Despite your best attempts to besmirch my reputation, the good officer recognized me as the upstanding citizen that I am."

"We wouldn't have been pulled over in the first place if you hadn't been driving like a maniac. I should never have trusted you. Never again."

Spencer ignored Jasmine's complaints, driving the rest of the way with much higher spirits. When they arrived at Vanessa's condo, he motioned for Jasmine to stay in the car.

"You can see me from here. I just need a minute to explain you to my date." He expected an argument, but Jasmine simply shrugged.

"Fine, but stay in the doorway where I can see you."

He rang the bell, smiling with anticipation.

The door opened. "Spencer, hi. You're right on time."

He smiled at the woman before him and started to ask for Vanessa . . . until he realized he was looking at her.

"Vanessa?" He couldn't believe this was the same woman he'd met last night.

She laughed, looking down at her green-and-white floral print jumper. She looked like she'd just stepped off *Little House on the Prairie*. "I know this isn't what you were expecting. You were such a gentleman last night, I knew you were different from most of the men I meet at clubs. I thought I'd take a chance and show you the real me. Is this okay?"

Spencer nodded vigorously, trying to hide his stupefaction. Saying she looked different was an understatement. After seeing every curve outlined in red spandex, he'd never expected her to show up in this schoolmarmish, shapeless outfit complete with a little white sweater that had a lacy collar.

Reading his eager head bobbing as approval, Vanessa beamed back at him. "I wanted you to meet my son, but the baby-sitter is upstairs putting him to bed."

"You have a little boy?"

"Yes, he's four, and he's the love of my life."

"Oh, well, maybe I can meet him next time."

What was he saying? There couldn't be a next time. He'd made a terrible mistake. Vanessa wasn't turning out to be the superficial, good-time girl he'd thought she was. His gut ached with guilt—he'd just have to show her the best time he could and leave it at that.

Pressing a hand to his churning stomach, he asked, "Are you ready to go?"

"Sure, just let me get my purse."

Spencer threw a glance over his shoulder and saw Jasmine sitting in the car. Damn! During his mental breakdown, he'd forgotten that she was sitting out there waiting for him.

Vanessa came back with her purse over her shoulder and began locking up.

"Uh, Vanessa . . ."

"Yes." She turned around, looking past him. "Who is that in your car?"

"I forgot to mention that my cousin is passing through town. I didn't want to leave her home alone, so I invited her to join us. Is that okay?"

"Of course." She tucked her arm through his. "I think it's so sweet that you brought a chaperone. I bet you weren't sure you could trust yourself alone with me, were you? Well, don't worry. Despite my current occupation, I'm really just a small-town girl at heart."

"Great. That's *just* what I wanted to hear."

Spencer led Vanessa to the car, gazing heavenward. This was going to be one very long night.

Jasmine followed Spencer and Vanessa to their table, grinning smugly at Spencer's back. She'd anticipated a miserable evening as the official third wheel, but she was actually beginning to think she might enjoy herself.

Too bad she couldn't say the same for Spencer. He'd barely said two words since they'd gotten in the car, giving Jasmine and Vanessa a chance to chat. To her surprise, she was getting along with the other woman very well.

Jasmine had toyed with the idea of using some of her contacts to run a background check on Vanessa, but now she doubted that would be necessary. At only twenty-two, the girl had led a very colorful life, and she didn't seem to have any qualms about sharing the highlights with them.

After ten minutes in a car with Vanessa, Jasmine had learned that the woman had been divorced twice, had a four-year-old, and had worked an array of jobs, including hand-dipping candles, selling funeral plots door-to-door, and her current position: silhouette dancing at a gentlemen's club.

It was Jasmine's job to read people, and she concluded that Vanessa was harmless. Still, she wasn't going to allow Spencer to let his guard down. She was holding her position that he shouldn't have made this date in the first place.

The waiter handed out menus, and Jasmine nearly fell out of her seat when she saw the prices. With wide eyes she stole a glance at Spencer. He didn't seem fazed in the least by the pricy items.

Shaking her head, Jasmine realized she shouldn't have been surprised. Spencer's house was located in one of the most expensive neighborhoods in Maryland. Though his taste in furniture ran toward the basic utilitarian necessities, when it came to stereo equipment, televisions, and other electronic appliances, it seemed Spencer had spared no expense.

Clearly, he hadn't grown up watching every dime as Jasmine had. Even though she made more than enough money for a comfortable living, she still couldn't bring herself to spend a penny more than was necessary.

Vanessa didn't seem to be having any problems with the prices, either. When the waiter came for their orders, she asked for the most expensive item without batting an eyelash. Though this was the perfect opportunity to stick it to Spencer, Jasmine ordered a salad.

After the waiter left them, Vanessa began to fiddle with the cloth napkin that was arranged in the shape of a rose at her place setting. "So what do you do for a living, Jasmine? I talked about myself so much on the drive over, I didn't get a chance to find out anything about you."

Spencer sat up straighter in his seat, shooting Jasmine a warning glance. Obviously, he was afraid she would blow his cover story as she had with Officer Rabinowitz. The fact was, she didn't know *what* to say.

"Actually, I'm—"

"Psychic," Spencer finished.

"What?" Jasmine and Vanessa asked in unison.

Vanessa pinned Jasmine with an expectant look. "You're a psychic?"

Jasmine chewed on her lip. Here was another opportunity to bust Spencer, but her job was to blend in, not cause scenes. "Uh, actually . . . I prefer the term clairvoyant." She didn't dare meet Spencer's eyes. "It's not so much a career as a . . . uh, hobby."

"Don't be modest, Jasmine," Spencer said, clearly recovering his mischievous spirit. He turned to Vanessa. "She's really very good. It's amazing. Back in Spokane—where she lives— she has her own telephone hot line."

Vanessa's eyes lit up. "You mean like the Psychic Friends Network? Wow, I've never met a real psych—I mean clairvoyant before."

Jasmine pressed her lips together. It was time to change the subject. She should never have gone along with Spencer's outrageous story in the first place.

Spencer was smiling slyly. "Go ahead, Jasmine. Read her palm."

"Spencer!"

Vanessa was already stretching her hand across the table. "Would you please?"

Jasmine cursed Spencer under her breath. He would pay for this. She'd show him not to put her on the spot, she thought, taking Vanessa's hand.

Taking a deep breath, Jasmine prayed that Vanessa didn't know any more about palmistry than she did. The long one was the life line, right? "You've got a very strong life line. You've had some struggles in your past, but you came through them just fine. Um, you're coming to a crossroads in the future. One path is a dead end, but the other will lead you to happiness and prosperity."

Great, now she sounded like a fortune cookie.

"What about my love line?" Vanessa grinned, shooting Spencer a coy smile.

Jasmine swallowed. Which one was the love line? She glanced at Spencer, who was grinning broadly. "Ah, your love line . . . I see that you still haven't found Mr. Right. You're more compatible with a professional man, like a doctor or a lawyer. Someone with a stable career. Stay away from the creative types, rock stars, artists, and the like—they're not equipped for long-term relationships."

Jasmine threw in a few other pithy phrases she'd heard on television to round out her predictions.

"How exciting," Vanessa said after Jasmine finished. "Thank you."

"No problem," Jasmine said, turning to Spencer. "Now, it's your turn Spencer."

His smile was stiff. "No, that's okay. I don't want to exploit your craft."

"Oh, no, I insist." Jasmine grabbed Spencer's

wrist and jerked it roughly across the table. "I'm sure you're eager to find out what the future holds for you."

"I think I already know," Spencer answered, loud enough for only Jasmine to hear.

As soon as Jasmine pulled into Spencer's driveway, he darted out of the car. They walked to the house in the same silence they'd driven home in. She entered the house first so she could make sure everything was secure.

Normally, once she completed her walk-through, it would be time for Jasmine to leave. Instead, she went to find Spencer in the kitchen.

He was halfway into one muffin and held a second in his hand. Considering that he'd barely touched his dinner, it didn't surprise her that he was starving.

"Why haven't you left yet?" he asked, chewing.

This time Jasmine didn't need to call upon any of her temper-management techniques. She felt eerily calm inside. "I need to talk to you."

He rolled his eyes. "Save it. Can't a brother eat a muffin in peace?"

Jasmine ignored him. "I think it was really cruel of you to use that poor girl the way you did."

He dropped the muffins on the counter. "Oh, now she's a 'poor girl.' This afternoon you thought she was a skanky tramp."

Jasmine chewed her lip. "I never said that."

"You thought it."

She felt her cheeks heat. "That was before I got to know her better."

"She's still a stripper."

"She's also a single mother trying to make a living the only way she knows how. She thought she was going out with a man who was interested in *her*, not in trying to make another woman jealous."

Spencer stared at her for a moment, then went to the refrigerator to retrieve a milk carton. Jasmine waited as he filled his glass and returned the carton to the fridge. Finally, he looked up at her. "I wasn't trying to make you jealous."

"That's a lie and you know it. Ever since I rejected your kiss this afternoon, you've been acting moody. Then the next thing I know, you've made yourself a date."

"Oh, you didn't reject my kiss. As I recall, you were kissing me back with everything you had."

Jasmine swallowed, not sure how to respond to that. She had enjoyed the kiss, and she'd thought of little else since it had happened—but that was only because she knew she couldn't let it happen again.

"You can't keep playing these games, Spencer. I'm not here as your sexual plaything, I'm here because your life may be in danger. This isn't a joke."

"Give me a break, Jasmine. The station is wasting its money. There haven't been any attacks on my life and there aren't going to be."

"You know, I hope you're right about that, but until we know for sure, my job is to keep you safe. You've got to start taking that seriously. I know I might have encouraged your bad behavior and childish antics by my own lapse in professionalism, but that ends now."

Jasmine shook her head, trying to find the words to get through to him. "I'm not here to cramp your social life, but you can't play any more games like the one you played tonight. No more setting up dates for my benefit. You could have put yourself and Vanessa right in the line of fire."

"You didn't have to send Vanessa into a panic by telling her that you're my bodyguard."

"I had to tell her the truth. How else could I explain the gun? She saw it in my purse while we were in the ladies' room. Maybe I could have played it off if you hadn't already told her I was psychic."

"I was just trying to keep things interesting."

"You didn't have to insist that I read her palm. I didn't know what the hell I was doing."

"Well, you sure were eager to read mine, telling her I was a fickle playboy who was reckless with money."

She shrugged. "What can I say? I can only use my powers for good." Since he'd been making up stories at her expense all night, she'd decided to use her role as his "cousin" to her own advantage. Jasmine had told Vanessa a few embarrassing stories about Spencer's childhood that she'd made up on the spot.

"I just wanted to go out and have a nice dinner. There might have been hope for the evening if you and Vanessa hadn't ganged up on me."

"Did you expect her to thank you for lying to her and making her feel like a fool? In the end, she thought we were both so crazy that she refused to ride in the same car with us. The poor girl was forced to take a cab home by herself."

"Look, I already apologized to Vanessa, and I'm apologizing to you. Now, will you please go home? I have a headache, and I'm going to bed."

He walked out of the kitchen and jogged up the stairs to his bedroom. Jasmine followed, hot on his heels.

"Don't walk away from me."

Spencer whirled around and threw his hands up. "What?"

"I need to know that you won't pull any more outrageous stunts. Every time I think we're making some progress, you pull something like this. You might as well admit that you did all of this because of that kiss."

He raised his eyes to hers, looking weary and defeated. Jasmine almost backed down, wondering if she'd done the right thing by forcing the issue. It was getting late. She could have brought this up tomorrow.

Spencer shook his head. "Fine. I'll admit it. That kiss threw me for a loop. After you blew me off as though it had absolutely no effect on you, I lost my head for a minute. I called Vanessa on an impulse. I thought your reaction to my going on a date would somehow prove that you'd felt something when we kissed."

Jasmine sucked in her breath.

He paced the floor in front of her. "Instead, I had a nightmarish evening, you and Vanessa got gourmet meals, and I ate peanuts at the bar. So the answer is no. I will not be pulling any more outrageous stunts like this one."

Jasmine started to speak, but Spencer held up his finger and said, "Now I want to know something."

He advanced on her, and Jasmine backed up against the wall. "What is it?" she whispered.

He caged her in with his arms. "Are you going to stand there and deny that you wanted that kiss just as much as I did?"

She swallowed hard. "I didn't say . . . It's just that we can't—"

He leaned in closer. She could feel his breath on her chin. "Can't what?"

Jasmine blinked, trying to clear her fuzzy brain. Suddenly she couldn't remember what the question was. "Can't . . . we can't—"

Ah, to hell with it. Why couldn't she . . . just this once?

Sliding her arms around his neck, Jasmine

brought her face up to meet Spencer's. She pressed her lips against his, and instantly the kiss deepened. The rhythm of the kiss was both quick and slow. Quick nips at the lips. Slow strokes of their tongues.

Not wanting to think about anything at that moment, Jasmine let herself become absorbed by their kisses. Warm, tingling heat spread down her abdomen.

The phone was ringing, but Spencer made no move to answer it. Instead, he pulled her more tightly against him, and she could feel his arousal.

The answering machine clicked on in the background, and Jasmine's mind vaguely registered the sound of a strange voice singing.

A warning signal went off in her brain, overriding her sensually charged nerve endings. Jerking out of Spencer's embrace, she dashed across the room to the answering machine and hit the rewind button.

Spencer stood motionless in the middle of the room. "What the hell is wrong now?"

"I'm not sure. Let's find out." She hit the play button. She recognized the sexless voice she'd heard on the air the other night:

Mr. Sandman, bring me a dream,
I want to wake up and hear you scream.
I want to see the fear in your eyes,
And when it's over . . . everyone dies.

5

Spencer stood frozen as Jasmine rewound the tape and hit play again. A chill ran down his spine as he listened to his stalker's words.

"My God, she knows where I live. My phone number isn't listed."

"You said 'she.' Do you have any idea who this person might be?" Jasmine was back in professional mode. He could hardly believe this was the same woman he'd been making out with not two minutes earlier.

Spencer shrugged, lowering his body to the edge of the bed. "I always just assumed it was a woman. Why? Do you think it's a man?"

Jasmine played the tape again, and Spencer winced. He'd be hearing that creepy voice in his sleep.

"It's hard to tell the sex of the caller from this recording. According to Tali, all of the calls have had this same kind of voice distortion." She punched a couple of numbers into the phone. "The call's out of range for star sixty-nine. It was probably coming from a pay phone anyway. Tomorrow I want you to order caller ID."

Spencer nodded, running his hands down his face. This was the first time he'd received any kind of threat at his personal residence. Over the years, he'd gotten telephone calls of every kind at the station—95 percent were from women offering sexual favors. The only phone number he ever distributed or allowed to be published belonged to his answering service. Up until now, that had been enough to prevent anyone from contacting him at home.

Jasmine walked over and knelt in front of him. "This call raises the stakes, Spencer. Now we know that your stalker has access to you. With today's technology, it's not a giant leap from a telephone number to an address."

He swallowed hard. For the first time since Jasmine showed up on his doorstep, Spencer was at a loss for words. He took what she was saying to heart. Maybe there really was someone out there who wanted to hurt him.

Jasmine moved to sit beside him on the edge of the bed. "I know what you're thinking right now. It's very hard to accept that someone may want to do you harm. We've gone over this before, but this is very important. Can you think of anyone you know personally who might have a reason to want to scare you or worse?"

Spencer tried to focus on Jasmine's question, but his mind was darting all over the place. Was someone watching him? Standing outside his house at that very moment? What could he possibly have done to make someone want to hurt him? Did this person really want him dead?

"I don't know," he answered.

"Think. Ex-girlfriends? Any of them still lingering around?"

Normally, that would have been the perfect setup for Spencer to tease Jasmine about her interest in his love life, but for once he wasn't in much of a joking mood.

"Ex-girlfriends? The last woman I dated seriously was Angela Bowers. It ended almost a year ago."

Jasmine retrieved her purse, taking out a pad and pen to write down the name. "How did it end? On good terms?"

He released a halfhearted chuckle. "Yeah, we're still on good terms. In fact, she's invited me to her wedding in August."

Spencer had fallen hard for Angela. She'd actually broken up with *him*. As something of a local celebrity, he'd been able to take her wherever she'd wanted to go and buy her whatever she'd wanted.

That had been good enough, until Angela

caught herself a bigger fish swimming in a deeper pond. Once she'd started dating a host of BET's late-night talk show, she'd wanted nothing more to do with Spencer. After all, TV was a lot more lucrative than radio.

"What about before Angela? Any bad breakups? Any women whose feelings might have been unrequited?"

He rubbed his temples. His head was throbbing. "I don't know. I just can't think about this right now."

Spencer held his breath, expecting Jasmine to try to push the issue, but to his surprise she just nodded. "Okay. It *is* getting late."

Spencer's gaze strayed over to the answering machine.

"You know, I'm a little too tired to get on the road," Jasmine said. "Do you mind if I crash on your couch?"

Spencer opened his mouth to make a lewd suggestion about where she could sleep, but the words never made it past his lips. "I have a spare bedroom down the hall. Sheets and towels are in the linen closet outside the bedroom door. Help yourself to whatever you need."

"Thanks, well . . . um, good night."

She turned and left the room, leaving Spencer to stare after her. He would never admit it out loud, but he would sleep a lot easier that night just knowing that she was nearby.

Jasmine woke up the next morning feeling disoriented. Spencer's guest room was more than comfortable, but it wasn't home. For instance, her home was a lot more modest.

The four-piece modern bedroom set was simple but expensive, as were the combination TV/VCR across the room and the clock radio and CD player on the nightstand. As she'd noticed at the restaurant last night, Spencer didn't worry about money, and he spent it as though he'd never had to.

The rest of his house reflected the same unconscious opulence of the guest bedroom. Jasmine shook her head as she entered the bathroom to brush her teeth and wash her face. She was sure it must be nice to spend money so carelessly, but growing up the way she had, she knew it wasn't something she'd ever get used to.

When she came out of the bathroom, Jasmine inhaled the unmistakable scent of bacon. Obviously, Spencer was up early. She hoped he hadn't had any trouble sleeping.

Dressing in a fresh change of clothes, thanks to the overnight bag she kept in the car for just such an occasion, Jasmine went downstairs to join Spencer in the kitchen.

"Good morning," she said, watching his face carefully.

He gave her a bright smile that came across as forced. "Good morning, Jasmine. Sleep okay?"

She nodded, taking a seat at the table. "Just fine. What about you?"

He waved off her question as he hustled to scoop a healthy serving of scrambled eggs, bacon, and fried potatoes onto a plate for her. "I slept like a rock. I must have been tired."

Jasmine continued to study Spencer. He was bouncing around the kitchen with a happy-go-lucky attitude, but she suspected that it was all an act. Nevertheless, she was going to take advantage of his positive mood and try to clear the air between them.

"Spencer, maybe now would be a good time for us to talk about what happened last night."

He started to sit across from her, then popped up at the last minute. "Oh, I almost forgot." He left the room for a minute, returning with a sheet of paper. "This is a list of my ex-girlfriends dating back to high school, if it helps any. I don't think any of them are out to get me, but what can I say? I can be a hard guy to get over."

Jasmine glanced at the list, then set it aside. "This is great, thanks. I'm sure it will help, but that wasn't what I meant. I think we should talk about what happened before the telephone call."

Spencer paused with his mouth full of eggs. Finally, he shook his head and continued to chew. "You're not getting all worked up over a few kisses again, are you? Look, if you want to pretend it never happened, fine. We'll pretend it never happened."

"Spencer, I don't think—"

"What?" he snapped.

Now it was Jasmine's turn to pause. Judging by the look in his eyes, his happy-go-lucky mood had changed to happy-go-homicidal. Clearly, he didn't want to talk about this.

"Um . . . I just don't think it's that simple," she finished quietly.

"Why not? It's that simple if we make it that simple. If you want to pretend there's nothing between us, go right ahead. I don't care. How are your eggs? I made them with two kinds of cheese."

"Delicious . . . uh, thanks." Jasmine let him change the subject. She wasn't going to get anywhere with this discussion right now. He had a lot to deal with. Her presence was supposed to give him peace of mind, not add to his stress level.

Maybe he was right, anyway. Maybe things *didn't* have to be so complicated between them. If they both agreed that things wouldn't go any further, then they wouldn't. It was as simple as that.

Early in the afternoon, Jasmine packed up her things to leave Spencer's house. He kept assuring her that he was fine, and though she wasn't quite convinced, she didn't have any excuse to stick around. Plus, there were some chores around her own home that she'd been neglecting. She left reluctantly, telling Spencer to call if he needed her.

By the time Jasmine reached her town house, her emotions were in such turmoil that she went straight to the kitchen and baked a pan of brownies. There was something about the sweet scent of baked goods filling the air that was comforting. She'd just set the pan on the counter to cool when the telephone rang.

"Hello?" she answered.

"Minnie! How's my girl doing?"

"Coby, are you back in town?"

At thirty, Coby was the youngest of Jasmine's four older brothers. Since he was only two years older than she was, he was also the brother she felt closest to.

"Yeah, New York isn't all it's cracked up to be. So, it looks like I'm going to be around for a while."

"What about your music video?"

"It's on the shelf for now. LinkStar Records didn't come through with the money after all. I think the label's going under."

"Oh, no. I'm sorry to hear that." But Jasmine wasn't surprised. Coby wanted to be a rap singer, but he had a short attention span. He wasn't the best at completing projects. Thankfully, his deejay business pulled in just enough money for him to get by.

She wedged the phone between her ear and her shoulder, so she could cut herself a brownie.

"Listen, where are you staying? We should get together."

"Uh . . . yeah, that's why I was calling. I was wondering if I could crash at your place until my apartment's ready?"

Jasmine shook her head, smiling at the phone. "Sure, I guess so. Where are you now?"

"I just got off the highway. I'll be turning onto your street in two minutes."

Jasmine opened her front door and walked onto the porch to wait for him. "Pretty confident, aren't you? What would you have done if I wasn't home?"

"Gotten back on the Beltway. The Tinman's only forty-five minutes away."

"The Tinman" referred to their older brother Justin. Their mother had thought it would be cute to give all of her children names starting with the letter *J*. But it soon became clear that having five people in one household with *J* names could be quite confusing. Even their mother couldn't keep the names straight.

Finally, after too many episodes of having Jason appear when she really wanted Jerome, the family devised a nickname system. Jerome, the oldest at forty-two, went by the name Rome. Next in line was Justin, at thirty-six, who became the Tinman. Then there was Jason, who, at thirty-four, thought he was too old to be known as Sonny and refused to allow anyone outside the family to call him by that name.

Jacob, the youngest of the four boys, had been nicknamed Coby. And Jasmine was affectionately referred to as Minnie. Like Jason, Jasmine, too, felt she'd outgrown her name, but old habits died hard. When it came to the family, she was stuck with the name.

"Why would you drive all the way to Baltimore? Sonny's closer and much more likely to be around now that school's almost out."

"Because Sonny would probably make me sleep in the bathtub. That is, if he let me through the front door."

"Don't tell me that the two of you are still arguing about what to do with Grandma's house?"

"You know how Sonny is. Mr. College Professor, thinking he knows everything. He doesn't like it when anyone disagrees with him, and since my idea is more . . ."

"Extreme?"

"*Forward-thinking* than everyone else's, he's trying to bully me into siding with him. Don't you think—"

"Oh, no, I'm not getting in the middle of this one. I already told you, whatever the four of you decide, I'll go along with."

Jasmine's brothers were always squabbling about something, and it seemed it always fell to her to straighten things out. This time she was determined to be Switzerland.

Their family had never had anything of value, so when their grandmother died and left her house and the surrounding land to be divided among her five grandchildren, chaos broke out among the brothers. Coby wanted to turn it into a bed-and-breakfast, Sonny wanted to preserve it for posterity, the Tinman wanted to sell the property and split the money, and Rome wanted to remodel the house and move in with his family.

Jasmine simply wanted the whole mess to go away.

A few minutes later, Coby's red sport utility vehicle rolled into her driveway. "Hey, kiddo," he called as he jumped out and bounded toward her.

Coby had a handsome baby face that appealed to the ladies. He was also the brother who most resembled Jasmine. Judging features alone, they could have been twins if not for Coby's rugged jaw and his burly, muscled physique.

Within seconds she was engulfed in a giant bear hug. At five foot nine, there weren't many occasions when Jasmine felt short, but being around her brothers could make her feel like she was twelve years old again.

"Mmm, brownies," Coby shouted, rushing into her kitchen. He stacked three in his massive hands and headed to the refrigerator for milk.

"Coby! Ugh, don't drink out of the carton."

"Sorry, Sis. I'll replace it." Coby took the milk carton and his handful of brownies into the living room and sprawled out on her sofa. Brownie crumbs marked his trail.

"I'm warning you, Coby. My house had better be in the same condition you found it in when you leave. I don't want you burning cigarette holes in my couch or spilling margaritas on my carpet like you did at Rome's house."

"Man, he's never going to let me live that down. I replaced the cushions. Besides, I've quit smoking."

"That's not the point."

"Okay, I promise not to trash your place," he said, with his mouth full of brownies. "So what's new in the P.I. business?"

"How many times do I have to tell you? I'm not a private investigator, I'm a close protection specialist."

Coby burst out laughing. "That's right, you're a bodyguard. How's that going?"

She rolled her eyes. "Just fine. I'm on a case right now. That's why I won't be home until late tonight. My client is a radio host at WLPS. He works the late show."

"Which one? The Sandman?"

"That's right."

"Cool. I listen to that show all the time when I'm in D.C. Hey, you should hook me up with him. I can mix him some funky new intro music for his show." Coby started rapping freestyle while he stomped out a beat with his size-thirteen boots.

"Uh yeah, if I'm not too busy, I don't know—

keeping him alive—I'll be sure to put in a good word for you."

Coby laughed. "No problem. I have my deejay equipment in the truck. I'll make a tape and you can just drop it off."

It was Jasmine's turn to laugh. Coby, the family schemer, was impossibly self-centered, but he was so sweet and lovable that she could never hold it against him. She'd bet he and Spencer had a lot in common.

"Okay, Coby. If I get the chance, I'll see what he says, but don't get your hopes up. I don't think he's going to want to hear any tips about his show from me."

"Why not? You're the woman standing between him and, you know, rat-a-tat-tat." He pretended to shoot a machine gun.

"Yes, I know, but our relationship is kind of . . . complicated."

He propped his combat boots on her glass coffee table. "Whoa, I know that look. What's up, baby girl?"

Jasmine sighed heavily. "I think I'm about to really screw up this assignment."

"Why do you say that? You can do the job. We taught you how to kick some ass. What's wrong? Is he giving you a hard time?"

"It's more than that. I think he's attracted to me."

Coby grinned. "How do you know?"

"He kissed me."

"You can't blame a guy for taking a shot. It's an ego thing, having a beautiful woman around . . ."

"He kissed me twice."

Coby rubbed his hands together. "Well, now, things are getting interesting, aren't they?"

Jasmine hung her head. For the first time in the last few days, she let her guard down. "No, they're getting *confusing*. I broke down my boss's door one morning and demanded a better assignment. He reluctantly let me take Spencer Powell's case, but he made it clear that if I blow it, he'll fire me." She slumped back on the couch cushions. "News flash—I'm blowing it big time. Clearly, there's a reason for the shortage of female bodyguards. And a reason why we always get assigned to women and children . . ."

Coby rolled his eyes. "Quit whining. When did you turn into such a crybaby?"

Jasmine looked up at her brother. "Would it kill you to give me just a tiny bit of sympathy for a minute here?"

He stood up. "I'm getting another brownie." By Coby's definition, "another brownie" meant six. He returned with two handfuls and started filling his mouth and taking swigs from the milk carton. Jasmine made a mental note to go grocery shopping. By the end of the day, her refrigerator would be empty.

"I would give you sympathy," he said between

bites, "if I felt you needed any. But I don't really see the problem. The guy's still alive, isn't he?"

"Yes, but—"

Coby popped an entire brownie into his mouth. "And no one has shot or stabbed him in the last few days, right?"

"Right, but—"

"So what's the problem? Sounds like you're doing a good job to me. If he hasn't gotten so much as a bruise since you've been on the job—"

Jasmine bit her lip. "Well, I didn't say that . . ."

"What? He's gotten bruises?"

"Okay, let me start from the beginning. My first day on the job, I showed up, and Spencer wasn't taking me seriously. So I challenged him to an arm wrestling match."

"That's my girl. Show him who's boss. You won, didn't you?"

"You know it, but, unfortunately, I didn't leave things there." She crossed her arms over her chest, feeling herself starting to get worked up over the whole thing again. "He was just such a smart-ass, you know? You should have heard the rude, sexist, and degrading comments he was making. He purposely set out to objectify me."

Coby's eyes went wide. "Oh, no. What did you do?"

"He took things too far . . . and then I made things worse. After I won at arm wrestling, I held my hand out for him to shake and—"

Coby was already shaking his head.

"—then I swept his legs out from under him and dropped him on his butt."

Her brother roared with laughter. "Are you crazy? You could have been fired."

"No kidding. But since he'd behaved badly as well, he wasn't in the mood to make a big deal out of it. We agreed to call a truce."

Coby's smile was full of pride. "You're still a little spitfire, I see. I'm sure the Sandman didn't know what hit him. In fact, what were you saying? He's in love with you or something?"

"I certainly wouldn't go that far. Lust is more like it. Just when I thought we'd come to some sort of understanding, he kissed me. I was really nice when I tried to explain that it was unprofessional for me to have any kind of romantic involvement with him, but he didn't take it well."

"What do you mean?"

"Just to spite me, he made a date with a stripper, knowing that I would have to come along."

Coby slapped his hand to his forehead, then doubled over, his chest rumbling with laughter.

"His plan backfired. His date showed up dressed more like a Sunday school teacher than a stripper. The whole night was a disaster. His date finally got into a cab and went home by herself."

"Whoa, you two have really been living dangerously. How long have you been working with him?"

"Today's my third day."

"What? You did all that in just two days?"

"Yes, and I left out a few details. For instance, after the date last night, Spencer and I started arguing, and before we knew it, we were kissing again. Actually, this time, I think *I* kissed him."

Coby groaned. "Okay, *now* you get my sympathy, kiddo."

"You see what I'm telling you? I'm blowing it. If my boss, Nathan, knew about half the things that have gone on in the past two days, I'd be booted right out of there. And to make matters worse, I think the threat to Spencer is beginning to escalate. He can't afford to have a bodyguard protecting him who can't even control herself."

"Don't be so hard on yourself. Just because the two of you have a mutual attraction doesn't mean you can't do your job. Have you talked to him about this?"

"I tried to this morning, but he blew me off." Jasmine stood and began pacing the room. "Things have been spinning out of control since day one, and I don't see it getting any better. I have to do what's in my client's best interest. Maybe I should resign from the case. At least if I do that Nathan won't fire me."

Coby started to open his mouth, but Jasmine wasn't finished.

"But if I do that, I might as well admit to Nathan that I can't handle high-profile clients. I'd be sentencing myself to high school senior proms for the rest of my career. I can't afford to go back into private practice, so if I give up—"

"Stop right there, Minnie. Do you want my opinion?"

"Of course." She sat back down on the sofa and folded her hands in her lap. "What do you think I should do?"

"Well, you've only been working with this guy for three days. I don't think it's too late to get things back on track. But the first thing you have to do is figure out how you feel about him."

"What's to feel? I hardly know him. I guess he's attractive—if you like that overrated, sexy body sorta thing. He can be charming, but only after he's been pushing my buttons. He's also arrogant, vulgar, and infuriating."

"Are you sure you're not just letting your bitterness about your ex-boyfriend cloud your judgment?"

"I am *not* bitter."

Coby snorted. "Oh, no? Then why haven't you had a serious relationship since you and Nick broke up?"

Jasmine's cheeks heated. She hadn't had much of *any* kind of relationship since Nick, and with good reason. He was the biggest mistake of her life—and one she could have avoided if she'd stuck to her principles. She didn't date pretty boys for a reason. Nick had been a liar and a user. And he'd also been married.

"Maybe I *was* bitter, but I'm not anymore. Nick has nothing to do with my current situation. My job is on the line. This isn't the time for me to suddenly become concerned about my love life."

Coby took a gulp of milk. "Why not? Plenty of celebrities date their bodyguards."

"Oh that's just great. So then I can get a reputation at Core for sleeping with my clients. All the rules about office romances apply here and then some."

"Fine. I give up. There's nothing going to happen between you and the Sandman, is that what you're telling me?"

Jasmine nodded. "That's exactly what I'm telling you."

"You've both agreed on this?"

She nodded.

"Then what's the problem? Go about your business."

Jasmine repeated her earlier words to Spencer. "I'm afraid it might not be that simple."

He shrugged. "Why not?"

"Because the last time I tried to establish boundaries, he pulled that stunt with the stripper. I don't want to keep inciting him into erratic behavior that could put him in danger. Besides, after I kissed him last night, he may think I was leading him on."

Coby grinned. "Just tell the guy the truth. It's been a long time and you were kind of hard up—"

"Hey!" Jasmine hurled a throw pillow at him. "I'm not hard up."

"Then what do you call it?" he asked, catching the pillow and tucking it behind his head.

"Waiting for the right guy."

"Then why did you jump the Sandman's bones?"

"One kiss is not jumping his bones."

Coby laughed in that typical annoying way men have when it comes to sex. "Okay, whatever it was. You just need to convince him that he needs you more than you need him. He's probably feeling pretty insecure about his safety right now. Make it clear to him that the only way he's going to stay alive is to play it your way. Distractions will get him killed. Even in the face of his own pride, he's not going to be able to argue with that."

"That's a good point," she said, mulling over his words. Every now and then, Coby really came through for her. With that settled, she was free to focus on her brother's visit. "I've got some time before I have to go to work; do you want to do something?"

"Actually, I have, like, two month's worth of laundry in the truck. Wanna help me out with that?"

Before she could answer, he was already halfway to his car.

6

*J*asmine glanced over at Spencer as she pulled into the parking lot in front of the radio station later that night. He was still cracking jokes and making silly comments as though nothing unusual had occurred. If she hadn't been there, she'd swear that the phone call hadn't affected him at all.

But she had been there, and she'd seen the look on his face when the truth of his situation had finally sunk in. Whether he would admit it or not, she knew he hadn't wanted to be alone in the house afterward. He'd been shaken up. Maybe even enough to start cooperating with her.

Jasmine just wished she had some clue as to what she was up against. Many of her previous clients had known exactly who had been after them. It was a lot easier to guard against a known enemy.

Spencer had a large audience. His stalker could be someone he knew or a stranger with no ties to him at all. She knew it wasn't her job to figure out who might be out to get Spencer. It was her job to keep him safe. Period.

This was the hardest adjustment to make from her former role as a police officer. She couldn't resist the lure of a good mystery, and her first instinct was to interrogate Spencer and everyone around him until she got a clearer picture of what she was dealing with.

Unfortunately, Nathan would have her head if she did any such thing. For now, she just had to keep her eyes and ears open. Protecting Spencer was her only priority.

Spencer bounded into the building, introducing her around as though she were his new best friend instead of his "personal assistant," but his false cheer didn't fool her. She'd seen this type of reaction before.

In the light of day, many clients went overboard trying to convince themselves, and everyone else, that nothing had changed. It was a natural defense mechanism, and without it they would probably stay huddled up inside a protective cocoon, afraid to face the world.

As she followed Spencer down the hall toward the studio, a head poked out from a doorway. "There you two are."

Spencer stopped short. "Tali? What are you still doing here? You're usually long gone by now."

"I've been waiting for you." Talibah Arkou was an incredibly tall woman; her height rivaled Jasmine's five feet nine inches. Her features were as indicative of her African heritage as her name.

The woman glanced down at her watch. "You have thirty minutes before you go on the air. Come in and tell me how things are going." She stepped aside, making room for them to enter her office.

Spencer's posture stiffened. "There's nothing to tell. Everything's fine."

Jasmine moved over to Tali, admiring her simple, casual style. She wore a long-sleeved T-shirt with a hand-woven vest and faded blue jeans. Deep brown lipstick was her only makeup, and she wore her long hair in a smooth knot at the back of her head.

"It's nice to finally meet you in person, Tali. Actually, it would be a good idea if we talked. Spencer received a call at home last night. It was from the same person who threatened him on the air."

Tali sighed heavily, walking into her office and taking a seat behind her desk. Jasmine followed, forcing Spencer to trail after her, reluctantly.

Tali shook her head. Her smooth ebony skin wrinkled over her wide forehead. "Sandman, why didn't you tell me this? I told you to keep me informed."

Spencer shrugged, slumping into a chair beside Jasmine's. "What do you want me to say, Tali? It was just a phone call, not much different from the other one."

Jasmine had heard Spencer's blasé routine before, and this wasn't it. His casual demeanor was an act.

Tali rolled her eyes, exasperated. "Do you see what I have to put up with?" she said to Jasmine. "This man thinks he's invincible. You can see why we need you."

Jasmine was grateful to finally have an ally. "I've been wanting to talk to you about Spencer's schedule. I noticed that he has some remote broadcasts planned locally, as well as one in Ocean City in a few weeks. I don't think it's wise to give Spencer too much public access right now."

Tali fished through some papers on her desk, finally finding what she was looking for. "I understand what you mean. Some of the club dates are no problem. I can have another host fill in for the Sandman, but there's nothing I can do about the Ocean City gig. We've already been paid, the arrangements have been made, and they specifically requested the Sandman."

Jasmine frowned. That wasn't what she'd been expecting to hear. Especially since Tali had told Jasmine she was willing to cooperate however she could. "I can understand your reluctance to cancel such a big and expensive event, but it's going to be much more difficult to control Spencer's environment in that kind of situation. He would require twenty-four-hour coverage. Are you willing to pay for more guards during his travel?"

Tali frowned. "We're already outside the budget on this one. No one ever anticipated that we'd need to hire bodyguards for our on-air personalities."

Jasmine leaned forward, pressing her point. "Then maybe it would be best if you got another host for the beach event. Someone who isn't in such a precarious position."

Spencer must have begun to fear that she was making some headway with Tali, because he finally spoke up. "Don't I get any say in this? This is my life and my career we're talking about here."

Tali turned to Spencer. "I'm trying to do what's best for you *and* the station. We've had a good year, that's why I'm able to invest a little money in a bodyguard, but I don't see how I can afford any others. At the same time, I can't risk hurting our reputation by breaking our contract."

She gave Jasmine a pensive look. "I really need the Sandman at that event. Can you give me a few days to work something out? In the meantime, Jasmine, is it a problem for you to accompany him to Ocean City?"

Jasmine released a resigned breath. "No, it's not a problem—"

"Good, then I'll get back to you soon." Tali rolled around to face her computer screen, effectively dismissing them both.

Instantly, Spencer popped up out of his seat and headed down the hall. Jasmine could tell he was brooding, but his sulky mood disappeared when he entered the studio.

There was another woman already inside. A wide grin spread across his face when he saw her. "What's up, Dr. G.?"

Dr. Gina was nothing like Jasmine had imagined. On the air, she had a cool, even voice that Jasmine had assumed belonged to a dry, scholarly type. She'd pictured an older, conservative woman like Dr. Joyce Brothers.

Instead, Gina was cover model beautiful with pale champagne-colored skin and long hair that fell in waves around her face. The only thing that fit Jasmine's expectations was the glasses. The trendy, narrow, wire frames added an intellectual look to her elegant beauty.

It would have been easy, in the natural order of feminine envy, to hate Gina on sight. She was clearly smart and clever, and to top it all off, she looked like she belonged on the cover of the swimsuit edition of *Sports Illustrated*.

But Gina made it impossible to hate her. After she returned Spencer's friendly greeting, she walked over to Jasmine and extended her hand.

"You must be Spencer's new . . . *assistant*. I'm Dr. Gina Hill. Since Spencer and I work so closely together, Tali thought I should know the real reason you're here. She didn't tell me you were a woman, but now I know why she said that I would be impressed. Has this guy been giving you a hard time?"

Jasmine laughed, returning Gina's handshake. "Oh, you know Spencer. He's not happy unless he's stirring up trouble. My name is Jasmine White."

"Well, Jasmine. Have you figured out how to deal with him yet? He's a handful."

"You can say that again. We had a very *interesting* first day. The second day was an adventure, too, but I think we're finally coming to an understanding. I can just imagine what you must go through, working with him each night."

Dr. Gina smiled. "*Adventure* is a good word. I guess you've noticed that he likes to have things his own way. One night he decided that we needed a special studio guest, so he sent three interns to Dupont Circle, promising a hundred dollars to the first one to bring back a transvestite. Can you believe that?"

"I can believe it. In fact, on my first day, he made me drive him to an after-hours club in Baltimore, complete with strippers."

"Enough!" Spencer held up his hands. "Stop talking about me as though I'm not in the room. I've got a slow jams show to do in fifteen minutes. I need some time to get into the mood, so if you don't mind . . ."

He took Jasmine's elbow and guided her toward an empty chair in the corner. Jasmine shrugged and shot Gina a conspiratorial smile.

Gina laughed in return. "Why don't we compare notes after the show, Jasmine? We can go for coffee at the IHOP down the street."

"It's a date."

Spencer frowned. "I'm assuming that I get to come along. After all, she's supposed to be guarding *my* body, might I remind you."

Gina smiled wickedly. "Sure you can come. We need someone to pick up the check."

Spencer leaned toward the studio mike as a commercial for a local car dealership went off the air. Gina was at the microphone directly across from him, and Jasmine was sitting on a stool in front of the third guest mike, so she could see what was going on.

"It's twenty minutes to eleven, and you're listening to the Sandman on WLPS. Dr. Gina is our licensed psychologist, specializing in dream interpretations. Caller, you're on the air."

"Hey, Sandman, what's up, player? This is Derrick from Temple Hills."

"Hey, Derrick, what's on your mind tonight?"

"Is Dr. Gina in the house?"

"Hi, Derrick."

"Dr. Gina, I saw you at Iverson Mall two

months ago, and I just wanted to tell you that I think you are so *fine*."

"Well, thank you, Derrick. Do you have a dream you'd like us to help you interpret?"

"Yes, I do. I had a really wild dream about two nights ago. In the dream, I discovered that my girlfriend is an alien."

Spencer chimed in. "Sounds like you're taking that *Women Are from Venus* stuff a little too seriously."

"Well, it's more than that. In the dream she wanted to take me away in her spaceship to her home planet."

Dr. Gina nodded slowly. "Derrick, there are a lot of elements in this dream to be analyzed. Usually, aliens represent our fears. The fact that you dreamed that your girlfriend is an alien either means that you're afraid of losing her or afraid of losing yourself to her. I tend to think it's the latter since you talked about her taking you away in her spaceship."

"Either that or you've developed a kinky fetish for big eyes and green skin," Spencer quipped. "We're talking role-playing for the new millennium. No more kinky doctor-and-nurse scenarios. Today it's the star fleet captain and his sexy alien seductress."

The caller laughed. "Nah, man. I'm not into that."

"Derrick, what's going on in your relationship right now?" Dr. Gina asked.

"What you were saying kinda made sense, Dr. Gina. I've been going out with Denise for two years, and now she's been hinting around about getting married."

"And you're not ready for that kind of permanent commitment?"

"What man in his right mind is?" Spencer asked, jumping in. "Marriage definitely bears a resemblance to a galaxy far, far away. It's not worth it, buddy. Just because she tells you no man has gone there before, don't you believe it."

Derrick laughed. "I hear ya, man. I love my girl, and all, but I'm just not ready yet. We're the only couple in our circle of friends who isn't married. Now she's trying to rush me toward wedding bells."

Dr. Gina nodded her head. "What's the problem, Derrick? Are you afraid that Denise isn't the one?"

"No, I'm sure she's the one. That's my point—we both know we're going to spend the rest of our lives together. What's the rush?"

"Something's holding you back. Either you're not ready to commit to anyone, or you're not ready to commit to Denise. That's what your dream is trying to tell you. If you want this relationship to have a future, you're going to have to figure out what you're afraid of and face it."

"Okay, thanks, Dr. Gina."

"One more thing, Derrick," Spencer added,

suddenly more serious. He could see the women in the studio holding their breath. "Even E.T. eventually phoned home. If you can't find a way to give the lady what she needs, she's going to find someone who can. Don't let her slip through your fingers just because you're afraid of change."

Spencer could feel Jasmine's eyes on him, and he knew she was waiting for the punch line. He couldn't have her thinking he'd suddenly gone soft. "Whatever you decide, just don't make her angry. The earth can't afford to fight an alien invasion."

Spencer queued up the next love song, preparing himself for the inevitable attack from Gina and Jasmine. He looked over, and the two women were whispering like old friends. He shook his head; the first part of the night they'd ganged up on him, and now, apparently, they'd decided to simply ignore him.

This wasn't fair. Not only was he outnumbered, now he was invisible. Well, not for long.

He smiled devilishly as the song went off and it was time to take more calls. "That was Mariah Carey's latest ballad, and now we're going back to the phone lines. We have a special treat for you all tonight. Sex therapist Dr. Jasmine dropped by the studio and has agreed to take a few of your calls." Before anyone could react, he hit the phone line. "You're on the air."

"Hi, my name is Christy. Is this live?"

"That's right, Christy. Do you have a question for our sex expert, Dr. Jasmine?"

"Wow, I can't believe I actually got through," the girl gushed. "I was just calling to request a song, but I guess I do have a question for Dr. Jasmine."

"Sandman!" Dr. Gina stared at him with wide eyes.

He flipped on Jasmine's mike. "Don't worry, Dr. Gina. We haven't forgotten about you. What's your question, Christy? We have two doctors in the studio to help you out."

Jasmine stared at the mike as though it were a snake about to leap out and bite her. She started to stand, but Spencer grabbed her arm, holding her in place.

"Dr. Jasmine, my boyfriend howls like a coyote during sex. I know he thinks it's sexy, but it actually turns me off. In fact, I've started faking my orgasms because of it."

Spencer poked Jasmine in the arm to get her to speak up.

"Well, um, Christy," Jasmine began. "Is th-this something that he . . . he's always done, or is it something that he picked up recently?" She turned and gave Gina a pleading look.

"It's something new," Christy answered. "I don't know where he got it from, but it's annoying. He thinks it makes him sound more masculine and primitive, but, really, it's just lame."

"Have you told him how you feel about this?" Dr. Gina asked.

"No. I don't want to hurt his feelings."

"You shouldn't be worried about hurting his feelings, Christy," Jasmine said. "There are two issues here. First, you need to be able to be honest with him. Second, you should *never* fake an orgasm. He needs to know when he's not pleasing you."

"Very good point, Dr. Jasmine," Gina said, winking at her. "I couldn't have said it better myself."

The caller thanked everyone and hung up, and Spencer queued the next commercial.

"Are we off the air now?" Jasmine asked, and Spencer nodded. "Good, now I can cuss you out. What the hell did you think you were doing?"

"I just didn't want you to feel left out. Besides, you did great. Ever consider a career in radio?"

Before Jasmine could retort, Gina interrupted. "Spencer, Tali's on the line. She's calling from home."

"Uh-oh," Spencer said, picking up the line. *Women. Why were they all so sensitive?*

After the radio show, Jasmine sat across from Gina and Spencer at the International House of Pancakes. She and Gina had decided it was too late for anything other than decaffeinated coffee, but Spencer had ordered the works.

At that moment, already knee-deep in cheese

eggs, hash browns, and bacon, he was pouring blueberry syrup over a stack of buttermilk pancakes. Her stomach hurt just looking at the food he shoveled in.

Spencer showed no signs of the sulky mood he'd fallen into after Tali had bawled him out on the telephone earlier. She'd made it clear that the consequences would be extreme if Spencer put Jasmine on the air again.

". . . so this three-hundred-pound woman sees us eating lunch outside, screams 'Sandman, I love you' at the top of her lungs, and throws her panties over the balcony." Gina scooped a long curl out of her eyes. "They landed in his coffee! Spencer nearly overturned the table, he jumped back so fast." Gina shook her head at the memory, laughing so hard tears filled her eyes.

Spencer paused to lick syrup from his thumb. "I had to move fast. Those bloomers were so big, I thought someone had thrown a parachute at my head."

"Wow, it's amazing what people will do," Jasmine said thoughtfully, sipping from her coffee mug. "So, Gina, it's safe to say that Spencer attracts some crazy fans, but do you know anyone who might want to crank-call him or play some kind of elaborate practical joke on him?"

Spencer's fork clattered on his plate. "Don't start this again, Jasmine. If I don't know anyone who'd want to do this to me, then Gina doesn't, either."

Jasmine shot him a dirty look. "Sometimes it helps to get another perspective. The smallest detail can make a difference."

He sighed heavily. "I'm going to the bath-room."

Jasmine started to stand.

"Uh-uh," he said, pressing her back into the booth with a hand on her shoulder. "You can see the bathroom door from here."

Jasmine watched, shaking her head as he disappeared into the mens' room.

Gina leaned forward, lowering her voice. "He can't stand talking about anything related to these stalker incidents. They're bothering him a lot more than he's letting on."

Jasmine nodded. "I think so, too."

"I've tried to get him to open up to me, but he keeps telling me to drop it."

Jasmine twirled a spoon around in her luke-warm coffee. "I don't want to upset him. I know that call last night really got to him, but at the same time, I can't stand working blind. The more information I have, the better I can protect him."

Gina gave her a commiserating smile. "I'll help if I can. The trouble is that I don't know any more than you do. The only thing I can tell you is that the person making these threats probably isn't one of Spencer's friends."

"How can you be so sure?"

"Reading people is my business. I know you think Spencer is just a wisecracking smart-ass, and I haven't helped that image with the stories I've been telling you, but the bottom line is that Spencer's friends are loyal. For every outrageous story, I can tell you something incredibly kind he's done."

Jasmine wrinkled her forehead. "What do you mean?"

"When my mother's house went into foreclosure last year, I couldn't afford to bail her out. One night I cried on Spencer's shoulder. The next morning, he mailed my mother a cashier's check for five thousand dollars and signed my name to the card."

"You're kidding."

"No, I'm not. For weeks, he denied sending the money. And get this, when I finally got him to admit it, he refused to let me pay him back."

"That's crazy."

Gina nodded. "That's not all. Over the holidays, after working a full shift, he drove three hours to pick up Tali when her boyfriend left her stranded. And, last summer, he baby-sat Carl Barnhardt's kids for a week so Carl could take his wife on a surprise vacation."

Jasmine shook her head. "You're making him sound like some kind of modern-day hero."

"He doesn't like to admit it—he even tries to hide it—but the fact is, Spencer Powell is one of the good ones."

"Are you sure everyone feels so strongly about

him? Can you think of *anyone* who might feel jealous or vengeful?"

Gina leaned back against the booth, smoothing her hair behind her ears. "Obviously, I don't know every person in Spencer's circle of friends, but everyone at the station is pretty close."

Jasmine chewed on her lip, tracing the edge of her paper placemat with her finger. "This is going to sound stupid, but my job would be a whole lot easier if the stalker were someone he knew. At least then I could narrow down the pool of suspects. Having to keep an eye out for his entire listening population makes things a lot trickier."

"If you want my opinion as a psychologist"— Gina waited for Jasmine to nod before continuing—"I'd say the letters and the call I heard on the air came from someone in a state of rage."

"Yeah, no kidding."

"Somehow, Spencer has become the focal point for someone's hostility. Maybe he represents everything this person hates about radio personalities, or black men, or just men in general. At this point, I don't think the threats are racially motivated, but I wouldn't rule out the possibility entirely. In this day of being politically correct, even psychos don't tip their hands too early."

Jasmine nodded. "I hadn't thought about it that way. Interesting."

"I didn't specialize in criminology, but my guess is that these threats don't have anything to do with Spencer. The stalker is simply making an example of him."

Jasmine watched as Spencer exited the men's room and headed back to the table. "Thanks for your input, Gina. Do you mind if I run a few things by you from time to time, just to get a psychologist's point of view?"

"Of course not, any time. Like I said, there isn't a single person at the station who doesn't owe Spence a favor. He's been a good friend to me personally. I'd do anything to help him."

Jasmine smiled at Gina as Spencer slid back into the booth. Finally, she had an ally.

Spencer was quiet on the drive home, giving Jasmine time to mull over the things Gina had said. She'd raised some interesting points. It might not hurt for Jasmine to give some thought to Spencer's public image and the attention it garnered. That brought Jasmine's mind back to his attempt to humiliate her earlier that evening on his radio show.

"Why do you keep pulling these stunts, Spencer? I'm your bodyguard. I'm supposed to be anonymous. Just a shadow in the background. Instead, you keep pointing me out. I know having protection wasn't your idea, but at this rate you may as well stand in the street and shout 'Come and get me.' "

"I'm sorry. What more do you want?"

"I want to know if you're just wasting my time," Jasmine said. "If you're going to paint a target on your back, I may as well give up. What can I do for you if you don't care about your own safety?"

"Who said that I don't care about my safety? Do you think I *like* knowing that someone is out there watching me?"

"I don't know how you feel, but I know how you've been acting. You're not exactly making choices that are in your best interest."

Spencer was silent. He continued to stare out the window as Jasmine pulled into his driveway. "Thanks," he mumbled. "Good night." He got out of the car, and she was forced to follow behind him to check out the house.

On the drive home, Jasmine planned her next move. She had a lot riding on this assignment, but it seemed as though everything was conspiring against her. Spencer kept trying to put her on the spot instead of letting her do her job. Even Tali, whom she'd been certain would see things her way, refused to cooperate on Spencer's schedule. The only person who seemed willing to help was Dr. Gina.

It probably had something to do with Gina's training. Psychologists always knew how to put people at ease. Jasmine had been very tense when she'd gone to see the police psychologist for temper-management counseling, but in the first five minutes Dr. Jeffries had gotten her to lower her guard and speak freely. Those ten sessions had set Jasmine on a path of self-discovery that eventually led to her decision to leave the force.

She hadn't regretted that decision, and she vowed to never look back.

Emotionally exhausted, Jasmine was relieved to finally pull up in front of her house. She could see that the lights were on in the living room. Coby was probably up watching television. It was somewhere around three-thirty in the morning, but that man kept a vampire's hours anyway.

Despite that fact, Jasmine was unprepared for what she found when she entered the house. Coby had his deejay equipment spread out on a fold-out table with two huge speakers stacked up on her living room floor. Two couples were sprawled around the room, smoking cigarettes and bobbing their heads to Coby's mellow club mix.

He waved a hand when he saw her standing in the doorway. "Hey, Sis, join the party."

She shook her head. "I don't believe this. What are you—sixteen? I'm gone for a few hours and you turn my town house into an after-hours nightclub?"

Coby pulled off his headphones. "Come on, Minnie, don't be mad. I'm doing this for you."

She put her hand on her hip. "How do you figure?"

"I'm making a tape for you to give to the Sand-man. Hey, do you think he'd ever add a mix show to his program? That would be really live on a Friday night."

Jasmine rolled her eyes. She just couldn't deal with another self-centered man at the moment. "Coby, I'm going to bed. Right now. If anything wakes me up, and I mean *anything*, you're going to be sleeping in your truck tonight. Is that understood?"

Before he could answer, Jasmine spun on her heel and trudged up the stairs.

Coby's voice carried up after her as he spoke to his friends. "See, I told you she wouldn't mind."

*S*unday afternoon, Spencer shuffled through the aisles of the Blockbuster Video store until the titles blurred before his eyes. He snorted as he read the time from the clock on the wall. He'd been circling the store for twenty minutes, and in all that time, not one damn thing had caught his interest. Though he didn't know why that should surprise him. These days, nothing excited him much.

Ever since he'd resolved to be a good little soldier, things had become pretty dull—especially between him and Jasmine. She'd said bodyguards were supposed to remain in the background. Spencer had taken that to mean he was supposed to ignore her. And that's exactly what he'd been trying to do.

No more wisecracks. No more come-ons. He'd been going about his business as though she wasn't even there. That's what she'd wanted from the start, but it was easier said than done.

How the hell was a normal, healthy, *straight* guy like himself supposed to ignore a woman like Jasmine? He'd finally established that there was a mutual attraction between them, and he'd been forced to abandon it.

After all, a brick wall didn't have to fall on his head—at least not literally. He'd had to face the truth. His life really *could* be in danger. If he made things tough for Jasmine, he could be digging his own grave.

So he'd been keeping a low profile as ordered. Now, he never saw Jasmine outside the radio station because he never went anywhere else. Tali had canceled all his appearances, including his promo day. Usually, on Thursdays, he was required to drive around D.C. in the WLPS van handing out freebies and greeting fans. Now instead of hitting the streets, he had to make up his time taping extra promo spots and public service announcements in the studio.

In a flash, Spencer's social life had gone up in smoke. But no matter how much he missed living *la vida loca*, living the hermit's life had been paying off. Two weeks had passed, and he hadn't heard a peep out of his stalker. With any luck, that maniac had gotten bored with him and had moved on to some other poor sucker.

Another week like this one and he could send his bodyguard packing. He could go back to having a normal life—maybe even a sex life. At the thought of sex, Spencer's mind strayed back to Jasmine. Maybe when she was no longer on the payroll . . .

That thought process was just an exercise in frustration, so Spencer turned his attention back to renting a video.

He was determined not to leave the store empty-handed. He'd played every Sega Dreamcast game cartridge he owned at least fifty times, and he'd seen every tired old movie playing on satellite. Though he'd done his best to turn his home into every bachelor's dream, after being cooped up all weekend even his personal den of iniquity felt like prison.

He'd had no choice but to escape. It felt good to be out in the light of day, among people again.

Spencer skimmed through the horror section and bypassed the drama rack altogether. He'd had enough of his own drama lately. He'd already seen everything good available on DVD and was on the verge of raiding the kiddie section for cartoons when an old screwball comedy caught his eye. Just what he needed. He chose three movies guaranteed to make him laugh and moved through the checkout line.

After dropping his videos on the front seat of his car, he decided to dash into the convenience store for chips and soda. He was pacing the snack food aisle when someone came up behind him.

"I'd go with the Cheddar-doodles. I think they may have some actual cheese by-products, as opposed to the Cheezios, which only have chemically manufactured cheese flavor."

Spencer's body went still at that familiar soprano. He couldn't mistake the accompanying floral scent that gave him the same gag reflex he experienced every time he passed the Potpourri Boutique in the mall. "Angela Bowers—soon to be Angela Travis. What are you doing in this neck of the woods?"

"I just bought one of the new condos across the lake."

He scratched his stubbled chin, puzzled. "You and Guy are moving out here? I'm surprised you talked him into leaving that fancy penthouse in the District."

Angela's glossy lips formed a pout designed to garner sympathy. "Don't be cruel, darling. I'm sure you've heard by now. Guy Travis and I are yesterday's news."

"Sorry." Spencer grunted. "I haven't been keeping up with the headlines lately."

"Don't worry about me, honey. I'm doing just fine. I pawned the rock he gave me, and now my living room doubles as a showroom for IKEA."

"Aren't you supposed to return the ring after an engagement is broken?" Spencer asked this more for reaction than anything else. Asking Angela to part with anything of material value was like asking a mouse to relinquish his cheese.

"Give it back? To that bastard? He owed me at least that much for sleeping with that bitch from the ten o'clock news. You can best believe I'm keeping the ring and the new wardrobe I bought on his credit card."

A laugh burst from Spencer's lips as he suddenly remembered why he liked Angela. On the outside, she registered French cuisine and Saks Fifth Avenue, but inside, she was French fries and Wal-Mart to the bone. Strip away her materialistic obsessions and social climbing, and there was real potential.

Unfortunately, he'd never had that much patience. "Oh, Ang, you haven't changed a bit, have you?"

"What do you mean? In all my depression I've gained two pounds. Can't you tell?" She laughed, mocking herself as she patted her ridiculously flat stomach.

He snickered. "I was trying to be polite, but now that you've mentioned it, I can admit that you've really turned into a sloppy cow."

Angela frowned prettily. "Men, you're a lousy lot, every one of you." She let her gaze travel the length of him, and without missing a beat, added, "Now that we're neighbors, we really should . . . I don't know . . . get together."

Spencer pivoted, snatching an oversized bag

of Cheddar-doodles off the shelf to go with the soda he'd picked up. "I'm sure we'll run into each other again," he said, deliberately vague. "A guy never knows when he'll need emergency snack food advice. It was good to see you, Ang."

He tried to sidestep her, but she stopped him with a hand on his arm. "Just in case you have a late-night processed-cheese-food crisis. Here's the number to my 'hot line.'"

Spencer took the card she offered and backed away, nodding his good-bye. Of all his ex-girlfriends, Angela was by far the . . . most recent.

As he stood in the checkout line, he replayed their encounter. If possible, she was even more beautiful now than when he'd last seen her, but somewhere in the elapsed months his taste in women had dramatically changed. Suddenly he was more attracted to faces that were striking without looking like the entire contents of a cosmetic counter.

Now he craved tight, athletic curves instead of more obvious voluptuous ones. He preferred short sleek hair over long extensions. Gamine features, including a pert nose and . . .

Realizing Jasmine had somehow invaded his brain, contaminating all his thoughts, Spencer swore savagely under his breath.

The young cashier before him froze, staring at him aghast. Apparently, that curse had come out more over his breath than he'd thought.

Muttering an apology, Spencer left the store

and started across the parking lot toward his car. He rolled his eyes when he noticed that someone had placed a flyer on his windshield. He couldn't stand it when people did that.

He snatched the white sheet of paper off his car, balling it up with one hand as he deactivated his alarm system with the other.

"What the hell?" Just as he started to slide behind the wheel, he noticed some dirt on his butterscotch leather upholstery.

"How did sand get in here?" He brushed off the seat, then smacked the back of his sweatpants in case he'd carried the dirt in on his clothes.

As Spencer moved to enter the car again, his eyes strayed to the car beside his. It didn't have a flyer on the windshield. He turned around, surveying the other cars in the lot. *None* of them had flyers. There wasn't anybody walking around, passing them out, either.

Pricks of sweat formed on his upper lip.

Holding his breath, Spencer unfurled the crumpled paper in his hand and smoothed it out. Feeling his heart drop through the bottom of his stomach, he read the large block letters:

Early to bed and never to rise
makes a corpse old and cold where it lies.

Spencer had never fainted in his life, but suddenly he was gripping his open car door as if this time would be the first. Head swimming, he inspected the parking lot again. Was the stalker still there . . . watching him?

Bounding into the car, he jammed his key in the ignition and stomped on the gas, almost hitting a parked car as he shot out of the lot. He picked up his cell phone and stabbed out a telephone number.

"Hello?"

"Jasmine? This is Spencer. I got another message from my stalker."

"Where are you?"

"I'm in my car, headed home from the Potomac Valley shopping center."

"Get straight in the house and lock up. I'm on my way."

Jasmine stood in the doorway of Spencer's kitchen as he spoke on the telephone, muttering responses and grunting periodically. Finally, he slammed down the receiver.

"Well, that was a colossal waste of time." He faced her with his hands on his hips. "Why did you even bother getting them involved?"

Jasmine had forced Spencer to call the Montgomery County Police Department as soon as she'd walked through the door.

"I know you're frustrated. Stalker laws are still very primitive. All the police can do at this point is take your report." She retrieved her legal pad from the counter, then seated herself across from him at the kitchen table. "The important thing right now is to start a paper trail."

He rubbed his eyes with the heels of his hands. "What for? The officer made it pretty clear that they practically had to catch the bastard with his hands around my throat before they could help me."

Jasmine sucked on her lower lip. She wanted to make excuses, but it was difficult to do that when she could see both sides. It would be hard for Spencer to accept that, living in Montgomery County, he was receiving more support from his local police than people in the bigger cities with higher crime rates were receiving. Who could appreciate that comparison when, in the end, he still came up short?

Jasmine let out a breath. "Down the line, if there are other incidents reported in the area, the police may be able to connect what's happening to you to other crimes committed by the perpetrator. We're just covering our bases. If they do catch this guy, then these police records will give you a stronger case in court."

"All these what-ifs. I keep forgetting that you were one of them." Spencer looked her in the eye. "Do you miss being a cop?"

Jasmine scribbled on the edge of the pad. "Occasionally. I don't miss the politics that went with it. But at times like this, I miss being able to take action. As your bodyguard, it's not my job to try to figure out who's after you. My only responsibility is to make sure that nobody gets to you."

Spencer stood, clearly restless. "Couldn't you protect me better if you knew who to watch out for?"

"Yes, but if I pour my energy into solving this little mystery, then my energy isn't focused on your safety."

He paced to the window and back. "Then why are you taking notes? Or is that pad and pen some kind of James Bond–style weaponry? Do you have a gun hidden in that ballpoint?"

"Very funny." It had been a while since she'd had the benefit of Spencer's sense of humor. Even lukewarm, she was glad he hadn't lost it completely. "I just want to stay on top of things— make sure there aren't any details we missed."

His lips curled into his trademark wicked grin, charging the room with electricity. "Doesn't that contradict everything you just told me?"

She gave him a stern look, but her heart wasn't in it. "Look, I may not be able to handle things the way I would like to, but that doesn't mean I'm going to sit around and wait for this nut to knock on your front door. If that means sliding into a few gray areas, so be it."

He nodded. "Now you're speaking my language. You and I are more alike than you care to admit. We only follow the rules that suit us."

Jasmine looked up and their eyes met. For just

a moment, something passed between them. Then Spencer abruptly turned away and it was gone.

He jerked open the refrigerator door. "I need a soda. Do you want one?" he called over his shoulder.

"No thanks."

That had been the most personal moment they'd shared in the last two weeks. Out of the blue, he'd decided to cooperate with her. He'd done exactly as she'd asked—he'd let her fade into the woodwork. No more verbal sparring or sexual innuendos. She'd been able to abandon her temper-management exercises completely.

Jasmine couldn't complain about Spencer's behavior anymore, but privately, she had to admit that she missed the attention. She hadn't realized, until just now, how much she'd missed his crude comments and devilishly charming expressions.

Spencer sat back down at the table with a three-liter bottle of cola and no glass. Jasmine opened her mouth to say something as he took a swig directly from the bottle, but she caught herself just in time. She would have been commenting simply to provoke him. She wasn't that desperate for his attention.

What bothered her most was that she was almost grateful for this latest event. If another week had passed without incident, Tali would have been forced to let her go. She could try to convince herself that she would have been disappointed solely because she hadn't proven herself to Nathan yet, but another part of her knew it was more than that.

Jasmine shook her head. She couldn't let her mind go there. What was wrong with her anyway? She had work to do. Picking up her pen, she began writing fast and furiously on the pad.

Spencer moved to look over her shoulder, taking another long pull from the bottle. "What are you writing anyway?"

"I've written down everything I know about each of the incidents from the time they began. I'm looking for patterns. So far, we know all the messages end with a little nursery rhyme or poem with the theme of sleep."

Spencer took another sip of his drink. "You're brilliant at stating the obvious."

She ignored him. "The stalker is aligning himself or herself with your radio identity—the Sandman. Each message also contains a death threat. I guess that's considered the ultimate slumber."

Jasmine tapped her pen against the edge of the pad as she thought. "He hasn't made any physical attempts on your life yet, but we don't know if that will change. Leaving that note on your car was a warning. The stalker was letting you know that he's close."

Spencer was quiet for several moments, moving back to his chair across the table. Jasmine watched him, wondering what was going on in his mind.

He'd been content to keep a low profile lately, and that was because he'd finally begun to take his stalker seriously. She knew when things had gotten quiet he'd been hoping the ordeal was over. But as soon as he'd dipped his toe in the water, he'd been reminded that it was still infested with sharks. That couldn't be an easy thing for him to cope with.

Spencer surprised her by changing the subject. "I rented some videos. Are you going to stick around, or what?" He didn't wait for her answer as he headed into the living room.

Jasmine got up and followed him. "That depends. What did you rent?"

Spencer hit the rewind button on the remote when the movie credits started rolling. Jasmine's lithe body was curled on the sofa beside him, with her long legs tucked beneath her. She clutched a throw pillow to her stomach.

"That was funny," she said, "I've never seen a Monty Python movie before."

He winked at her. "Stick with me, kid. I'll show you the world."

If he said too much more, he might spoil the congenial mood they'd fallen into. They'd never been able to remain sociable for this long before. If it weren't for the unsettling events of the afternoon, he could almost pretend she was a friend instead of a hired protector.

Hoping Jasmine wasn't in a hurry to rush off, he stood. "When the tape is finished rewinding, put in the next one. I'm going to microwave some more popcorn."

To his relief she just smiled and nodded. Maybe she was having a good time, too. Of course, there was always the possibility that she was just doing her job. He had no idea how she billed her hours, but getting paid to watch a couple of movies and baby-sit a radio jock wasn't bad for a day's work.

Spencer stared at the microwave as the bag started popping. A niggling of resentment sprang up. He didn't like the idea of Jasmine's being with him just for a paycheck. If the station wasn't paying her, would she spend time with him voluntarily? He knew they liked to lock horns, but that was part of the fun.

Suddenly, he wondered what it would be like to have a real date with her. If he asked her, he already knew she'd say no. No dating clients . . . unprofessional . . . blah, blah, blah. Nevertheless, he really wanted to know what things would have been like if they'd met at a party instead of their current circumstances.

He had a feeling they would have had some wild adventures together.

"Hey, Spencer, I think you got this one mixed up with one of your home movies."

"What?" He went into the living room. "What are you talking about?"

She pointed at the screen. Instead of the latest Martin Lawrence release, Jasmine was watching a video showing the outside of Spencer's house.

"You must have gotten this mixed up with the rental. Should I cover my eyes?" she joked. "You seem like just the type to videotape yourself having sex."

Spencer picked up the remote and started to fast-forward the tape. "I've never seen this video before. Where did you find it?"

Jasmine sat up straight, the smile disappearing from her face. "You've never seen it before? But it was in the cassette case from the video store. Are you sure you didn't mix up the tapes?"

His whole body was ice-cold, but he felt sweat beading on his upper lip. "I never took that tape out of the bag. Just now, you took it out for the first time."

He stared at the screen as the camera moved around his house, from one window to the next, zooming in on each room. His mind slowed, numb with disbelief. The only thing that registered was the fact that this was terribly wrong.

"This doesn't make any sense. How did a video recording of your house get into the Blockbuster case?" Jasmine knelt on the floor in front of the TV screen, for a closer look. "Look at the date in the corner."

It had been taped three days earlier. "Shit."

The numbness was receding, replaced with white-hot rage. Spencer released a violent stream of expletives. When he ran out of new words, he spewed a creative combination of old ones.

Jasmine ignored his tirade. Instead, she stopped the tape and pushed eject. She examined the outside, careful not to handle it too much. "The note on your windshield wasn't the only message the stalker left for you."

He stopped his frantic pacing and faced her. "No, obviously it wasn't."

"When you left the video store, did you take the tapes into the convenience store with you, or did you leave them in the car?"

"I left them in the car."

"That's when he switched them. How long were you in the store?"

"Not long . . . well, actually, I ran into someone I know, so we took a few minutes to catch up."

She came to her feet. "Who did you see in the store?"

"Angela Bowers."

Jasmine frowned. "Your ex-girlfriend?"

He rubbed his pounding temple. "Yeah. She just moved into the area. She broke things off with her fiancé. That's one wedding gift I won't have to buy."

Jasmine seemed to mull over his words. "This is the same woman you said wasn't thinking about you because she was in a new relationship?"

"Right." His head jerked up. "I know what you're thinking, but you don't know Ang. Stalking, fixing a flat tire, making a sandwich—whatever, this girl won't do anything that might cause her to chip a nail."

"You'd be surprised what a person is capable of if he has the right motivation."

Spencer shook his head. "That's just it, Angela doesn't have any motive for something like this. As much as it bruises my ego to admit it, she dumped *me.* But we parted on good terms. In fact, she gave me her number with the implication that we should get together some time."

"I can't believe you didn't mention this sooner. We've got a woman you used to date in your local shopping center at the same time as your stalker. That supposedly chance meeting in the store could have been a ploy."

"That's crazy. You're reaching."

"Of course you'd never suspect her," Jasmine said. "Maybe you weren't the guy who did her wrong, but if she just ended a relationship with a man she planned to marry, chances are she's a little bitter." Jasmine paused to sniff the air. "Spencer, what's that smell."

"Shit, the popcorn's burning!" He raced into the kitchen, grateful to have something fairly mundane to focus on. The kitchen became overpowered by the acrid scent of burnt popcorn as he delicately removed the smoking bag from the microwave.

With the blackened bag safely disposed of, he leaned against the counter, taking a moment to catch his breath. He didn't know how to take all of this in.

After a cold beer, and when his heartbeat had returned to normal, he joined Jasmine in the living room again.

By the time Spencer returned, Jasmine had had time to carefully review the videotape and was jotting notes on her legal pad. She was glad to see that Spencer's normal rich color, which had previously turned three shades lighter, was restored. He seemed to have taken some time in the kitchen to calm down a little.

That was important, because she needed him calm for what she had to say.

"What are you writing?" he asked.

She put the pad aside and put the videotape on pause. "Well, based on this video, we now know a couple of important things about your stalker."

He sat on the sofa beside her. "Like what?"

"For starters, it's definitely a woman."

"How do you know?" Spencer asked.

"A videotape like this is classic passive-aggressive behavior more typical of a woman. Male stalkers tend to get violent and aggressive right away. Even if they're just toying with you, the messages would have escalated in a much more rapid pattern."

"Is that it? You think it's a woman because this fool hasn't tried to shoot me yet?"

"No, that's not it." She ran the tape back, then hit pause. "Look here. You can see most of her hand in the lower left corner. Even though it's covered by black gloves, it's way too small to belong to a man."

"So, I suppose you think this proves that Angela—"

"Not necessarily," Jasmine interrupted. "Despite what I said earlier, her presence in that store could have been purely coincidental. We just don't know yet. But the most important thing I learned from being a cop is that you never dismiss a suspect without investigating first."

"Fine," he said with a resigned sigh. "What else?"

Jasmine released the pause button and let the video play. "Well, whoever this woman is, she's been watching you very closely. The tape shows her here last Thursday at eleven twenty-two A.M."

"That's the day I was in the studio taping public service announcements all day."

Jasmine nodded. "Exactly. The rest of the week you were home, so she must have been very aware of your schedule."

"So this means some wacked-out chick has the hots for me."

"It means a bit more than that. You have a car

alarm, Spencer. How did she break in to switch the videos without setting it off? Just because we know it's a woman doesn't mean she's not dangerous. She's very determined."

Jasmine watched Spencer's face change. Clearly, he hadn't grasped the full impact of what was going on here.

"No kidding," he said, his index finger boring into his temple. He stood. "Look, I've got a headache. Do me a favor and let yourself out when you get ready to leave."

With that, he left Jasmine sitting alone in the living room.

Spencer lay on his bed, staring up at the ceiling. His mind was whirring too fast for him to get to sleep any time soon, but he'd needed some time alone to think.

He knew Jasmine wanted to help him, but he hated seeing her eyes cloud with concern. Did she think he was a victim? That was the last thing he wanted. Yes, it was her job to protect him, but he wasn't going to let her see him cowering behind closed doors. If he continued to do that, how could a woman like Jasmine possibly respect him? How could he respect himself?

During these past few weeks, he'd turned his life upside down because he'd been afraid. He'd even convinced himself that he was doing himself a favor by hiding out inside his house.

Well, he wasn't going to hide anymore. It was time to call this bastard's bluff.

If this stalker wanted him, he—or she—was going to have to come and get him, once and for all.

$\mathcal{T}$he next night, Jasmine drove Spencer to the studio early so he could tape some commercial spots before his show. While he worked inside the glass compartment next door, Jasmine sat in the studio with her portable computer on her lap.

Since she needed to have a variety of information at her fingertips, her laptop had become one of her most valuable pieces of equipment. In her line of work, plans changed without warning. She had to be ready to reserve alternate hotel rooms, map backup driving routes, and most important, play solitaire when things were slow.

Right now, she wanted to look up the Sandman's web site, which she'd seen listed on some promotional material lying around the station.

She needed to know what kind of information about Spencer was publicly accessible.

Jasmine hooked her cell phone to her modem, connected to the Internet, and typed in the URL. Home pages ran from the amateurish, with clumsy homemade graphics, to flashy high-tech presentations. As the page loaded, she noted that the Sandman's web site was closer to the latter.

The screen started out black and then animated, gold-flecked sand began to sprinkle from the top of the page. The particles drifted slowly downward until they materialized into the grinning image of Spencer Powell. It was a sexy publicity photo fit for the cover of one of the teen magazines her nieces read.

Jasmine laughed to herself. This was just the type of slick, self-promoting exhibition she should have expected from Spencer. And the pages that followed didn't disappoint her.

She clicked through bios for both Spencer and Gina, transcripts of some of the more interesting dream interpretation call-ins, audio clips, games, screen savers, and tons of delectable pictures of the Sandman. All in all, it was the perfect kindling to feed the fire of any card-carrying, love-struck stalkerette.

Jasmine had just taken note of the E-mail link at the bottom of the page when Gina entered the studio.

"Hi, Jasmine." Gina strolled up to her looking fabulous as usual. The station was fairly casual, especially the late shift, but Gina always looked cool and professional. Today she wore a cream silk tank top with a matching blazer and cream-colored jeans.

Jasmine smiled up at her new friend, suddenly feeling boyish in her Orioles jersey and shorts. "Hey, how was your trip to Richmond?"

"The drive was exhausting, but my mother had the time of her life. We stopped in on some relatives and spent the rest of the trip shopping at outlet malls. I thought we were going to need a U-Haul to bring back all the stuff she wanted."

"That sounds great. I can't tell you the last time I've been shopping. I could use a few new things," she said honestly, eyeing Gina's sharp ensemble—simple and feminine.

"You live in Virginia, don't you?" Gina asked.

"Yes, Vienna."

Gina smiled. "Perfect. The next weekend you're off we can go shopping at the Tyson's Corner malls."

"I'd love that." Jasmine had missed out on shopping and lunch dates with the girls growing up. She was ready for all that to change.

Gina's gaze drifted over her head to Spencer, in the next studio. "What's he up to?"

"Taping a commercial spot."

Gina tucked her purse in an empty drawer. "Another one? Since when did he become the official WLPS ad announcer?"

"While you were away, Tali canceled all of

Spencer's remotes. He's on PSA duty in the studio for a while."

"That must be killing him. You know what a ham he is. What's he going to do without all of that attention from his adoring fans?"

"I think he'd like a little less attention from his adoring fans right now, especially one in particular."

Gina looked concerned. "Don't tell me something else happened? . . ."

"Things were quiet for a while, but yesterday, Spencer had another visit from his stalker."

Gina's face fell. "Oh, no. I talked to Tali when I got back into town last night, and she told me she thought the stalker had moved on."

Jasmine shook her head. "Unfortunately, it's getting worse. This time she broke into Spencer's car."

"She? Do you know that it's a woman?"

"She left behind a videotape. She'd been spying on Spencer's house. I noticed a hand in one of the shots. It definitely belonged to a woman."

"Well, hey, that's progress. Did you give it to the police?"

Jasmine nodded. "They took everything to check for evidence, but nothing turned up. She managed to get in and out of Spencer's car without breaking anything or even setting off the alarm system."

Gina gasped, gripping her chest. "That gives me the chills."

"No kidding. Watching the tape was even creepier. She walked around Spencer's entire house peeping in windows. Luckily, he wasn't home. The video recorded the date. It was only four days ago."

"That's a little too close for comfort."

"She didn't have any problem getting into his car," Jasmine said. "It's only a matter of time before she gets inside his house, too. We've already had all the locks changed, and I'm not letting him drive his car anymore. I think she wants us to know that she has access to Spencer. The tape may have been a warning. What do you make of it?"

Gina raised her eyebrows. "I think you're right about the warning. Now that we know Spencer's stalker is a woman, we can make a few more assumptions. Twenty percent of all stalkers are women. Women tend to be passive as stalkers. Instead of getting violent or vengeful, the woman is usually seeking intimacy. If the feelings are unrequited, the behavior can escalate to erotomania."

"*Erotomania?* You kidding! They actually have a name for it?"

"You bet," Gina said. "With this disorder, the woman believes the object of her desire is in love with her, even if they've never met. Celebrities run into this frequently. Half of these stalkers have some sort of mental or personality disorder."

"Wow, Gina, you're full of useful information."

"When Spencer started having problems I read up on the topic. I also have a somewhat photographic memory."

"That must come in handy."

"Spencer must be losing his mind. Maybe I should try to talk to him. Coping with this kind of situation can be difficult. Especially for a man with a lot of pride, like Spencer."

Jasmine nodded. "Maybe that might help. I can't read his moods. One minute he seems absolutely paralyzed, the next minute he's bopping around like nothing ever happened. It has to be some form of denial."

Gina nodded, her eyes full of concern. "I'll see if I can't get him to open up to me. The sooner he faces his fears, the better off he'll be."

Jasmine let her eyes stray back to her computer screen. "I was just browsing Spencer's web site."

"Pretty flashy, huh? Can you believe he designed it himself? He didn't like the one the station put up for him, so he took a six-week class in web design and came up with this one."

"It's impressive," Jasmine agreed. "It's easy to see what got our girl so fired up. It could also make him a bigger target. This site is an open door into his life. His bio page talks about where he grew up, his goals, and his hobbies."

"Enough to really whet the appetite of an overzealous fan."

"Exactly." Jasmine clicked on the E-mail link. "Do you know if he checks his E-mail regularly?"

"I doubt it. He rarely checks his personal E-mail, so I doubt he keeps up with that one."

Jasmine wrote down the Sandman's E-mail address. "Nevertheless, I think I'll have him check it later."

Gina stood. "I'm going to the break room for a soda. Do you want anything?"

"No, thanks. I have bottled water with me."

Gina came back a few minutes later with a bright yellow flyer in hand. "Have you seen this?"

Jasmine turned off her laptop. "No, what is it?" She reached out for it.

"I can't believe this. What on earth is he thinking?"

"What now?" Jasmine took the flyer Gina held out to her. "He's insane. He can't do this!"

Just then Spencer appeared in the doorway. "Don't worry, you're both invited. I can't have a backyard barbecue without my two favorite girls."

Jasmine crumpled the paper in her fist. "This Saturday? What's the matter with you? Have you forgotten about last night already?"

"That's exactly why I'm having this little party. Staying holed up in my house for days didn't get me anywhere. I refuse to keep hiding. If this girl wants something from me, let her come and get it."

"Spencer, I don't think you've thought this through—" Gina started.

His eyes narrowed. "Oh, believe me, I've thought it through. This crazy woman had been hanging around my home and spying in my windows. She broke into my car. She may find this whole thing amusing, but I'm not going to stand for it. My life has to go on."

"So, what does this mean?" Jasmine asked. "You're making things even easier for her? Inviting her to come to a party and make herself at home?"

"Not exactly," Spencer said. "But it is an invitation."

Gina sighed heavily while Jasmine started grinding her teeth.

"It could be anyone," Spencer continued. "A friend, a casual acquaintance, someone I passed on the street, or someone I've never met. Whoever she is, I'm sick of her hiding. I want this out in the open. I want to know who I'm dealing with."

Gina slapped her forehead. "Aye, aye aye! Spencer, you're dealing with a social deviant. Someone with emotional and personality abnormalities. What makes you think you can control this situation? Suppose she does just walk up and introduce herself, then what will you do?"

Spencer raised his eyebrows. "We'll see."

"This is ridiculous," Jasmine protested. "My job is to protect you—even from yourself, if nec-

essary. I will not support your making yourself
an open target."

"That's up to you, but you can't change my
mind." He moved over to the mike, staring at
Gina. "Are you ready? We have a show to do."

Jasmine leaned against the wall, shaking her
head. Spencer's insolence was becoming com-
monplace, but this was something new. He
wasn't just being difficult this time. She knew
from the stone-cold expression in his eyes that he
was serious.

Wiping her hands down her face, Jasmine
blew out a heavy breath. How was she going to
explain this latest development to her boss?

"He's having a party?" Nathan's voice exploded
in Jasmine's ear like a gunshot. "That's ridiculous!"

"I know that, but I couldn't talk him out of it.
It's just a barbecue," she said. "Just a few of his
co-workers from the radio station." She hoped.
He hadn't run the guest list by her.

"I don't care if it's just a handful of senators
from Congress. It's your job to make sure things
like this don't happen."

"Believe me, I did the best that I—"

"Maybe that's the problem. You don't have
enough experience with a client like this. Kirklin
or Rudy—"

"Wouldn't have had any luck changing
Spencer's mind, either," Jasmine spat out.

Why'd he have to mention Ted Kirklin? Just the sound of his name was enough to make her right eye twitch. He was the office hotshot at Core, and he never let her forget it.

He took every opportunity to be condescending to her, dropping the names of his prestigious clients and then asking with a smug grin how her assignments were going.

When she'd gone into the office to pick up her paycheck last week, she'd taken great pride in talking up her assignment with Spencer Powell. But he'd still grinned down at her from his nearly seven-foot height, and all but patted her on the head. "That-a-girl. Let me know if you need a hand. Pruitt mentioned that you might be in over your head on this one."

It was bad enough that Nathan didn't have confidence in her, but did he have to let the entire office know about it?

"Look," Jasmine said, "this is not the first time Core has dealt with a stubborn client. If one of the men had to work with Spencer you wouldn't undermine him by putting the office on notice that he might be in over his head."

She heard Nathan grumbling under his breath. "Core isn't about building personal careers, it's about providing security for our clients. You represent the entire company when you're out in the field. If I have to put an extra man on the job to make sure our clients are taken care of, I'll do it. If your feelings get hurt, then you're in the wrong business."

Jasmine rolled her eyes. What had happened to the congenial man who'd been so anxious to have a woman on the team? Part of her wanted to tell him what he could do with the job and his attitude. But if she did that, all those men who were sitting back waiting for her to crack would win. She was through quitting.

"I've got the situation under control," she said with clenched teeth.

"Well, it's my job to make sure of that. You say that this barbecue is on Saturday? I'm sending Kirklin over as backup. You can't cover that many people on your own."

Jasmine swallowed hard. He was right, but she hated to admit it. She would have welcomed the extra help if he hadn't been such a jerk about it.

And why, of all people, did he have to send Kirklin? "Why not Rudy?"

"He's on vacation this week. Either you work with Kirklin or not at all."

That was just great. She wasn't in the mood to deal with *another* giant ego.

Saturday afternoon was perfect for a barbecue, Spencer thought as he carried extra chairs out to the deck.

He knew Jasmine thought he'd lost his mind. Instead of lying low, he'd invited every woman he knew to a party. She was running around like a wet hen trying to make sure all her security measures were in place. She was doing her best in the face of his disobedience. She wanted to do whatever she could to make sure nothing out of the ordinary occurred today.

It might be twisted, but part of him hoped something *would* go down. He wanted to catch this psycho chick in action. He actually hoped she wouldn't be able to resist this opportunity to make her move. He was in good hands with Jasmine and the extra bodyguard on duty.

Jasmine seemed nervous today. Something told him it wasn't just the party he was having. The fact that another guard from her agency was going to be around seemed to have something to do with it.

His theory was confirmed when the man arrived thirty minutes later. Ted Kirklin fit Spencer's classic bodyguard image. With a massive square jaw and a square crew cut, he had a profile that seemed to be chiseled out of granite. He had a thick trunk of a neck, stemming from a block of steel in a polo and Khakis.

According to Jasmine, he was a former Secret Service agent, which was evident from the way he took charge the minute he walked in the door.

"We need to make sure we keep the party contained in one area," Kirklin announced. "Discourage anyone from hanging around in the house. They'll have to go back and forth to the bathroom, but that's it. We'll lead people into the yard from the side of the garage instead of through the house. That should encourage them to stay outside."

"There may be a few people bringing food," Spencer volunteered. "They'll want to have kitchen access."

"White can collect food and escort guests to and from the kitchen," Kirklin decided.

Spencer noticed Jasmine bristle. "But I need to stay close to Spen—" she began.

"While she's monitoring the inner parameter," Kirklin interrupted, "I'll cover the southern quadrant of the yard behind the pool."

"No, listen," Jasmine said, her voice even. "I've got this all worked out. Kirklin, you should man the barbecue grill; that way everyone who enters the house will have to pass by you. Since everyone knows me as Spencer's assistant, I'll shadow him. You and I can rotate counter-clockwise. That way Spencer will always be between us."

Kirklin blatantly turned his back on Jasmine to face Spencer. "Better do as she says, otherwise we'll never hear the end of it. Know what I mean?" He clapped Spencer on the back, then moved through the room.

Spencer could feel the tension radiating from her. He tried to catch her eye to express his sympathy for her having to put up with a jerk like that, but she wouldn't meet his gaze. He started to reach out to her, but they were interrupted by the doorbell.

"I'd better get that," Jasmine said, already halfway to the door.

"Gina, hi." The two women embraced as though it had been weeks instead of hours since they'd last seen each other. Clearly, Gina felt the tension in Jasmine's body, because Spencer heard Gina whisper in her ear, "Are you okay?"

"Hanging in there. It's good to see you." It must have felt good to see a friendly face. Between him and Kirklin, she was going to have her hands full tonight. Spencer knew she had no choice but to keep her cool, no matter how much Kirklin tried to undermine her.

"I thought I'd come early and see if you-all needed any help setting up," Gina said.

"I can always use an extra pair of hands," he said, taking one of Jasmine's hands and one of Gina's. "You put yours here and you put yours here."

Their two free hands punched him in either arm.

Jasmine looked at her watch; it was only seven-thirty, but things were still fairly tame. Guests had been arriving steadily, and she and Kirklin were keeping them in the designated areas.

She looked up, and, next thing she new, her brother Coby had walked up and clapped

Spencer on the back. "Great party, man. Great house, too. It has excellent feng shui."

Spencer grinned with mild curiosity. "Thanks, and do you mind if I ask what you were doing checking out my funky sway?"

Coby shrugged without missing a best. "Feng shui," he repeated. "I figured if you could make out with my sister, I could take a quick tour of your pad."

"Touché, but I still don't know what shwing shway is." Spencer glanced over and caught her eye, clearly amused.

"Feng shui, man. Feng shui—"

Jasmine massaged her temple. Didn't she have enough to worry about? "Coby, what are you doing here?" she interrupted before her brother could elaborate.

"I crashed, Sis. I hadn't heard anything on my demo, so I figured you hadn't given it to him." He wiped a compact disc out of his baggy jean shorts pocket. "Luckily, I happen to have one on me."

Spencer took the CD Coby offered him. "What's this for?"

"You see, I'm an entrepreneur. I was hoping you and I could do business together. Have you ever considered getting a theme song for your show? Check it out and let me know what you think."

"Coby! I can't believe you had the nerve to barge in here." She took the disc out of Spencer's hand and tried to hand it back to her brother. "Spencer doesn't want to be bothered with this."

Spencer took the disc back. "Yes, I do. If I move to the morning slot in the fall like I'm hoping, I'll definitely need a new theme song."

"See! Relax, Minnie. I told you the man would be interested."

Spencer did a double take, then burst into laughter. "Who is Minnie? You?" he asked, looking Jasmine up and down.

She pursed her lips. "Shut up. It's a family nickname."

Spencer laughed harder. "I think it's cute. Minnie."

"Don't you start." She glared at him.

Spencer leaned on Coby's shoulder, suddenly fascinated by her brother. "Glad you could make it, man. So tell me, are you *Minnie's* older brother?"

"That's right."

"Cool. Why don't you tell me more about this feng shui business," Spencer said.

"Word. Feng shui is the practice of keeping harmony with the natural energy forces of the environment. I just did my new apartment and . . ."

Jasmine rolled her eyes. She should have know they would get along. They were cut from the same cloth. Knowing Spencer was in good hands with her brother, she took the opportunity to survey the party again. She knew they wanted her to leave so they could talk about her anyway.

Now she had a chance to really observe the crowd. Was Spencer's stalker there? She'd made sure he identified every guest. There had been only three women Spencer didn't know personally. Two were the dates of guys who worked at the station; one was a friend of Tali's.

Spencer had said he invited a few ex-girlfriends, but only one had shown up so far. Angela Bowers. Jasmine planned to keep a close watch on that one.

Jasmine took in the woman's black sarong skirt and snakeskin halter top. So this was his type? Why did men always go for women with so much makeup and flash?

Gina came up to stand beside her. "Which woman are you giving the evil eye to?"

Jasmine laughed, embarrassed at having been caught in the act. "Where's your date?"

"He's over there in the pool with Carl's kids, but no changing the subject. Which one are you glaring at?"

"Not glaring, observing," Jasmine insisted. "Angela Bowers—do you know her?"

"I met her briefly when she and Spencer were dating. She's nice to look at but nothing much going on upstairs. Not Spencer's usual type at all."

"Really? What's his *usual* type?"

"Oh, he likes them pretty, but they usually

come with brains, too. Before Angela, he dated
an aerospace engineer. She spent her days monitoring satellites."

Jasmine nodded. Great, his tastes ranged from
bimbo to rocket scientist. He could have any
kind of woman he wanted. She felt some alarm
at the wave of jealousy she felt coursing through
her. She studied the woman beside her. Gina was
everything men dreamed of having in a
woman . . . beautiful, smart, successful.

"Speaking of Spencer's taste in women, I'm
surprised you and he never dated. You two have
so much in common."

Gina nodded, silent for a moment. "That's
true, we never *dated*. Tali brought homemade
sushi. Have you tried it?"

Jasmine could tell by Gina's tone that she
wasn't giving her the full story. She couldn't let
her get away with changing the subject. "Why
am I getting the feeling that something did happen between you two?"

Gina hesitated.

"Come on, we're friends, aren't we?"

"I don't think I should say anything."

Jasmine started at her. "Oh, my God, did you
two have an affair?"

"It wasn't an affair . . . more like a fling."

Jasmine's whole body went hot. She blinked,
trying to keep her face straight. "When was
this?"

"Oh, a long time ago. At least a year."

Only a year? Jasmine's mouth was dry. "When I asked him about his past relationships, Spencer never said anything."

"Believe me, it was nothing," Gina said. "A rebound weekend and then it was over. I'm sure he didn't mention it because it was so brief. I'm embarrassed about the whole thing, if you must know."

Jasmine swallowed hard. When people said things were nothing, they were usually *something*. "Rebound? For you or for him?"

"For him. He and Angela had just broken it off. WLPS was sponsoring a ski trip in the mountains. One night in the bar he made a move, which was nothing new, you know what a flirt he is, but this time it was different. He was sweet and vulnerable. That reeled me in. We spent the rest of the weekend together, but after that I had to call a halt to it for the sake of our working relationship and our friendship. We talked it out and agreed not to let it come between us. It was awkward at first, but we got past it eventually."

Jasmine wasn't thrilled to learn that Spencer hadn't been the one to end things. Gina was definitely the kind of woman a guy could carry a torch for. That was probably the reason he'd never mentioned the fling in the first place.

On a personal level, she knew it shouldn't matter to her what Spencer had done in the past and whom he'd done it with. Professionally, this new information technically made Gina a suspect. As

quickly as that thought popped into Jasmine's
mind, she discarded it. Gina had been on the air
with Spencer at the same time Jasmine heard the
stalker threaten him. Even if she could stretch
their brief fling into a motive, Gina had an airtight alibi for his "encounters" with the stalker.

Jasmine shifted, looking down at her feet. Suddenly she felt awkward around Gina. The
woman was going out of her way to reassure Jasmine that it was no big deal. Easy for her to say.
Before Jasmine could formulate an appropriate
reaction, they were interrupted.

"Where are all the single men?" Tali asked,
walking up with her friend Anne, whom Jasmine
had met earlier.

Gina's brows rose. "I didn't know you were
looking. What happened to Calvin?"

"Girl, that's over. I don't know why I'm in a
rush to get another one. The last one was such a
disappointment." It was clear that Tali had been
hitting the cocktails pretty hard. "I'm on the market again. In fact, it's a shame Spencer works for
me, because he's looking pretty good right about
now."

As the girl talk continued, Jasmine fell into a
pensive silence. Her gaze wandered back over to
Spencer.

He was hugging a woman she didn't recognize. They embraced for a long moment, then
with his arm still around the woman's waist, he
led her over to the buffet table.

Jasmine watched for a minute, her heart rate increasing with each passing second. Was this another one of his ex-girlfriends? He was obviously close to this woman. His eyes softened in a way Jasmine had never seen before.

She was attractive, but not with the same cosmetically enhanced perfection Angela had. She was very petite and feminine. Her shoulder-length brown hair was french-braided at her neck, and she wore crisp white overall shorts. She was . . . adorable, Jasmine thought bitterly.

Clearly, Spencer thought so, too. He was constantly stroking her arm or playing with her braid.

"Excuse me," Jasmine said to no one in particular as she broke away from the cluster and headed across the lawn.

It was time for Jasmine to introduce herself.

9

"There you are," Spencer said, seeing Jasmine crossing the yard toward him. "I want to introduce you to somebody."

"Fantastic," she muttered through tight lips as she watched him squeeze the girl affectionately. "I'd love to meet your new friend."

"New friend," he repeated, then the two of them looked into each other's eyes and giggled.

Jasmine felt her fists clenching at her sides. "What's so funny?"

Spencer must have noted her stiff posture, because he threw his head back and laughed. "Jasmine, I'd like you to meet my baby sister, Dina."

Tiny flames of embarrassment licked at Jasmine's cheeks. She tried not to meet Spencer's gaze as she shook his sister's hand and exchanged pleasantries. She couldn't hold out long. When her eyes darted in his direction, he winked knowingly.

Suddenly, Jasmine didn't know what was worse, thinking Spencer's sister was an old girl-friend or having Spencer know she'd thought his sister was his lover.

Dina's smile was warm as she glanced from Spencer to Jasmine. "So are you and my brother dating?"

"Nope," Jasmine said.

"Nooo," Spencer added emphatically.

"Oh, really. I thought I saw something going on there for a second," Dina teased.

"Come on, Dina," Spencer said. "You know I can't confine myself to one woman. I've gotta spread the love."

"Yeah, right." Dina rolled her eyes, then turned to Jasmine. "So the two of you are co-workers?"

Spencer moved a stray tendril of hair away from Dina's ear and stage-whispered, "She's my bodyguard."

Dina's eyes went wide as she tried to compre-hend his words. "Wow, I didn't realize his body-guard was a woman. That's incredible. Spencer glossed over the details on the phone. I just as-sumed when he mentioned the party everything had been resolved." She turned worried eyes on her brother. "Are you still in danger?"

Spencer drained the beer bottle in his hand. "That's why I didn't go into detail on the phone.

I didn't want you to worry. We've got everything under control. Don't let Jasmine's soft exterior fool you. She can be a brute when she needs to be."

Dina still looked concerned, and Jasmine wanted to put her mind at rest. "It's okay, Dina. Spencer's in good hands."

The woman nodded and they fell into a moment of awkward silence. Then Dina perked up again. "I wish I could introduce you to my husband, Tim, but he's sacked out on Spencer's bed. He's got a little bit of a summer cold. The drive down from Philly wiped him out."

Jasmine nodded. "I'm sorry to hear that. Are you two staying in town long?"

"We were going to stay overnight. But since he's not feeling well, I'm going to let him rest up and then drive him back home. I can't stand being away from the baby anyway."

"Oh, do you have a boy or a girl?" Jasmine asked.

"She has a puppy," Spencer broke in. "I keep trying to tell her that Jane is *not* a good dog name."

Dina punched him in the arm. "I keep telling him, a dog will tell you what its name is, if you know how to listen. Mine says her name is Jane. Who am I to argue?"

Spencer laughed. "Who's going to argue with a dog? You say, 'Hey mutt, your name is Fido.' Period."

"That's stupid, Spencer. You just introduced me to Jasmine. I didn't say, Hey, I like the name Jambalaya better, so that's your name from now on."

"It's a dog, Dina. I'm sure she doesn't even know—"

"I can see you two must have had a very interesting childhood," Jasmine interrupted.

Dina giggled. "Girl, you don't know the half of it."

Seeing her chance for payback, Jasmine slung an arm around Dina's shoulder. "Well, I'd love to hear all about it."

"Dina, don't you need to run upstairs and check on Tim," Spencer interrupted.

Dina smiled. "No, I'm sure he's fine."

Spencer looked at the two of them. "Oh, hell. I don't suppose there's anything I can do to keep this from happening, is there?"

"Nope," Jasmine said with a grin.

"Noooo." Dina added emphatically, and she and Jasmine burst into giggles.

Spencer knew he was beat. "Fine, I'm going to the john."

Jasmine caught Kirklin's eye, and he moved into position to follow Spencer.

Around ten-thirty, Jasmine circled the lawn doing a mental count of the remaining guests. The party was winding down, and just about everyone was heading home. The only people left beside herself and Kirklin were Gina, her date, Tali, and Tali's friend, Anne. Spencer had just returned from walking Dina and Tim to their car.

Gina patted Spencer on the back. "Well, I've got to hand it to you, buddy. You made it through the party despite your best efforts to invite trouble."

"Yep, I guess Nightmary decided to stay home," Spencer said.

"Who?"

"What?"

"Nightmary?" They all asked at once.

"That's what I'm calling her. The Sandman's nightmare. Get it? Nightmary."

"Very clever, Spencer," Tali said. "It's just that kind of mocking attitude that's going to get you in trouble. When are you going to take this seriously?"

"Oh, I'm taking it seriously . . ." Spencer's voice trailed off as he busied himself clearing away empty cups and plates. "Everyone loves a party, but no one ever wants to clean up."

Gina tugged on her date's hand, leading him to the buffet table. "What are Dan and I, chopped liver? We stayed to help."

"Hey," Spencer said, "I don't have room for all this food in my refrigerator. Eat up, guys."

"Just bring it in to the station. It will be gone in minutes," Gina suggested.

Spencer's arms were filled with food. "That will take care of the chips and side dishes. What am I going to do with all these leftover hamburgers? I can freeze the turkey burgers, but you know I don't eat beef."

Dan spoke up. "If the grill is still going, throw a few on. You can eat one, can't you, Gina?"

"Yeah, cook whatever's left and we can divide them up."

Jasmine held her stomach. "I know I can't eat another thing, but more power to all of you."

Kirklin walked up to Jasmine. "Think you can handle a crowd this size?" His tone was condescending as usual.

Jasmine resisted the urge to roll her eyes. "Oh, Kirklin, are you leaving so soon?"

"I'm working with Senator Braddock early tomorrow morning . . ." He continued to brag, but Jasmine allowed her thoughts to wander.

Something caught her attention from the corner of her eye. Spencer was tending to the grill, but his head was turned toward her as he called across the deck to Tali, who was explaining how she wanted her burger.

Suddenly, the world seemed to move in slow motion. Jasmine saw the flames leaping out of the grill like an outstretched hand about to grab him.

Her mouth opened to shout his name, but she could already feel the material of his shirt between her fingers as she tried to jerk him back. Spencer had turned toward the grill and the flames climbed high, narrowly missing his face.

Jasmine stumbled backward, bringing Spencer

down on top of her. A chorus of startled screams and gasps buzzed in her ears. She could feel Spencer's body trembling above her.

Seconds later, Kirklin was hoisting Spencer off her. "Are you okay? Geez!"

Gina's date pushed the lid of the grill closed from behind, extinguishing the flames. Suddenly everyone was buzzing around, tending to Spencer.

Jasmine's knees felt weak. She sank back into a lounge chair. Gina knelt beside her. "Are you okay? You didn't get burned, did you, Jasmine's?"

"No, I'm okay. Just catching my breath." Jasmine's gaze searched the deck, but she didn't find what she was looking for. "How is Spencer?"

"I think he's okay. The front of his hair got a little singed."

Her eyes sought him out again. "Where is he?"

"I guess we were hovering," Gina said. "He broke away and went upstairs."

Jasmine took a deep breath, coming to her feet. "Now that everything is under control, maybe we'd all better go and give Spencer a chance to relax," she said, loud enough for everyone on the deck to hear.

Kirklin came over. "Maybe I'd better stick around. This may not have been an accident. I need to check over the grill and make sure the grounds are secure."

"I'll take care of that. Why don't you go home and get some rest. You have to work tomorrow, remember?"

"Yes, but—"

Jasmine was in no mood to argue, so she walked away.

Tali and Anne were standing at the gate to the front yard, whispering and looking worried.

"Ladies, why don't you head on home now?" Jasmine said.

For the first time since Jasmine had met the confident, capable woman, Tali seemed to be at a loss. "Are you sure he's okay? Maybe I should go talk to him."

"He just needs to rest, and I need to do the job you're paying me to do," Jasmine said firmly.

Jasmine walked around front to make sure everyone was on their way. Gina was walking hand in hand with her date out to their car. When she caught Jasmine's eye she waved good-bye, then held her thumb and pinky to her face, mouthing the words "Call me."

Jasmine nodded and waved before going back in the house. She thought about checking out the grill, but she realized that she didn't know what she would be looking for. Plus, she'd never used a grill in her life.

Picking up her purse, Jasmine walked upstairs to find Spencer. His bedroom door was closed, so she knocked gently, fully expecting to be turned away.

"Come in."

Not sure what she would find, she eased the door open a crack and peeked inside. Spencer was sitting on the edge of the bed, shirtless.

"I just wanted to let you know I sent everyone home and set the alarm. The place is secure. Are you okay?"

He finally looked over at her. "You're not leaving, are you?"

The disappointment in his voice caught her off guard. "I can stay . . ."

He nodded, inviting her into the room with his hand. She pushed the door all the way open and walked over. She noticed his Hawaiian shirt crumpled at his feet.

"Is your shirt ruined?" she asked, picking it up to examine it.

He shrugged. "You ripped off a few buttons when you jerked me away from the fire."

"I'm—"

He held up a hand. "No, don't apologize. You saved my life." He stood, bringing his body inches from hers. He looked down, into her eyes. "Thank you. If you hadn't been there—"

"Don't think about it. The important thing is that—"

"Do you think it was an accident?" he asked.

Jasmine sighed, unprepared to answer that question. She knew this wouldn't be the first time a grill had blown up in someone's face. Still, there was something about the way it happened. The timing of it.

"What do you think, Spencer? You were tending the grill; did you let the coals get too hot or something?"

"I don't think it was an accident. That's not my ego talking. If I screwed up, I'd admit it."

He reached up and fingered the lightened hairs above his forehead. They crumbled in his fingers, and he stared at the dust in his hand for several seconds.

"I didn't believe she wanted me dead."

The words hung between them. Jasmine wasn't sure what to say. This wasn't the time for an I-told-you-so, and she could see he was more shaken than ever.

He released something between a sigh and a laugh. "I thought maybe she just wanted to get close to me. Steal my underwear, take my picture, stuff like that. Creepy, sure, but ultimately harmless. I never expected—" His voice broke.

She reached out and took his hand in hers, squeezing gently. "You don't deserve this. It's not your fault."

He reached out with his other hand and cupped her neck. Their lips met slowly. The kiss was brief but filled with emotion.

When they parted, Jasmine looked at Spencer's face and saw into his soul for the first time. He no longer had the energy to hide behind his slick, cool radio image. The cocky smart-ass had been replaced by a real man she could finally connect with.

He must have misinterpreted her pensive expression, because he reached out and shook her shoulder gently. "Don't . . . please? Please don't overthink this moment. Just let it happen. I need you."

Even if Jasmine hadn't been ready to let go, his emotional words melted her heart. Unable to find any words to convey her feelings, she leaned forward and took his head between her hands.

Their lips met softly like a whisper at midnight. His arms instantly encircled her body, holding her close. Raw emotion that Jasmine had been holding back for weeks spilled into her kiss.

Letting go of her reservations in such a forceful rush nearly made her light-headed in the same terrifying way extreme heights did. As his tongue entered her mouth, Jasmine's stomach pitched and dropped away as though she'd just gone over the first hill of a roller coaster. There was no turning back now. And she didn't want to.

Spencer's hands roamed over her bare back as though he couldn't get enough of her. The sound of his ragged breathing and the low growl in his voice quickened her heartbeat. But she couldn't revel too much in her feminine power over him because she was feeling overpowered herself.

Needing to feel his skin, hot under her hands, Jasmine reached out for him. He gasped, trembling slightly as she dragged her fingertips over his taut pectoral muscles.

She giggled, watching his reaction. "Mmm, I don't think I've ever noticed that a man's nipples could get that hard."

He grabbed her hands and pulled them away from him. "What kind of woman are you to laugh at a tortured man? Two can play this game." He stripped off her top, baring her breasts. "I've been wanting to do this all night." He dipped his head and lightly skimmed his lips over her sensitized skin, carefully avoiding the tips of her breasts.

With each delicate brush, sensation ebbed and flowed in intensity, suspending her in exquisite torture. Her back arched over his arm, which firmly supported her weight. She couldn't help herself as a tortured moan escaped her lips.

Immediately, she felt her face heat. She'd always been the quiet type when it came to sex. But there was no time to dwell on that. Spencer's tongue darted out of his mouth and gently flicked her nipples.

Her knees started to give out, and he lifted her, the two of them falling onto the bed together. Needing him close, Jasmine immediately locked her legs around his waist as their lips met again in an urgent kiss.

Spencer's hands found the waistband of Jasmine's shorts and eased them over her hips. As she arced against him to allow him to pull them free, she felt herself rock into the hardness of his arousal. It was her turn to gasp.

Seconds later, he'd removed her underwear, and she was naked, crushed under his powerful body.

"You're falling behind," she whispered into his ear as he bowed his head to suckle her neck.

His head came up in confusion. "What?"

She laughed, gesturing toward the shorts that still covered his lower body.

His grin was masculine. "Getting anxious, are you?"

"Why? Are you suddenly feeling shy?" she asked, turning the tables on him.

He planted a hard kiss across her mouth. "I'm anything but shy." With that, he unfastened his belt and backed away enough for his shorts to slide down his muscular legs.

"I see you're a briefs man. And red ones at that."

"Don't get used to them." His midnight velvet voice made her shiver as he quickly stripped off the red briefs and made them disappear.

Jasmine took her time admiring his body. She didn't care if her obvious pleasure swelled his head . . . or other parts. In the past, she'd tried to convince herself that looks weren't important; according to theory, average-looking guys treated women better than handsome men. But this was one moment when Jasmine could admit how good it felt to be close to a handsome man with an above-average body. She could hardly believe that she had all this to herself.

Her cheeks heated when she realized that she wasn't the only one appreciating the view. Spencer had been taking in an eyeful, and the look on his face said he was enjoying what he saw.

Spencer held his eye contact with her as he lowered himself to her, covering her body.

"You're so beautiful," he said, his voice thick.

Sensations layered in her body, building in intensity. Every breath she took seemed to take on a note.

"I know, baby. I feel it, too. Just hold on." He rolled away from her, returning with a foil packet that he pressed into her hand.

She ripped it open with her teeth and made short work of putting it on him. Spencer leaned down to kiss her as he lifted her legs around his waist, joining their bodies.

Jasmine's head fell back as every nerve ending responded to the feel of him inside her. She bit down on her lip, tasting blood as she tried to control herself.

Spencer rocked into her, leaning down to her ear. "Let go, baby. You don't have to fight it. It's just you and me here."

Her legs tightened around his back, driving him deeper inside her. "Mmm."

He retreated from her, dragging his fingers down her sides. "Ooh."

Their bodies came together. "That's it, honey. Let me know if you like it."

A loud scream filled the room, punctuating the liquid explosion between their bodies.

Jasmine must have drifted off for a while, because when she woke, she and Spencer were nestled under a lightweight sheet, spooning. The clock radio showed it was after midnight, and the only light in the room was a table lamp on the nightstand beside her.

She smiled to herself, enjoying the feeling of his arms wrapped around her. Her body felt languid and relaxed. She wasn't ready to return to the real world, so she closed her eyes and cleared her mind.

Spencer leaned over, placing his head in the crook between Jasmine's neck and shoulder, so his lips brushed her ear. "Jasmine?"

"Yes," she murmured.

"Why didn't you tell me you were a screamer?"

Her eyes popped open, and her back went rigid. She buried her face in the pillow, muffling her response.

He gently rolled her over. "What did you say?"

She pressed her eyelids shut. "I said, I didn't know that I was."

Spencer turned her onto her back, grinning down on her smugly. She braced herself for the moment when he would beat on his chest and yell like Tarzan. "So, I'm the first guy who ever made you—"

"Don't go getting all cocky on me." Jasmine, blushing, hid her face in her hands. "It had nothing to do with you."

He snorted. "Nothing to do with me, eh? Well, then I'd love to know who it *does* have to do with, because right now, I'm only counting two people in this bed. You and me."

She groaned, finally turning to face him. "I just mean that you shouldn't read anything into it. That's all."

He nodded, leaning back on his elbow. "I see. You're saying that just because our lovemaking was so spectacular that you saw fit to scream uncontrollably like a horny porn queen—which, might I add, you've never done before—I shouldn't feel that my incredible, masculine prowess had anything to do with it."

Jasmine batted at his head with her pillow. "I should have known you were going to be immature about this."

Spencer must have decided he'd teased Jasmine enough, because he wrapped his arms around her. She suspected that it wasn't just to enjoy the feel of her skin, but to keep her from taking another shot at him as well.

"You don't have to be embarrassed, sweetheart. I've never felt anything like this before, either. I know my reputation as a raging stud precedes me, but . . ." He released a self-deprecating laugh, and his joking tone slipped away. "Nobody's ever gotten under my skin the way you do."

Unsure what to do with the strong emotions flooding her, Jasmine tried to lighten the mood. "You mean, nobody's ever gotten on your nerves the way I do."

She'd suspected that Spencer never resisted an opening for a joke, but he did this time. "If we get on each other's nerves, it's only because we're so much alike. Tonight we've proven that we work well together in at least one way." He stroked her shoulder softly. "I bet there are other ways, too," he said seriously.

Jasmine swallowed a lump in her throat. "Maybe," she whispered. "I don't know. I'm not sure about anything right now. It's been a long time since I've . . . been like this with anyone."

He studied her face. "Really? How long?"

Suddenly, Jasmine felt shy. Her eyes locked on the ceiling fan above the bed. "A year and a half."

Spencer nodded, propping his head on his hand. "You know all about my past loves. In fact, you met half my ex-girlfriends last night, but I don't know anything about your love life. Did you have your heart broken? Is that why you waited so long?"

Jasmine knew it was an innocent question, but she still had mixed feelings. He hadn't told her *everything* about his love life. Still, it was true that he didn't know as much about her. Maybe if she confided in him . . . "I haven't had a lot of time for relationships. I've been working, fixing up my condo, and trying to—"

Spencer touched her shoulder to slow her down. "Who was he, Jasmine?"

With a deep sigh, she tried to relax. He was right; she did know all about his relationships. She owed him some kind of an answer, no matter how difficult it was for her to talk about.

"Nick. That's his name. I met him on a job I was working just before I left private practice to work for Core."

"Was he your client?"

"No, his wife was."

His jaw dropped. "He was married?"

"Actually, they were separated. Amy had moved into her own apartment in the District. She was a criminal lawyer and she was getting threats from the family of a client whose case she'd lost."

"So how did you get started up with the husband?"

"As things were calming down in Amy's life, I started running into Nick more when he came to visit their four-year-old son—"

"They had a kid!"

Jasmine winced. "I know. I know. Please don't judge me, otherwise I won't be able to finish the story."

"Sorry. Please finish. I'll be quiet."

"Both Amy and Nick confided in me that the marriage had been over for a long time and that they were both ready to move on. Still, don't get me wrong, I had no intention of getting involved. Even when I sensed Nick's attraction to me."

Jasmine sat up straight, leaning against the headboard as all the old emotions came flooding back to her. "The affair started by accident. Nick called to tell me he might have a job for me. I was living paycheck to paycheck, and by then I considered him a friend, so I agreed to meet him.

"We met for drinks and he told me about a friend of a co-worker who might need such and such, but it was all pretty vague. Nevertheless, we got to talking and he said he was going through a really hard time and it helped to have me as a friend. He gave me this sob story about how Amy looked down on him because she was a lawyer and he was a construction worker without a college education. He told me he'd found out that she'd cheated on him shortly after they'd been married and that she'd been lying to him all along. How he was going to leave her until he found out she was pregnant and blah blah blah.

"Anyway, I fell for it. He seemed to really need a friend, so when he called to talk, I always gave him my shoulder to cry on. Well, one night we went out for dinner and he insisted on buying. He ordered a bottle of wine, and he kept my glass full throughout dinner. I told him my limit, but when he kept pouring, I didn't want to waste his money.

"Needless to say, by the time we left, all that wine really hit me. I couldn't drive home, and he insisted I stay in his guest room. One thing led to another, and I woke up in his bed. That morning I freaked out and gave him a list of reasons why this couldn't go any further.

"But he told me he was falling in love with me. He said all the things I needed to hear, and talked me into giving it a shot. Next thing I knew I was knee-deep in a torrid affair. He even said he'd told Amy about us and that she didn't care. Just when I thought it might all work out after all, he dumped me."

"Why?"

"For all the reasons I'd had for not getting involved in the first place. The divorce wasn't final, he'd been on the rebound, their son might become confused, blah blah blah. He'd just been using me. After he didn't need me anymore, he dumped me, leaving me feeling like the world's biggest fool. I'd known better, and if I'd followed my head instead of my heart, none of it would have happened."

"He's a prick. He used you; it wasn't your fault."

"Oh, it was my fault all right. I knew better than to let it happen. He wasn't even my type."

"What *was* your type?" Spencer asked.

"Mature scholarly types. You know, well-dressed, well-spoken. Conservative. Not exactly handsome, but—"

"Safe."

"That isn't what I was going to say."

"And what was this Nick character like?"

"Handsome, well-built. Very masculine. Very attractive, but—"

"Anything but safe," he finished for her.

"Well, you can see what my walk on the wild side cost me."

"Everyone's heart gets broken."

"It was more than that. I lost respect for myself. For a while, I couldn't even trust my own judgment. I fell into a very deep depression after that. It took a lot for me to come back from it."

Spencer didn't speak; he just wrapped his arms around her and held her close. They lay that way for a long time, Spencer stroking her hair. Jasmine didn't want the mood to linger on that last conversation.

"I really enjoyed meeting your sister tonight," she said softly.

"Yeah? I'll bet." Spencer grinned. "What were the two of you talking about while my back was turned?"

"Actually, I couldn't get much dirt out of her. She mostly sang your praises. Clearly, she adores you. Dina seems really sweet."

"I adore her, too, but she wasn't always that sweet. She was the original wild child. In high school she had dyed hair, tattoos, piercings, black nail polish. The works. She was into that whole gothic thing."

"Interesting. So while your sister was into 'that whole gothic thing' you were into the whole all-American boy thing?"

"She told you about that?" Spencer sighed dramatically, clutching his heart. "Yes, it's true. I confess." His tone sobered. "My sister and I took opposite tactics to get our parents' attention when we were young."

"Uh-oh." She heard the same tone in Spencer's voice that came to hers when she spoke of her father.

"Oh, don't feel sorry for us. Dina and I grew up with proverbial silver spoons in our mouths. Our parents made sure we wanted for nothing, including the best nannies money could buy. It was years before either of us figured out that our parents couldn't stand the sight of us. They'd had children just because it was expected."

"So your parents weren't around much when you and Dina were growing up?"

Spencer laughed. "Hardly at all, but that's a good thing. They both have toxic personalities. Imagine how screwed up the two of us would be if they'd actually had some influence over our lives."

"Clearly, you both were affected, though. You said Dina acted out and you . . ."

"I tried to be the perfect son—but not for my parents' benefit. I did it for Dina. She needed to have someone in her life to look up to. I toed the line so that she would know she could always depend on me."

"She told me that you practically raised her."

"Oh, don't give me more credit than I'm due. We had excellent nannies. They raised us both, but they weren't family. Dina needed someone who could understand what she was feeling."

Jasmine's gaze wandered back to the photo on the dresser. "Well, your influence paid off. She's clearly grown into a lovely woman."

"Yeah." Spencer smiled, his face full of affection for his younger sibling. "She turned out okay. Me, on the other hand . . ."

Jasmine smiled, deciding she could be generous with him for a change. "You turned out fine, too. But what happened to that all-American boy?"

"It was all an act. Haven't you guessed that by now? Once Dina was in college, and I knew she was going to be okay, I moved out of the family house and got a job at WHOT one hundred as a shock jock. I knew my parents would *love* that. But I didn't have to toe the line anymore, so I didn't."

"So you're a bad boy now?"

One eyebrow rose. "I can still be good when I want to." He pulled the sheet away from her breasts, revealing her erect nipples. He slowly lowered his head. "But when I'm bad, I'm very very bad."

Jasmine gasped as his lips closed around her. "And that's good."

The next morning, Jasmine woke to Spencer snoring in her ear. She carefully slid out of bed. She found her clothes scattered around the room, and slipped into the bathroom to change.

Eyeing the square tub with bubble jets enviously, she opted for the glass shower stall in the corner instead. Twenty minutes later, she was feeling slightly more human and Spencer was still sound asleep.

As she watched him sleep, curled on his side and hugging the pillow where she'd been, doubts began to creep up on her. After all, she'd just slept with a client. If anyone found out, she'd get the boot for sure. But it wasn't really her job she was worried about. It was her heart.

In the harsh light of morning, she wasn't sure if what had happened between them had been a one-night stand or something more. Spencer had certainly behaved tenderly toward her afterward, but last night he'd been vulnerable. Today he might wake up his old cocky self and act differently.

She slipped out of the room with her things in hand. Part of her considered leaving before he woke so she wouldn't have to face him. But the other part of her knew that would be a mistake.

She would have to wait and confront this thing head-on. That was the only way they could salvage a working relationship, if that was all they were meant to have.

Entering the kitchen, Jasmine knew she needed to stay busy. After a quick peek in the refrigerator, she decided to make biscuits to have with breakfast. Lining items up on the counter, Jasmine went to retrieve the milk, noticing that the carton felt heavier than normal.

"I hope it hasn't gone bad." She opened it, discovering the contents were dark. "What the hell?"

Jasmine started pouring out the carton in the sink. "Oh my gosh, it's *sand*."

She heard something behind her and looked up to find Spencer standing in the doorway.

"Nightmary strikes again."

10

Spencer exited the bathroom to find Jasmine sitting at the kitchen table with her infamous notebook. For a moment he'd been afraid he was going to empty his guts, but he'd managed to pull himself together at the last minute.

"What are you writing now?" he asked, determined to put on a brave face. He'd woken up feeling pretty good for a guy with a stalker who'd been upgraded from psycho to homicidal. His main focus for the day had been to romance Jasmine to the point that she'd forget those doubts he knew were spinning around in her active mind.

He'd braced himself for a lecture on how unprofessional she felt it was for her to sleep with a client, and all the reasons why they should pretend last night had never happened.

But he'd had no intention of letting her get away with it. He'd made cautious, conservative Jasmine scream with passion, and he wasn't going to let her forget it. That was, until he'd watched that stream of sand flow out of his milk carton into the sink a few minutes ago.

"I'm making a list of suspects," Jasmine said.

"Is that right. And just how many people do you have on that list?" He went to the refrigerator and pulled out half a cheesecake that was left over from the party.

Jasmine eyed him sternly. "Are you going to eat that for breakfast?"

"Of course. It's pretty much been decided that there'll be no cereal and milk for breakfast. So, cheesecake's the next best thing. After all, I still need my dairy."

Jasmine shook her head but didn't comment. "I've listed every woman's name who was at the party last night. Until this morning, there was still a possibility that the grill fire was an accident. Now that I've seen the sand in the milk carton, we can be sure that Nightmary was on the premises."

"Want some?" he asked, dishing cake onto a plate. He knew it was important to go over this stuff, but he was a fan of the no-making-lists-of-potential-murderers-before-noon rule. If he could, he'd serve up a healthy slice of denial along with his cake.

He opened the refrigerator door to put the cake back, only to be met with protests.

"Hey, where are you going with that?" Jasmine said. "When you asked me if I wanted a slice, I nodded yes."

Spencer nearly dropped the cake platter. Never in a million years would he have guessed Jasmine was the type to indulge in sweet empty calories for breakfast. "That just goes to show, just because you sleep with a person doesn't mean you know everything about her."

"What?" she asked absentmindedly as she poured over her list.

"Nothing." He placed a plate of cheesecake before her. "So, don't keep me in suspense. Who's on the list?"

"Just to be fair, I had to include everyone. I figured if we evaluate each woman on the same criteria, we can eliminate them with confidence."

"So, if everyone is on that list, did you include yourself?"

Jasmine gave him a dirty look. "I'm the list maker. What would be the purpose of pretending I'm a suspect?"

He shrugged. "I just thought you were being thorough."

"I wrote the names down by order of arrival. It was easier to remember everyone that way."

"Unh," he grunted around a mouth full of cheesecake. "Let me see."

She slid the notebook across the table and dug into her piece of cake.

"Who's Miranda?" he asked, examining the first name on the list.

"That's the waitress who came with the caterer."

He nodded, skimming the names again. Gina's name was next, followed by Duan's and Juan's dates. Then came Tali and her friend Anne. Most of the other women were identified by their husbands. Carl's wife. Richard's wife. His brows rose when he came to the big red star beside the name Angela Bowers. "What's with the star?"

She didn't hear him. Her eyes were closed as she savored a creamy bite of cheesecake. Her eyes fluttered open slowly. "Mmm." She blinked, coming back to earth. "Did you say something?"

Spencer swallowed, trying to remember. All the blood had just left his head and pooled in his groin. "Uh . . ." He pointed to Angela's name.

"Oh. Right now, she's my top pick."

"Why?" he asked.

"Because we can place her at the scene of at least two incidents. She has a reason to be bitter toward men after the nasty breakup of her engagement. Plus, in some twisted way, she may blame all of this on you."

"How can that train wreck be my fault? She dumped me for a guy with more money."

"I know. That fits into my theory."

Spencer gave her his best you're-out-of-your-mind expression.

"The person we're dealing with is not using the same kind of logic the rest of us are using. In her demented mind, if you had been everything she'd needed, she wouldn't have had to going looking somewhere else. Maybe she's become fixated on you now because you represent everything she's lost."

Spencer pushed his empty plate from him with a weary sigh. "Sounds like a stretch to me."

"As a cop, you're trained not to dismiss any potential suspects. People have sides that they hide from the rest of the world. You can never be sure."

He shook his head. "I think you hated her on sight and that's why you're picking on her."

Jasmine bristled. "Why would I hate her on sight?"

He folded his arms behind his head, preparing to bait her. "Because life imitates high school, and she's the fluffy-headed cheerleader type that smart, studious girls like you loved to make fun of."

"Are you implying that I was a nerd in high school?"

"Not at all, but correct me if I'm wrong. What kind of grades did you get?"

"Mostly A's and B's, but I was very well rounded," she rushed to add.

He nodded smugly.

"I played on the field hockey team and I ran track."

He winked at her.

"And I had lots of . . . friends."

He decided to let her off the hook. "Hey, I believe you. Never doubted it for a minute."

She reached over and took the list back. "Fine. If you think I'm not being fair, talk me out of it. While you were dating Angela, would you say she appeared to be stable all the time?"

He leaned forward and met her direct stare. "Let me put it this way. She didn't seem any *less* stable than you."

"Touché." Jasmine's lips puckered as though someone had just pushed a lemon between them. "Okay, then you look at this list and give me your top pick."

When the notebook came back across the table at him, Spencer folded it shut. "I say we give this a rest."

Jasmine immediately began sputtering protests as he came around the table toward her. "I know it's important, but other things are important, too."

"What's more important than this?"

He wrapped his arms around her waist and began backing her toward the stairs. "Making you scream again."

"I hate to disappoint you, but I'm pretty sure that was a onetime thing. It had been a while . . ."

"We'll see," he said, picking her up and carrying her to the bedroom.

Later that afternoon, Spencer's ears were ringing, but they were both very satisfied.

The phone rang as Jasmine entered the house later that day. She was still focused on what had happened at Spencer's when she picked up the receiver. "Hello?"

"Minnie, you're home. I was all set to leave you a message."

"Hey, Sonny, what's up?"

"*Jason*. For heaven's sake, I'm not twelve anymore."

"I'm sorry, *Jason*. But I notice you're still calling me Minnie."

"Habit."

"What's up?"

Jasmine had a lot on her mind, and she was anxious to get back to her thoughts. They'd searched Spencer's entire house from top to bottom, but they found no other presents from Nightmary, as Spencer called her. The sand in the milk carton had been enough to prove that she had been at the party the night before. The question was: How had she slipped past them?

". . . take a vote since Mom won't get involved. If you agree to vote with me, I think I can convince Rome to do the same, and we'll win with a majority vote."

"I really can't get into this right now, Sonny. I have a lot on my mind." She hadn't wanted to leave Spencer alone at the house, but he'd insisted that he was tired since he hadn't gotten much sleep the night before.

That had caused Jasmine to blush. Finding the latest calling card from Spencer's stalker had prevented them from discussing what had happened between them. Part of her had been grateful for the distraction.

". . . take this more seriously. We all have to agree on what to do with the house. Keeping it intact will give us something to share with future generations of . . ."

Jasmine held the phone away from her ear for a moment while she changed her clothes. Aside from an awkward moment at the door before he decided to kiss her, things seemed okay between her and Spencer. Once again she was having trouble reading his reaction to the latest chapter in their stalker mystery.

". . . listening to me? What are you going to do about this?"

"I already told you what I'm going to do. I'm going to stay out of it. If Grandma had known what a fuss this was going to cause, I'm sure she would have left the house to Aunt Lavita's kids. Now, did you have anything else? If not, I have to go."

"I should have known you'd . . ."

Holding the phone between her jaw and her shoulder, Jasmine pulled a pair of jeans over her hips. She was going to have to move on the assumption that the stalker was one of the women at Spencer's party last night.

". . . responsibility to the family . . ."

It was possible that someone from the outside had snuck in and rigged the barbecue and left the carton of sand, but that was too hard to fathom at that point.

". . . would have a lot on your mind after you broke that guy's arm."

"What?" Suddenly, Sonny had Jasmine's full attention. "Just exactly whose arm do you think I broke?"

"I talked to Coby this morning. He told me all about that jam you got into with your new radio jock client."

"He told you I broke Spencer's arm?"

"Yeah. He said the guy was mouthing off and you wrestled him to the ground and—"

"Stop right there. We arm wrestled, Sonny, that's all. His arm was still intact when it was over. I guess he did technically end up on the ground, but that happened later." She rubbed her temple, realizing she wasn't making it sound any better. "But he wasn't hurt . . . I mean, I didn't—Oh, it's a long story."

There was a long silence on the other end of the line. "Uh . . . okay. Why don't I call you back when things have calmed down. By the way, Mom wants you to call her."

"Okay, fine, I'll call her. Talk to you soon. 'Bye." Jasmine hung up the phone, feeling a slight headache coming on. This was not a good time to call her mom.

Popping a couple of Advil tablets and chasing them with a tall glass of lemonade, Jasmine found herself in the guest bedroom where she kept her dollhouse collection.

She had only three houses so far, but she'd enjoyed picking out the delicate furnishings for each room. Her favorite was a tiny Victorian dollhouse she'd found in Williamsburg, Virginia. For this house she'd picked out frilly lace curtains, dainty chairs with flowered coverlets, and handmade rugs woven from colored ribbons.

Her own house was simply styled with clean lines and neutral colors because that was practical, but she really let herself go when she decorated her dollhouses. She tried to imagine what it would be like to live in such a perfect little house with a husband and a family.

That was where her fantasies always broke down. She could see the husband and the children as clearly as if they were real. But when she tried to paint herself into the picture as wife and mother, the image faded.

Part of her was afraid she'd never have those things. She lived and worked in a man's world, and every day was a struggle to survive.

Jasmine could hit a target between the eyes shot after shot at the firing range, and she could take down a man twice her size without breaking a sweat. She knew she could do her job better than most men, but when it came to being a woman, Jasmine felt inferior. Compared to women like Angela Bowers and Gina Hill, she felt like a boy with her short haircut and tall frame.

It wasn't just her looks. She knew she had feminine features and that men found her face and body attractive. It was the little things other women did that she had trouble with.

She'd never learned to flirt or exploit her feminine wiles. She rarely made up her face. When she remembered, she'd throw on some lip gloss and mascara, but that was it. She couldn't remember the last time she'd worn nail polish or had shopped for sexy lingerie.

Spencer hadn't seemed to mind, though. He seemed genuinely pleased with her qualities, she thought, trying to pull herself out of her moment of self-pity.

But how long would his interest in her last? The element of danger had always spurred their romantic encounters. Would he have shown any interest in her at all if he hadn't been forced by the circumstances to spend so much time with her?

Who knew? By now he might be having regrets about the night they'd spent together. Jasmine fingered a spindly little wooden baby crib that had plastic lilacs wound around each bar. She made the tiny crib rock with the tip of her finger.

It wasn't like her to feel this insecure. Telling Spencer about her relationship with Nick had left her feeling vulnerable.

The telephone rang, interrupting her pity party. She retrieved her cordless phone from her bedroom. "Hello?"

"Jasmine, can you come over right away?" It was Spencer.

"What's wrong? Is it an emergency?"

"Yes."

"I'll be right there."

Spencer opened the door, and Jasmine flew into the room. "What is it? What's wrong? Did you find something else?"

He watched calmly as she circled the room. "No."

She stopped in front of him. "Then what is it? You said it was an emergency."

He reached out and pulled her against him. He'd missed having her close. "Not that kind of emergency."

She blinked. "Oh."

He bent his head toward hers.

"Wait a minute," she said, placing a hand between them. "I should be really mad at you for scaring me like that."

"Fine." He pushed her purse off her shoulder.

"Be mad at me later. Right now, I'm going to make love to you."

That night, Spencer had trouble sleeping. He'd wanted to ask Jasmine to stay, but he wasn't sure if that would have been for professional or personal reasons. He wasn't even sure what he'd prefer.

The idea that some woman hated him enough to kill him really put life in perspective. He mentally retraced every relationship and acquaintance he'd had with a woman. Not every one had run smoothly, but all in all, he felt he had more motive for murder than any of them.

Part of the reason he couldn't sleep was because he knew he had to go on the air the next night. He was afraid of losing his edge. If he guarded every word for fear of inciting Nightmary, then his show would suck. On the other hand, if he let it fly like he always did, who knew what Nightmary would do next.

He wanted Jasmine close, but he hadn't planned on calling her back that afternoon. He knew he'd complicated things for both of them by letting their relationship become physical, but he didn't regret it.

Jasmine had cautioned him not to mention the sand in the milk carton to anyone else. She said there was a strong possibility that Nightmary was someone he'd invited to the party, rather than some elusive stranger who'd slipped in and out without being noticed. And perhaps that person would give herself away by mentioning it first.

Spencer wasn't sure what his next move would be. But, suddenly, with Nightmary out there somewhere, he was grateful to have Jasmine at his back.

Gina was already in the studio when Spencer and Jasmine got there Monday night. "Hey, you two," she greeted them. "Spencer, you look like your old self again."

He ran his hand over the flat top of his hair. "Like my new do? It's shorter than I normally like it, but I had to get rid of the singed hair."

"It looks great," Gina said. "I never would have known you'd had an accident."

Jasmine smiled. He really did look great with his new haircut.

Spencer strutted toward the kitchenette like a model on a runway. "I'm going to get a cup of coffee. Anyone want anything."

Both women laughed and shook their heads.

Jasmine settled into her usual corner only to find Gina studying her closely. "What?"

The woman grinned. "That's what I want to know. What was that?"

"What was what?" Jasmine felt her face heat. She hoped it wasn't true that another woman could sense when a woman had had sex.

"That look you and Spencer exchanged. Is there something going on between you two?"

Jasmine swallowed hard. "That's ridiculous."

"No, it's not. Reading people is my job, and something has definitely changed between the two of you. Look, I hope you're not uncomfortable because of what I said the other night. That was a long time ago. We've both moved on."

Jasmine popped up to shut the door of the studio. She obviously wasn't going to be able to hide the truth from the other woman anyway. "This has got to stay between you and me, Gina. I don't know where this thing with Spencer is going yet. Plus, I could lose my job if it gets around."

Gina's eyes widened. "Say no more. Confidentiality is my specialty. What happened?"

Jasmine had just opened her mouth to tell her when Spencer returned with his coffee. The room was instantly quiet, and Spencer looked around suspiciously. "Why do I get the distinct impression the two of you were talking about me?"

Gina snorted. "That's only because you think everything pertains to you, Spencer. But, contrary to your beliefs, the world doesn't revolve around you." Gina seemed to realize her words must have come out more sharply than she'd intended, because she tried to soften the blow with a delicate laugh and a friendly slug in the arm.

"Touché," he said, sipping his coffee.

"Mmm, that smells good." Gina stood. "I'm going to go get myself a cup before we go on the air."

He shook his head. "I just asked if you wanted some."

"I didn't want any then, but I want some now. Be right back."

Spencer watched Gina leave, then he walked over to Jasmine and planted a juicy kiss on her lips.

She pushed him away with two hands. "Spencer, if anyone sees you doing that, I'll lose my job."

He grinned wickedly. "Every relationship needs a little danger to keep things interesting."

Jasmine shook her head, pushing harder on his chest. "You, of all people, should know that's not true. Please, now, go over there before Gina gets back."

Difficult as always, Spencer wouldn't go back to his seat until he stole another kiss. Jasmine couldn't pretend she was upset. She couldn't help enjoying the attention.

Gina came back, stirring her coffee with a strange look on her face.

"What's wrong?" Jasmine asked.

"It was really weird. I opened a new container of sugar, and when I poured it into my coffee, it was sand."

Spencer froze. "What?"

"Oh, my God!" Jasmine exclaimed.

"I know; it was strange. So anyway, I opened *another* one and that was fine."

"What did you do with the first container?" Jasmine asked.

Gina looked at Jasmine quizzically. "Well, I threw it in the trash. Why, do you think we should sue the manufacturers?"

Jasmine didn't stay to answer Gina's question. She raced down the hall to the staff kitchen. Sure enough, the sugar container in the trash was filled with sand. She put it into a plastic bag and brought it back to the studio.

"You're going to keep it?" Gina asked when she saw Jasmine with the bag. "It's the strangest thing. I feel like I'm being haunted by the sand monster or something."

Jasmine stared at Gina. "What are you talking about? Has this happened before?"

"Yeah, when I got into the car this evening, there was a big pile of sand on my driver's seat. I couldn't figure out how it got in there."

"No, Gina," Spencer said, speaking for the first time. "Nightmary is after you, too!"

It was nearly midnight when Jasmine's cell phone started ringing. She had to stand up and rush out of the studio before she interrupted the broadcast. "Hello?"

"Do you need a lawyer?"

"What? Tinman, is that you?" She could hear her ten-month-old niece crying in the background.

"I said, Do you need a lawyer? I can't imagine that there won't be some legal repercussions when this guy wakes up."

Jasmine rolled her eyes. This had to be some kind of joke. Her older brothers had been known to play some pretty cruel jokes on her while she was growing up. "Justin Cuthbert White, I don't know what you're talking about, but I don't have time for games right now. I'm working."

"I hardly think putting a client into a coma is a game. Now, do you have a good lawyer, or not? If you don't, one of the guys at the firehouse recommended—"

"What?" Jasmine shrieked. Then she took a deep breath, trying to bring her pulse back under control. "Don't tell me you've been talking to Sonny. I told him—"

"Actually, it was Coby. He called me late last night at the firehouse. He said you'd gone upside some disc jockey's head because he made some sexist remarks."

Jasmine rubbed the back of her neck, suddenly very tired. "That's not the exact story, but how did you get from there to a coma?"

"You know how Coby tells a story: 'She threw him over her shoulder . . . yadda yadda yadda . . . and he's still unconscious.' "

"Coby exaggerated, but I'm not going to go

into the details now. Like I said, I'm working. Suffice it to say, I haven't put anyone into a coma, and I don't need a lawyer."

"Okay, Sis. That's what I wanted to hear. Call me at the firehouse tomorrow. I want the long version of this story, hear me?"

"You got it."

"By the way, call Mom."

Jasmine hung up the phone, muttering under her breath. If her mother wanted to talk to her so urgently, why didn't *she* call *her*, instead of telling her brothers to deliver the message? *Family.*

Jasmine stepped out onto her front porch for the *Washington Post* to read with her breakfast. She went into the kitchen and started leafing through the paper as she sipped her coffee.

"Hmm, seems like a slow news day," she muttered as she turned to the Style section. When she caught sight of the huge black-and-white photo that stared back at her, she screamed and spilled her coffee all over Spencer's widely grinning face.

She had to run the paper under a blow dryer so she could read the article. The headline read, "SANDMAN'S DREAM GIRL: Local Radio Deejay Hires Female Bodyguard for *Close* Protection."

Jasmine clutched her chest to make sure she wasn't going into cardiac arrest. Her cover had just been broken in a major newspaper.

11

*J*asmine had just finished skimming the article when her telephone started ringing. She expected she would get several more calls before the day was out, but it was no surprise that Nathan got to her first.

"Before you say anything, Nathan, let me explain."

"You're damn right you're going to explain. Explain to me why the hell I shouldn't fire you right now."

"Well, I—"

"Not only can't you control your client, but you get your name plastered all over the *Washington Post* like some kind of sex scandal. I have a mind to—"

"Listen, Nathan, this was not my—"

"Never in all my thirty plus years in this business has anyone botched a job like this."

"Nathan! Will you please just listen. For heaven's sake, how am I supposed to explain myself if I can't get a word in edgewise?"

"Don't you disrespect me, Jasmine. I'm your boss, at least for the next five minutes."

"Look, there was obviously a leak to the press, but it didn't come from me. Since a few people at WLPS, and even fewer people at Core, are the only ones who even know enough to tell, why don't you give me some time to get to the bottom of this? I'll call the station manager and see what she knows, then get back to you."

"You'd damn well better get back to me. I want answers and I want them today!" With that, he hung up on her.

This is not going to be a good day, Jasmine thought, hanging up the phone.

As soon as the phone made contact, it started ringing again. "Here we go." Taking a bracing breath, she picked it up. "Hello?"

"Jasmine, why didn't you tell us you were going to be in the paper? I just went out and bought ten copies."

"Mom, I didn't know I was going to be in the paper. Besides, this isn't a good thing."

"Well, I know they didn't include your picture, but they must have printed your name at least seventeen times. I counted," she said proudly.

Jasmine sighed. "No, that's not the problem. The problem is that I shouldn't be in the paper at all. I'm a bodyguard, remember? I'm supposed to remain anonymous."

"Oh." There was a brief silence that gave Jasmine just enough time to catch her breath. "Well, when you talk to Rome, can you tell him to stop by the house? I picked up some extra socks for the kids. I ordered them off the Internet."

Her mother was always ordering one thing or another off the Internet. Jasmine was afraid that the family would have to get together for an intervention soon, to cut up her credit cards. "Is that why you called me, Mom?"

"No. Of course not. I called about the newspaper article."

"But yesterday both Sonny and Tinman said you wanted to talk to me. The paper didn't come out until today."

"Hmm, I wonder what was on my mind?"

Jasmine shook her head. If this day got any worse, then she was going to go back to bed.

"Oh, now I remember. I'm cleaning out the attic and I have some boxes that need to be taken to the Salvation Army."

Jasmine didn't like where this was going, so she headed up the stairs to her bedroom. "Yes?"

"The boxes are filled with old books from Grandma's library. Can you come and get them for me?"

Jasmine groaned silently as she sank onto the

edge of the bed. "Mom, books are heavy. Why don't you get one of the boys to do it?"

"But you live the closest and you're the most reliable."

Gee, that's just great. She would have been home free if her mother hadn't thrown in that last bit about her being the most reliable. She stretched out on the bed, tucking her head into the pillow. "But you just said that Rome had to come by and get the socks. Why don't you wait for him?"

"Does that mean you won't do it?" Her mother had perfected the same pitiful voice she and her brothers had used when they wanted dessert before dinner.

Jasmine pulled the covers over her head. "I'm not saying that, it's just—"

"Perfect. I'll have them ready for you to pick up tomorrow. I have to run. Talk to you soon. 'Bye."

Jasmine stared at the buzzing telephone. "Very clever, hanging up before I could say no."

Just as she was about to drift off to sleep the phone rang again. "Who is it?" Jasmine barked crankily.

"Is this a bad time?"

"Gina! Oops, I'm sorry. This day just hasn't gotten off to a good start."

"I can imagine. Listen, I saw the article in the *Post*. Any idea how they got it?"

"Your guess is as good as mine," Jasmine said.

"There are only a handful of people who could have done it."

"I know. Anyway, since we didn't get to finish our conversation last night, and since that article probably sparked a few tempers, I thought you might want to get together for some coffee or something."

Jasmine was touched. "That sounds pretty good. It would be nice to see a friendly face before I have to face the lions."

"Great. Do you want to meet at the Starbucks in Union Station around one o'clock?"

"Sounds great. See you then."

An hour later, Jasmine was dressed and ready to head out the door when her phone rang again. "Hello?"

"Hey, kiddo, what's up?"

"Rome. I should have expected to hear from you next. You all are so predictable. Before you say anything, no, I haven't murdered, maimed, or mutilated any of my clients. I do not need a lawyer, and my health insurance is current."

"What are you talking about, Sis?"

"You mean you haven't talked to Coby."

"Sure, I talked to him a couple of days ago."

"And he didn't tell you that I broke Spencer Powell's arm or put him into a coma? Or any other such nonsense?"

"No. Why would he?"

"Oh, thank goodness!"

"But what's this about you having a three-way with the Sandman and a stripper?"

Jasmine ran out of the house cursing under her breath. If she wasn't already late, she'd call Coby and give him a piece of her mind.

That would teach her to confide in him. There was no way he'd botched the story that much by accident. He must have thought it was really funny to make her family think she was even crazier than they already thought she was.

She made a mental note to return the practical joke at his expense when her schedule cleared up.

Jasmine got to the radio station just after eleven-thirty. She was hoping to go straight to Tali's office, but everyone she met in the hallway wanted to talk about the article in the *Post*. Either they were shocked because they'd had no idea she was a bodyguard and wanted to discuss the business, or they wanted her to know how clever they had been in suspecting something was up, even though they couldn't quite put their fingers on it.

When she finally did reach Tali's open office door, she leaped inside and closed the door behind her.

Tali swung around from her computer. "There you are. I've been trying your number since ten A.M."

"Needless to say, my phone's been ringing off

the hook. If you've been looking for me, I guess I don't have to ask if you read the article in the *Post*."

"Any idea who leaked the story?" Tali asked.

"I was just about to ask you the same thing."

Tali shook her head. "I've grilled all my people and threatened them with unemployment, and they all swear they had nothing to do with it. I have to believe them. Most of them honestly believed you were Spencer's personal assistant."

Jasmine sank into a guest chair in front of Tali's desk. "So where do we go from here? Even though the public doesn't know what I look like, technically my cover's been compromised."

Tali rubbed her temple. "I've been thinking about this carefully. How important is anonymity to your job, really?"

"That depends on the client. We usually try to keep a low profile out of respect for the client's privacy."

Tali thought for a moment. "We'll be packing up and leaving for Ocean City this weekend anyway. Even if we were to get someone else at this point, the story's already been leaked. There's nothing we can do about that. Maybe acknowledging the fact that Spencer has a bodyguard will be an additional deterrent."

"That's possible. It's your choice, Tali. Nathan is prepared to send over someone else, if that's what you'd like."

"I know. When I couldn't reach you, I called him. Even though Nathan thinks it would be best to rotate, Spencer is used to you, and you know how temperamental he can be. With all the additional stress he's under with these threats and the barbecue explosion, I want to keep him calm."

Jasmine sighed in relief. So Nathan had tried to edge her out behind her back. So much for a fair shot. He could make her life very difficult if he'd lost faith in her. Even though Tali was still in her corner, she had to try to turn him around.

After she left the station, Jasmine headed straight to the offices of Core Group Protection. The bodyguards all had cubicles where they could fill out paperwork, make phone calls, and plug in laptops.

Since, until recently, Jasmine had spent the most time in the office, she'd gotten the biggest cubicle. It was beside a huge picture window and in a prime spot just outside Nathan's office. Even if that spot did mean running off copies for Nathan on occasion, the window seat was worth it.

She stopped by her desk to drop off her things and discovered that everything had been rearranged. In fact, she didn't even recognize most of the junk. "Whose stuff is this?" she called out to no one in particular.

A second later, Mike Rudy's head popped over the wall. He was her one true ally at Core. A thick, burly black man around six-six, he could have easily passed for one of her brothers.

"I tried to stop him, J."

She rolled her eyes. "Don't tell me."

"Kirklin bogarted your desk."

"Should I even bother to ask why?"

Rudy sipped from his coffee mug and shrugged. "Some lame excuse. They painted the hallway last week, and he said the fumes were affecting his sinuses since his desk is by the door. He said he had to have this desk because it was by the window."

Jasmine was seething. "So, let me guess. He moved all my stuff to that crappy desk by the door."

Rudy nodded. "I told him he was acting shady, but he wasn't trying to hear me. He said he cleared it with Pruitt."

"That's who I'm here to see anyway."

"Keep it real, J. Don't let him hate on you."

She nodded. "I'll try not to."

"Cool. I'll holler at you later."

Jasmine knocked on Nathan's door and waited for him to tell her to come in. He insisted on keeping his door closed. He claimed it was because he dealt with confidential issues regularly. She was pretty sure it was because he didn't want anyone to know he was playing solitaire all day.

He looked up as she plopped herself into a

chair. "What are you doing in today? It's not payday."

"I just came from WLPS. Tali said you tried to convince her to let me go."

His brows knit together. "I told you in the beginning—this isn't about your ego. We've got to do what's best for the client."

His complete lack of remorse for dogging her behind her back, in addition to Kirklin's shady move with her desk, had the little vein in her neck throbbing. In a perfect world, she could leap across his desk and choke some sense into him without repercussion.

Instead, she took a deep breath. *Temper Management Exercise No. 2: Convert Negative Thoughts into Positive Ones.* She was never going to get anywhere with Nathan if she flew off the handle. Somewhere in that blustery exterior was the man who'd hired her in the first place. The one who'd said that her unconventional style was an asset. She just needed to remind him.

"I was just wondering why you're so convinced that I'm not the best man for the job."

"You're letting this character run you," Nathan said. "You're supposed to have control of the situation. We're never going to see any results this way."

Results? Spencer Powell is alive. What more do you want? "Sir," she said calmly, "maybe I haven't done a good job of making you aware of the dangerous circumstances that I've maintained control over. In fact, I saved Spencer Powell's life Saturday night."

Nathan smirked. "Giving him a soft cushion to fall on as he leapt back from a flaming barbecue doesn't quite constitute saving a man's life. Kirklin was the one who secured the remains of the grill. He said you were sitting in a chair shaking like a leaf."

That low-down double-crossing liar. I'll kill him!

Jasmine bit the inside of her cheek. "I think in all the excitement, Kirklin missed a few details. Like the fact that I saw Spencer light the grill and noticed that the flame was not contained inside as it should have been. His back was turned, so Spencer didn't notice. If I hadn't pulled him back, he would have been flame-broiled. Both Tali and Spencer can confirm that."

Nathan was silent for a moment. "Kirklin didn't tell me that."

Damn right, he didn't. Because saving the target beat the hell out of retrieving a stupid grill from the pool. Stick that in your pipe and smoke it, Nathan!

"Well, I'm glad we got that straightened out," Jasmine said. "I want you to have confidence in me, sir. The radio station seems to be pleased with my performance, but none of that matters if I don't have your respect."

Nathan grumbled under his breath. "Yeah, well, I wouldn't have hired you if you weren't competent. Just, just . . . keep up the good work."

On her way to the door, Jasmine looked back over her shoulder. "By the way, Nathan. Do you mind if I move my stuff back to my desk? Now, that the painters are finished, I'm sure Kirklin would prefer his old desk."

Nathan nodded and waved her out.

Jasmine smiled when every paper clip and staple was back where it belonged. Not only had she gotten through to Nathan, she'd managed to stick it to Kirklin, even in a small way.

Jasmine caught the metro to Union Station and barely made it to the coffee shop on time. Gina was waiting for her out front, looking fresh and cool in her yellow linen shorts and matching tank. She had a periwinkle-blue sweater knotted over her shoulders and blue-tinted sunglasses shading her eyes.

Jasmine tried not to feel self-conscious about her own plain white jeans and peach T-shirt. She'd been happy with the summery outfit until she'd seen Gina.

The two women hugged hello, then found a table near the window. Jasmine had never been much for flavored coffees, but today she decided to tear a page out of Gina's book and ordered a raspberry mocha latte.

"You look really drained," Gina said, studying her face with concern. "How are you holding up?"

Jasmine had never had too many girl friends

growing up, and suddenly, she was beginning to realize just what she'd been missing. "I'm not used to people asking me that. Because of my job and the environment I grew up in, most people expect me to just deal."

Gina sipped her coffee. "You know, it's not uncommon for women working in predominantly male environments to feel a bit of an identity crisis."

Jasmine blushed. "Is it that obvious?"

Gina waved her hand. "Not at all. I don't want you to think that because I'm a psychologist I'm trying to psychoanalyze you. I called you because I'd like for us to be friends."

Jasmine smiled at her new friend. "I'd like that, too." Glancing around the coffeehouse, she wanted to make sure that no one was listening. That was the great thing about D.C. People had their own problems and weren't worried about anyone else's.

Even though she was grateful to have another female in her corner, Jasmine was out of practice when it came to confiding to a girl friend. She wanted to release all the overwhelming emotions that had been building inside her about Spencer, but she knew she was going to have to work up to it. Jasmine had a real fear of letting herself become too vulnerable, and she spent most of her time avoiding that eventuality, not inviting it in.

"Right now," Jasmine said, "the most important thing on my mind is keeping Spencer safe.

Have you talked to him this morning? I tried his number a few times before I came to meet you, but I kept getting his answering machine."

Gina shook her head. "I talked to him just after I called you. He did say he was turning off his ringer. I let him know that I would be seeing you, and he wanted me to tell you that he'll see you tonight."

Jasmine nodded. "What did he say about the article?"

"He has no idea where it came from, just like the rest of us. Tali called and raised holy hell with him because she thought it was another one of his irreverent pranks."

"Spencer likes to be the center of attention," Jasmine conceded, "but even I know he'd never take it this far. Especially now. I think he's actually a little afraid of what Nightmary will do."

"How's he holding up? You know Spencer, it's really hard to gauge his moods."

Jasmine nodded. "He's been more quiet than usual. After you found sand in the sugar container, he seemed to withdraw. I admire the way he carried on for his radio audience, but on the way home he clammed up. Nightmary wants us to know that she's close, and I think that's getting to him."

"Do you have any more clues to her identity? What about the police?"

Jasmine rolled her eyes. "We've been making regular police reports, but, of course, their participation is limited. I'm starting to think it has to be someone Spencer knows. We were all watching so carefully at the party, but Nightmary still managed to slip in and out undetected. Same deal with the radio station. Who else could slip into the staff kitchen and leave that sugar container?"

"That's very interesting. Obviously, the article in the *Post* was placed by someone who was intimately familiar with the recent circumstances. That means it was probably Nightmary."

"I hadn't thought of that," Jasmine said. "My first guess was that it was someone at the station looking to drum up publicity, but it makes sense that it could be the stalker. She's mocking my attempts to protect Spencer."

"How does that make you feel?" Gina asked.

"Angry!" Jasmine found herself shouting, and consciously lowered her voice. "Of course, it makes me feel angry. Especially since I don't know what this woman wants or what she hopes to gain from this. What do you think she's after?"

Gina stared down into the darkness of her coffee, contemplating Jasmine's question carefully. "That's really hard to say right now. There is a pattern emerging. Using the sand as a calling card, to both torment Spencer and be close to him. It's really hard to understand what level of dementia this person is functioning on."

"How can I keep Spencer safe now when all of the D.C. metropolitan area knows that I'm trying to do it?"

"The bright side is that they didn't print a picture of you in the paper," Gina reminded her. "Only Spencer."

"Yes, but they have my name. It's only a matter of time before they dig up my high school yearbook and splash my bad hairdo and pimples all over the front page."

Gina smiled. "I don't think that's going to happen. Don't worry about what the media is going to do. Until someone tells you otherwise, you've still got a job to do. How are things between you and Spencer anyway?"

Jasmine felt herself blushing again. "We've ventured into uncharted territory."

"What does that mean?"

Jasmine squirmed a bit in her seat. "Doors have been opened between us that can't be closed."

"What are you trying to say?"

"I'm saying that Spencer and I are dancing to a new tune now. I just don't know how long I can avoid stepping on his toes."

"You're driving me crazy." Gina smacked her forehead. "What's with the metaphors? Spit it out. Are you and Spencer a couple?"

"I can't say the words out loud because I don't know where we stand. We've definitely broken new ground—"

"Jasmine . . ." Gina warned with a sly smile.

"I mean we've definitely broken out of the client/bodyguard relationship. We've even surpassed friendship, but by how much, I just don't know. We haven't talked about it, and frankly, I'm afraid to. I'm not even sure if I'm ready to have it clearly defined for me. Besides, we've had a lot of other things to worry about. Suddenly the dynamics of our 'relationship' don't seem quite as important."

"That happens a lot in budding romance. The element of danger heightens the need for physical and emotional comfort. It's very easy to turn to the person you're going through that adventure with for release."

Jasmine's heart sank. "I'd been wondering about that myself. Would Spencer and I have anything to do with each other if we weren't caught up in the moment?"

"Is that all you think this is?" Gina asked gently.

"I don't know *what* to think about it. You're the psychologist. What do you think?"

"As a psychologist, I'd say you'll never be able to be sure what this relationship is based on until you've given it a try under everyday, ordinary circumstances. You know, the mundane, like dirty socks on the floor and panty hose on the shower rod. But, as your friend, I say screw that psychological crap. If you like him and he likes you, that's what matters. A lot of relationships get started under bizarre circumstances, but that doesn't mean they won't last."

Jasmine released a breath of relief. "Thanks,

Gina. Hearing that from you really helps. I mean, you know Spencer better than almost anyone."

"We've been friends a long time. I want him to be happy. And, right now, I can see that you're making him happy. Of course, if you hurt him, I'll have to rip your hair out." She laughed heartily at her joke.

Jasmine joined in. She'd *never* hurt Spencer. She only hoped that went vice versa, too.

That evening, Jasmine arrived at Spencer's to take him to the studio. But when he opened the door he was wearing his bathrobe.

"Why aren't you dressed?" she asked. "I know it's radio, but don't you think you should at least wear pants?"

"I'm not going to the station tonight," he said.

"Why not? Is something wrong?"

"I called in sick."

Jasmine reached up to feel his forehead. "You don't have a fever. What's wrong?"

He took her hand from his forehead and held it between both of his own. "Nothing's wrong. I just needed a break, and I thought it would be nice if you and I had a date."

Her mind went blank. "Date?"

"Yes. A date. You know, those things that regular couples have all the time. I know we shouldn't go out, so I thought we'd do it here."

For the first time, her eyes drifted past him, and she could see candlelight flickering from the living room. Her heart swung out of her chest and back like a pendulum. "Are we a couple?"

His smile was tender, devoid of its usual wicked tilt. "Yes. We are." He pressed a finger to her lips. "And I don't want to hear any protests."

She swallowed the "but" that teetered on the edge of her tongue. With it went the doubts and questions she'd been tossing around for the last few days.

He squeezed her fingers. "I know what you're thinking, but I'm not him, and you've got to take a chance again sometime. You've got to let someone in here eventually." He tapped her chest, above her heart. "I'm just letting you know, that person is going to be me. You're going to give *me* a chance."

"Mighty sure of yourself, aren't you?" she said with feigned hauteur, only because she couldn't handle the tide of emotions threatening to drown her at that moment.

He picked up her cue to lighten the mood. "Of course I am. I can't let you just use and abuse my body. I'm not that kind of guy. If you want the goods, you've got to wine and dine me."

"Well, in that case, wait until you see what I bought at Victoria's Secret today."

12

"**I** haven't been to Ocean City since college," Jasmine told Tali. They were sitting in the lobby of the hotel, waiting for their rooms to be ready. "A group of girls would live at the beach every summer, and sometimes I'd go down and visit for a weekend or two."

Tali shrugged. "I know this place like the back of my hand, I've been down here so much. Not only does the station come every year, but sometimes I make the trip for vacation in the fall."

Tali had had to come down early to supervise the equipment setup, and Jasmine had ridden with her to put security precautions into place. Two more vans would arrive later that afternoon, one with the hosts from the morning show and the other with Spencer, Gina, Kirklin, and Rudy.

On a good day Jasmine wasn't much of a beach person. So the added pleasure of watching out for a crazy woman while trying to keep Kirklin from muscling her out of the job made this particular trip even less appealing.

"You should take advantage of the fact that you'll have two other men on duty, and see the sights," Tali suggested. "You guys work in shifts, right?"

Jasmine nodded. "That's right. While Spencer's in the hotel, one of us will always be on duty. When he has activities, no less than two, sometimes all three of us, will be on duty."

"I find what you do really fascinating." Tali went on to ask her a lot of questions about the business. How she'd gotten started, what kind of training she'd needed, and how she maintained security during a crisis.

Jasmine was a little surprised by the depth of Tali's interest in her work, but since she represented the company that was paying her salary, Jasmine answered all her questions.

"Well, I'm hoping nothing will happen while we're out of town," Tali said, glancing at her watch.

"Me, too. This is where we find out just how determined Nightmary is." Unfortunately, their location wasn't a secret. Spencer's show would be broadcast live all week long.

Tali shook her head. "I can't believe you-all

gave her a name. Don't you think that gives her more dignity than she deserves?"

"It was Spencer's doing, but I have to admit that I got tired of referring to her as 'the stalker.' "

Tali shrugged. "I don't care what you call her just as long as you keep her away from Spencer. We have a lot riding on him."

These hotel arrangements stink! It took all of Spencer's willpower not to shout those words out of the balcony doors at the top of his lungs.

His bedroom suite had a king-size bed that he'd been hoping to share with Jasmine—at least on occasion. Instead, he discovered that he had one guard sleeping in the sofa bed in the sitting room, and another one on a roll-away by the windows! Jasmine was in a connecting room next door, but with this 24/7 surveillance, he'd never have any time alone with her.

He'd been hoping for the best when Tali informed him that there would be two more guards in the rotation during the trip. The new guy didn't seem so bad. Rudy even seemed to have a sense of humor, but the other guy, Kirklin—he was another story . . . and another story . . . and another boring story after that. Why didn't he ever shut up?

As he unpacked his suitcase, Spencer decided he was going to have to do something about this arrangement. A lot of his time was carefully scheduled, but that didn't mean there wouldn't be time to sneak off with Jasmine if he played his cards right.

Jasmine pushed open the connecting door between the rooms. "How's it going over here, boys?"

Spencer's eyes prowled over her like a hungry predator. He could just eat her up. Apparently, she had gone shopping with Gina for some new clothes for the beach. Part of him wished that she hadn't. She always looked tailored and professional around him. Nice. But today . . . he didn't know how he was going to keep his hands off her.

She stood in the open doorway dressed in pale yellow shorts that were practically see-through against her honey-gold skin. Her top, also pale yellow, looked like a wispy handkerchief that she'd knotted around her breasts.

He was dying to cross the room and peak under that filmy triangle. The worst part was the haircut. Spiky, short, and sexy. If he had a nickel for every person who'd said she looked like Halle Berry, he'd be a richer man.

"Great. Just great," Spencer said, closing the drawer on the last of his clothes. "I was just telling these two that I'd like to hit the boardwalk tonight."

Jasmine sank down on the bed with a big bounce. "I don't know if that's a good idea."

Kirklin started to interject, but Spencer spoke over him. "I already know what you're going to say, Jasmine. You want me to stay in the hotel every second that I'm not scheduled to do a show, right?"

"Well, I'm not trying to make you into a prisoner, but—"

"Good, then it's settled. Boardwa—"

"But," she interrupted, "it wouldn't hurt to stay close. The hotel has some nice restaurants and a game room for you to check out."

"The hotel's right on the boardwalk," Spencer reminded them. "I'd say that's sticking close."

Jasmine shook her head. "There are lots of people on the boardwalk. Crowds we won't be able to control. There's no sense in making things—"

"Dag!" Rudy said, shaking his head. "Do you two always go at it like this?"

Kirklin moved to the center of the room. "There's an easy solution to this problem. Maybe White wasn't capable of handling this type of situation on her own, but there are three of us now. We'll make one trip down the boardwalk and back. Each of us can take a hundred-and-twenty degree scanning sector."

Spencer grinned, watching Jasmine's lips press tightly together. Up until now, he'd been under the impression that was an expression reserved solely for him. "I have no idea what he just said, but it sounds like a plan to me,"

Spencer announced, jumping at the idea before Jasmine could protest.

"For the record," Jasmine said, folding her arms stubbornly across her chest, "I'm against this."

Nevertheless, thirty minutes later they were marching down the boardwalk. It wasn't quite what Spencer'd had in mind. Kirklin walked ahead of him, and Rudy and Jasmine were spread out behind him. Every time he stopped, the whole team would halt and rearrange their positions around him. He felt like he was a part of a broken-down high school drill team. All they needed were colored flags and a cadence.

"Okay, I've had enough of this bullshit," Spencer finally said when his frustration level reached its peak in front of a little beachwear shop. "I feel like a freak with the three of you circling around me like this."

Jasmine grinned knowingly, moving to his side. "Well, then you should have stayed in the hotel as I suggested."

"No! We're miles away from home, and I'm not going to spend this entire trip hiding out. Besides, it's so overcast right now, the boardwalk is half empty anyway. Either walk with me like normal people or head back to the hotel, but I'm not putting up with this crap anymore."

At first Spencer thought they were going to argue, but to his surprise, it was Jasmine who caved in first. "Okay, let's do this. I'll walk beside Spencer. The two of you flank us from a four-foot distance, covering the rear and sides. That ought to make him feel less conspicuous."

Kirklin looked like he wanted to protest, but Rudy jabbed him in the arm, and they started off in the new formation.

"Is this better?" she asked.

"Much better," Spencer said with a sigh. "At least this way we can talk without those two goons overhearing us."

"They're not goons. Well, *Rudy* isn't a goon."

"Yeah, I guess he's cool. I meant to ask you after the party, what's the deal with Kirklin?"

"He's a self-important, egomaniacal jerk. Next question."

"Ha, that's what I thought." They walked in silence for a moment, taking in the expanse of the sandy beach and the Atlantic Ocean. "So," he said, ready to discuss the topic that had been on his mind all day. "How are we supposed to find any alone time with this arrangement? I have no intention of going this entire week without making love to you."

Jasmine's eyes went wide and her head darted around to make sure Kirklin and Rudy hadn't heard him. He followed her panicked gaze. The two men weren't paying them any mind.

Nevertheless, she gave him a warning look. "Keep it down. If anyone finds out—"

"I know, I know. Don't change the subject. What's the plan? How do we get rid of these two goons when we want to be alone?"

"We don't get rid of them. They're here for your protection . . . just like I am. I'm afraid you're going to have to go without *intimacy*." She whispered the last word.

"The hell I will. If you won't help me come up with a plan, I'll do it by myself."

Jasmine giggled. "Doing it by yourself. You're right. That will solve the problem perfectly."

He rolled his eyes. "You know that's not what I meant."

"Look, we can't discuss this. Especially, not now."

"If you're worried that we'll make too much noise, I have ways of taking care of that."

Jasmine glared at him, clearly refusing to continue the conversation.

Spencer chuckled at her stiff profile. He loved it when she got all uptight and rigid. Making her loosen up was so much fun. "Don't worry, babe. When no one's looking, I'll make sure we both get what we need."

Jasmine stood on the balcony of her hotel room, staring out into the ocean. It was six o'clock in the morning, and the beach was still untouched and unpopulated, save an older man jogging with his dog.

Soaking in the sunshine and inhaling the fresh beach air almost made her wish this were a true vacation. But she couldn't pretend she hadn't wished they were home at least half a dozen times.

The week had passed quickly. They had only two more days left in Ocean City and then they'd be headed home. Despite her cynicism, Jasmine was pleased that the bulk of the week had passed without incident.

That is, if she didn't count the drunk and rowdy college girls she occasionally had to peel away from Spencer on the dance floor of whatever bar he was hosting his show from on a given night. And he was loving every minute of the attention, too. He'd flirt shamelessly while he was onstage, then he'd sidle up to her and whisper in her ear that he knew she was jealous.

And she was. Jasmine would never admit it out loud, but she was starting to crave that alone time Spencer had spoken of earlier that week. Each evening she'd sit through his sexy dream interpretation radio sessions, and then she'd toss and turn all night with erotic dreams of the two of them together.

She'd worked herself into such a state of frustration that she'd nearly taken some poor girl's head off on the beach yesterday because she'd dared to get too friendly with Spencer. Smooth as usual, the bum, he'd played it off by telling the girl Jasmine was his very jealous girlfriend. Jasmine was grateful that no one from the station or Core had been close enough to witness the scene.

Even though Spencer clearly saved his most flirtatious moments for her, he'd yet to make good on his promise to get her alone. Now Jasmine couldn't help feeling a bit insecure about the relationship. When she'd heard him say the word *girlfriend*, she'd started to wonder just what their . . . whatever it was they had . . . meant to him.

She was the one who'd been petrified that someone would find out about them, but now she'd give anything to know that his feelings for her—whatever they turned out to be—hadn't changed.

Jasmine turned and came back inside the room as she began to hear people stirring next door. She didn't know how she could be upset when she wasn't even sure what it was she wanted from her relationship with Spencer.

For now, she had a job to do. As long as she concentrated on that, she'd worry about the relationship when they got back home.

"So, how are things going?" Gina's question was leading.

"What do you mean?" Spencer asked cautiously.

"You know what I mean. With you and Jasmine."

He caught his breath. "She told you?" He couldn't hide his surprise.

"We're women, Spencer. Women confide in each other that way. Besides, I don't think Jasmine has very many female friends. She needed someone to talk to, and I lent her my ear. I really like her."

"So, you don't have a problem with this?"

Gina smiled. "Why should I? I think she's good for you. You have enough women in your life to feed your ego. You need someone who's going to keep you in line."

"So what did she say about me?" he asked slyly.

"I'm not telling. All I know is that she likes you. How do you feel about her?"

"Does this confidentiality work both ways? I know how you chicks stick together. Are you taking notes to run back and tell her what I said?"

"This is strictly between you and me," Gina promised.

"Okay, then, she makes me crazy."

"Good crazy or bad crazy?"

He laughed. "Both. With Jasmine I don't know which end is up. One minute she seems really into me, the next she acts like she can barely stand me. In the past, I've had absolutely no trouble knowing where I stand with a woman. In fact, more often than not, I've been the pursuee rather than the pursuer." He shook his head and smiled. "I can't say that I like it. I mean, nothing's easy with Jasmine. She makes me work for every inch she gives me. But I think she's worth it. She hasn't opened up to me completely yet, but I think she wants to."

Gina nodded. "Yes, in my conversations with Jasmine, I have noticed that she's a very private person. She's had to struggle for everything she's gotten in this world. Naturally, she fights hard to protect it."

"You're a shrink, Gina. Tell me how to get inside that protective shell she's wearing."

"There aren't any magic tricks, Spencer. You're never going to get inside."

"What?"

"I mean, you can't get inside her shell unless she invites you. It will probably take a lot of hard work and a lot of time. Are you up for it?"

"Are you trying to say I'm wasting my time?" he asked.

"I just don't want you hurt," Gina said. "Either of you. She's a lot more vulnerable than she lets on. I don't think she's the type for casual affairs. If you're not ready to go the whole nine yards—" She let the rest of her thought hang in the air between them.

Spencer sipped his drink, trying to take in Gina's advice. He knew she was right. After what Jasmine had told him about her last disastrous relationship and how low it had laid her, the last thing he wanted was to wreck her like that again.

"I hear what you're saying, Gina. I guess I have a lot of thinking to do."

Jasmine was reclining on her bed, watching cable, when the connecting door to Spencer's room jerked open and he dashed into the room.

"What's going on?" she asked, sitting straight up, startled.

He held a finger over his lips. "Shhh."

That's when she noticed that he was wearing only a big white hotel towel around his hips. Before she'd fully absorbed the impact of that fact, she was on her feet and being pulled into the bathroom.

"What are we doing?" she asked in a loud whisper.

He reached over and started unbuttoning her blouse. "We're taking a shower."

Grinning, she sniffed the air and wrinkled her nose. "Are you trying to tell me something?"

Her shirt slid to the white-tiled floor, and Spencer's fingers moved to her bra. "Yes, I'm trying to tell you that we need some time alone together."

An erotic thrill raced up her spine. "In the bathroom?"

Her bra landed on top of her shirt. He jerked her closer to him, holding the snaps on her jeans. "That's right. I'd like to see those two goons you work with interrupt us in here."

As Spencer began working her jeans over her

hips, Jasmine grabbed the towel around his waist. "Where are they?"

"Kirklin's next door talking on his cell phone, and I sent Rudy downstairs for *Playboy*."

Jasmine let his towel join her clothes on the floor. "Great. We won't be seeing either one of them any time soon."

He'd discarded her panties, pulling her naked body against his. "That's the idea."

Holding her close with one arm, he used his free hand to turn on the shower faucet. "How hot do you like it?"

She ran her fingers over the smooth skin of his back. "Is that a trick question?"

"Oh, I know you like it hot. But maybe I should turn on the cold water just to be safe. After all, bathrooms have echos, and we both know—oof!"

She'd punched him in the stomach lightly. "You're never going to let me live that down." She knew she was blushing profusely, but despite her embarrassment, Jasmine was rather pleased that Spencer could make her feel so sexually free. She'd never let him know it, but she'd been accused of being sexually uptight in the past.

As payback for her playful punch, Spencer picked her up and thrust her under the water. The cold shower inspired a startled shriek, followed by Spencer's hand over her mouth.

Not one to suffer alone, Jasmine jerked him inside the shower with her, relishing the frigid grimace on his face. She watched as goose bumps rose on his brown skin. His arms came around her, plastering her wet body to his.

Their lips met in an eager kiss. "Mmm, I've missed being close to you like this."

Jasmine giggled as he kissed from her earlobe to her neck and shoulders. She knew the shower spray was messing up her sassy new hairdo, but, at the moment, she didn't care. She'd let the hair salon downstairs deal with the aftereffects of their watery romp.

Right now she was enjoying this rare opportunity to have him all to herself. Grabbing the liquid soap from the corner of the tub, Jasmine filled her palm. She built up a rich white lather between her hands, then let them roam free over his slick wet skin.

She traced the outline of his biceps and tickled his abs with her fingertips. Her hands continued lower until she could tangle them in the forest below his waist. There it was clear she had his full attention as his manhood extended toward her.

Eagerly, she reached for the bottle of soap again.

"Mmm, give me some of that." He took the bottle away from her. Their hands slipped and slid, working their bodies into a soapy frenzy.

Jasmine pressed her lathered skin against his, letting it slide and slither against him. "Time for rinsing."

Reaching behind her neck, Jasmine adjusted the shower head until it sprayed directly onto Spencer. Getting behind him, she used her hands to wash away the soap suds in the water stream.

"Your turn." He pulled her forward, allowing the water to cascade over her. He meticulously tracked down every trace of soap that dared hide on her body. When they were both squeaky clean, he turned off the water and pulled her out of the shower with him.

He reached for a fluffy white towel and wrapped it around her shoulders. Jasmine started to rub it over her skin to dry off, but Spencer stopped her.

"That's my job. Just a second." He turned on the heat lamp overhead, and heat chased away the frigid air that chilled them. Red light cloaked the room with a sexy, steamy haze.

Spencer returned to her, taking the towel away from her, proceeding to rub it over her body. Carefully and gently, he dried her. He moved the towel lightly over her back, between her thighs, and down her legs. Then he returned to the top. Stray water droplets dotted her neck and shoulders.

He relentlessly pursued each one, kissing them from her shoulders or flicking them from her neck with his tongue. Finally, when Jasmine's body was completely dry, he wrapped the towel around her back and tucked it between her breasts.

Jasmine pulled a fresh towel from the rack. "Your turn." She applied the towel to his body with the same loving care he'd administered to her. It was a pleasure to take her time drying every muscle, slope, and hard curve of his solid body.

Suddenly a wicked thought leaped into her mind. "This area requires special attention," she whispered, kneeling before him.

Spencer threw back his head and groaned loudly as she took him into her mouth.

Ha! she thought. Something told her she could make him do a little screaming this time. Unfortunately, she couldn't afford to let them be overheard.

She paused to remove one of the hands that gripped her shoulder and pushed it up to his mouth. "Shhh."

He bit his knuckle as she continued to love him with her mouth. Occasionally, she'd glance up at his face, and the intense pleasure she saw there gave her enormous pride.

"I can't take this anymore," he said, setting her away from him. Hooking his hands under her arms, he lifted her back to her feet, pulling her face to his in a deep kiss.

Without breaking contact, he moved over to the commode and sat down, settling her on his lap. "I want to be inside you, baby," he whispered between kisses.

Feeling reckless and urgent, Jasmine was just

about to guide him to her when a loud noise startled them out of their passionate haze.

"You in there, Spencer?" Rudy called, banging on the door again.

Jasmine hopped off him as Spencer sprang to his feet. "Uh, yeah. I just got out of the shower. Hold on."

They shared a frantic look, and towels went flying as they scampered around the bathroom.

"You have a phone call, man. It sounds important."

Spencer pulled a bathrobe off the hook. "Tell whoever it is that I'll call back."

"The woman says it's urgent."

Jasmine, now wrapped in a towel, her clothes piled in her arms, nudged Spencer with her knee.

"Woman?" he called back to Rudy. "Do you know who it is?"

"It's Gina. That co-host lady."

"Shit," he said, only loud enough for Jasmine to hear. Once again they shared a look before Spencer pushed her behind the door as he slid out.

Jasmine pulled on her clothes in a rush while trying to listen at the door at the same time. She could barely make out Spencer's side of the conversation. From what she could tell, there were a lot of gasps and oh-nos.

Finally, she heard him hang up the phone, followed by a jumble of voices that were undoubtedly Kirklin and Rudy asking questions.

Now fully dressed again, Jasmine knelt at the door with her ear pressed against it. How the hell was she supposed to get out of there with Kirklin and Rudy two feet away?

There wouldn't be any way to explain her presence in Spencer's bathroom. Rudy had already seen Spencer leave it wearing nothing but a bathrobe. If she came out now, the conclusion would be obvious.

Jasmine took a towel and rubbed out a clear spot in the mirror. Damn, she looked like she had a giant fur ball on her head. The shower had slicked away her curls and the steam had crinkled her hair into a frizzy puff.

She ran her fingers through the tangled mess, but she only made matters worse. Great. Now, when she did get out of there, she'd have to explain what she'd been up to.

Swearing under her breath, Jasmine tried to creep back across the bathroom to the door. Instead, her sandal slipped on a towel on the steam-slick tile, and she came down with a distinct thud.

Spencer held his breath as every head in the room snapped toward the bathroom. Kirklin was the first to move, stalking toward the door. "Was someone in there with you?"

Gulping, Spencer strained to stay cool. "I wish. But I have been forbidden to pick up strange women on the beach these days. No one's in there," he said as Kirklin's hand went to the doorknob. "It's probably just my shampoo bottle falling into the tub."

"I don't know," Kirklin said, pushing open the door.

Spencer hung up the phone. "Someone needs to get to Gina's room," he said quickly. "She's terrified that someone followed her back to the hotel. Why don't you guys get up there?"

Kirklin poked his head into the bathroom, then turned at Spencer's suggestion. "One of us needs to stay here."

Spencer shook his head. "I need to get dressed. I'll grab Jasmine and meet you guys up in Gina's room. She's in 8023."

To Spencer's relief, Kirklin backed off the bathroom, apparently satisfied by a cursory glance inside that no one was in there. "Let me advise White that we have a situation and that Rudy and I will be taking the lead on this phase of the investigation."

He started toward the connecting door to Jasmine's room, and Spencer's relief evaporated into panic once again.

He opened his mouth to speak, but this time his normally quick-thinking brain let him down. No words came out.

Spencer's gaze darted to Rudy, who'd been silent and watchful during this torturous scene. Suddenly, Rudy's eyes took on a knowing glint. "Hey, yo," he called to Kirklin. "I'm going to head out now. No telling what's going on up there."

Kirklin, clearly afraid of being overshadowed, quickly followed Rudy to the door. "Spencer, you can give White the update. We've got to make sure Ms. Hill's room is secure."

Spencer released his breath as the two men filed out of the room. He rushed over to the bathroom and tugged open the door. She was nowhere to be seen. "Jasmine?"

Her head peeked around the edge of the shower curtain. "Are they gone?"

"Yeah, come on. I sent them up to Gina's room."

Jasmine hopped out of the tub. "Why? What's going on?"

"We've got to get up there. Gina thinks someone followed her back to the hotel. She sounded really frightened on the telephone."

"Did she see who was following her?" Jasmine asked.

"No, but she thinks it was Nightmary."

Jasmine let out a hard sigh. "So much for our quiet vacation. Get dressed and let's get upstairs."

13

When Jasmine and Spencer finally got up to Gina's room, they found her curled on the bed. Kirklin was pacing the room and Rudy sat at the desk chair, staring at Gina with rapt attention.

Clearly, Gina had just replaced Jasmine on the top of Rudy's list of romantic pursuits. Jasmine moved over to sit beside Gina on the bed.

"Are you okay? What happened?" Jasmine asked.

"Damn. Your face is cut," Spencer said, standing at the foot of the bed. "Was it Nightmary? Did she do this to you?"

Gina's hand went to the bandage on her forehead. "It's just a cut. I'm okay."

"How did this happen?" Jasmine asked again.

"Tali and I were shopping on the boardwalk

this evening. We were browsing the stores, and I wanted to walk back up the boardwalk to get a seashell necklace for my mom that I'd seen earlier. Tali decided that she didn't want to come with me and headed back without me. So I was alone."

"That's it!" Spencer paced back and forth. "From now on, no one goes out alone."

"I didn't think anything of it at first. It wasn't dark and there were plenty of people around. Anyway, I was crossing the street and a white van came out of nowhere and tried to run me over. Someone pulled me out of the way in time, but no one got the license plate. I couldn't even see the driver's face."

Spencer released a few more colorful expletives. "Now she's not just after me." He turned to Jasmine. "Can one of you keep an eye on Gina while we're here? Obviously, Nightmary isn't above going after her, too."

"Spencer!" Gina protested. "I don't want to take away from the team that's supposed to be guarding you. Now is not the time to lighten up your defenses."

"I'm sure we can work this out," Jasmine said. "Gina, it might not hurt for you to stick close. You and Spencer will be together most days anyway. It's not a big leap to extend our watch to you. Other times, we'll just make sure you're not alone."

Gina took a deep breath and nodded. "I want

to thank you all for coming up here to make sure I was okay. I feel a little better now."

Spencer, still agitated, continued to pace the room. "Do you want us to hang out here for a while, Gina?"

"No, that's not necessary. I feel silly for bringing you all running as it is. I'm sure I'll be fine."

Jasmine wasn't convinced. Gina still looked a little pale and very shaken. "Rudy, why don't you and Kirklin go downstairs. I'll stay up here with Gina for a little while. We have some girl talk to catch up on anyway."

After the men left, Jasmine sat down on the foot of Gina's bed. "Why do I get the impression that something else is on your mind? More than your near miss on the boardwalk today."

Gina ran her hands over her face, composing her features. "Call me crazy, but I think nearly being run down in broad daylight is more than enough to occupy my mind."

"Of course it is. But I could tell by the way you relayed the story that you're leaving something out."

"I told you all the facts. Anything else . . . well, it would just be speculation, and that's not enough to . . ."

"Not enough to what? Finish what you were going to say," Jasmine pressed.

"I don't want to open a can of worms."

"Look, I've had enough of this, Gina. Even if it's just your gut feeling, an instinct, I want to know what you're thinking. I don't care how far-fetched it may sound."

Gina shook her head, pulling her hair back from her face. "Fine, but you're going to think this sounds just as crazy as I do." She looked Jasmine straight in the eyes, then spoke. "There was something about the way things happened today that got me thinking maybe this wasn't a coincidence. I feel like I've been set up."

"Set up? By whom?"

"That's the crazy part. Tali and I were planning to shop all afternoon and then have a late lunch back at the hotel. But in the middle of our trip, she decides to head back, leaving me to walk alone."

Jasmine frowned, trying to grasp what Gina was trying not to say. "Do you think Tali had something to do with your nearly getting hit?"

"I don't know. But just that niggling suspicion in the back of my neck got me thinking about a few other things. If Nightmary were someone Spencer knows, it would explain a lot of things. That person would have access to his keys, his home, and his personal belongings."

Gina paused, biting her lip. "I feel terrible saying this, but Tali loosely fits the profile. She's had a lot of bad experiences with men, and she's expressed physical interest in Spencer."

"Wow," Jasmine said, trying to follow Gina's logic. "Do you really think that's enough—"

"This may be a bit of a stretch, but it's possible

that she's turned Spencer into an icon for her ideal man. His lack of interest in her could fuel the love/hate obsession that Nightmary has exhibited toward Spencer. She's also had access and opportunity during most of the incidents involving Nightmary."

"I can see where you get the motive, Gina, but she hasn't behaved suspiciously otherwise, right?"

"You're right. I certainly don't want to falsely accuse her of anything. But the fact that we caught her leaving Spencer's room when he wasn't there yesterday afternoon . . ."

"Gina, she told us that she was just picking up some extra promo T-shirts for giveaways."

"I know, but when I spoke with Spencer later, he said he'd never had promo shirts in his room. We never actually saw the clothes Tali had in that bag she'd been carrying."

Suddenly a memory came back to Jasmine. This morning, Spencer had been complaining that his favorite shirt was missing. Finally, he'd decided that he'd forgotten to pack it, but what if it had been stolen instead?

Jasmine chewed on her lower lip. "I hate to admit it, but you might be on to something, Gina. Be very careful around Tali until I can check this out further. Right now, I have to get back downstairs. Do you want to come down with me?"

"No, I'm going to try to get some rest. I'll be fine. I'll call down if I need anything."

* * *

A few minutes later, Jasmine walked into Spencer's room like a zombie. She didn't want to believe her suspicions, but the more she put the puzzle pieces together, the more startled she was at how well they fit.

She was so absorbed in her thoughts, it took her a moment to realize that the mood in the room was more tense than usual. She glanced around and noted that everyone looked agitated.

"What? What's going on?"

Rudy shook his head and pointed toward the bathroom. "Look for yourself."

Jasmine's heartbeat sped up. The bathroom? Had they found out about her and Spencer? Had she and Spencer left some sort of evidence of their afternoon romp behind?

Trying to maintain her dignity to the end, Jasmine marched stoically to the bathroom, expecting the worst. What she found when she pushed open the door caught her off guard. But it shouldn't have.

"What the—" There was sand everywhere. It filled the sink, half the bathtub, and was scattered all over the floor.

Spencer appeared in the doorway behind her. "While we were gone, Nightmary paid us a visit."

Jasmine shook her head. "This is just crazy."

"We weren't gone long. Obviously, she'd been watching, waiting for us all to leave. I can't imagine how she broke in here with all this sand and slipped out so fast."

Jasmine released a heavy breath, slipping past Spencer into the room. "Pack up everyone. We're changing hotels. Now."

They had only one night left, but Jasmine had no intention of spending that night in a hotel where security had been breached. They had backup reservations at another hotel, and she put those into effect immediately. This time she made sure no one knew where Spencer was staying, especially Tali, despite the woman's persistence.

Needless to say, the sand incident put a damper on everyone's spirits. Jasmine just wanted to get through the last day and be on their way in the morning.

Jasmine stood off to the side of the hotel ballroom admiring the decorations for the WLPS luau. Part of her wished she could free her mind enough to appreciate her surroundings. But, instead, her thoughts were intent and her eyes were alert. The false sense of security that had settled around them because they were out of town had vanished.

Today all of their illusions had been shattered, and Jasmine was determined not to let down her guard.

Gina came up beside her. "Can you believe this getup they're making me wear?" Jasmine turned to study her ensemble. Gina wore a grass skirt and a sky blue bikini with a matching lei. "I get to look like one of those tacky hula dolls off a trucker's dashboard."

"Well, I think you look great," Jasmine said. She herself was wearing her new white linen pants with a white linen tank top and a lei.

Gina took her elbow and pulled her even farther away from the party. "Listen, about what we talked about this evening . . ."

Jasmine's heart rate sped up. She'd been unable to think of anything else. "Yes?"

"I think I was out of line to say anything. I mean, the very idea that Tali could mastermind something like this is crazy. I think I was too shaken up to realize what I was implying. Can we just pretend the whole conversation never happened?"

"Don't be so hasty to disregard that theory, Gina. I've had more time to think on it, and the more I do, the more it makes sense."

Gina bit her lip, looking skeptical.

"Look," Jasmine said. "We can talk more about this later. But in the meantime, keep your eyes and ears alert. Watch your back."

A few minutes later, Gina had to rush up on-stage to start her set, and Jasmine went back to her role as the quiet observer.

Despite the harried events of the day, Spencer commanded the mike like the pro he was. His dry wit was as sharp as ever, and she never would have guessed he'd been through any traumatic events that day.

Gina and Spencer sat side by side on stools behind two mike stands. The deejay was on a large platform behind them; the platform sported a colorful banner and the WLPS logo, a pair of juicy red lips, puckered and ready.

"Now we've come to the dream interpretation portion of our show," Spencer announced. The crowd got rowdy, cheering and screaming. Clearly, they knew what was coming up next.

By now, Jasmine had sat through countless radio shows, but this was the first time she'd had a dream interpretation question of her own. She couldn't call attention to herself under the circumstances, but maybe she'd ask Gina in private.

Jasmine had just resigned herself to that idea when Spencer's voice pulled her attention again.

"We're going to do things a little differently tonight. We've noticed that people are much less inhibited on the radio because we can't see your faces." The crowd roared with laughter. "But, since this is a live show, we don't want to miss out on one juicy detail of those really hot dreams. So we've provided index cards, which are available at the bar or through your waitress, so you can ask all those sexy questions anonymously. But, if you're brave, or intoxicated, you can step up to the mike set up in the audience and ask your question directly."

Jasmine suddenly realized that she'd been handed an opportunity. But now that she'd be able to ask her question in this forum, was it a smart thing to do?

Before she could overthink the situation, she snagged a passing waitress. "Can I have one of those cards, please?"

Jasmine began writing, then halted mid-sentence. Would Gina or Spencer recognize her handwriting? Not wanting to take the chance, she scribbled quickly, spreading out her letters to disguise her normally precise script.

She gave the card to the waitress as the woman passed again. "No turning back now," she muttered.

A loud roar of laughter rippled through the crowd after the Sandman rattled off a witty quip in response to Gina's interpretations of an audience member's dream about a bathtub filled with low-fat cottage cheese. Jasmine continued to lurk in the back, deeply regretting her decision to write down her dream.

"Settle down, folks. I've got another question here," Gina said, holding up an index card. When the audience settled, she began to read: "Recently I dreamed I was at a party. A few minutes into the dream, I realized that it was a birthday party for me. Everyone surrounded me shouting for me to blow out the candles. I blew

them out, and when I looked up, the faces of the
people around me were all blank. No features. I
didn't recognize anyone. What does this mean?"

Jasmine blushed, glad no one knew it was her
question. After that point, the dream had
changed. The doorbell rang and it was Spencer.
They went upstairs together, and from there the
dream turned erotic. A few minutes later, Spencer
had awakened her for the real thing. She didn't
need any help figuring out that part of the dream.

Spencer laughed, bringing Jasmine back to reality once more. "A party full of blank faces,
huh? I think I've been to a few parties like that.
But, usually, it's the day *after* the party that people are afraid to show their faces."

Gina tapped the card against her thigh. "This
isn't a difficult dream to interpret. Parties in
dreams can often represent friendships. Clearly,
you feel there are people—or one person in particular—close to you whom you don't know as
well as you feel you should. Or it could mean
that you're trusting someone you shouldn't
trust."

Gina and Spencer exchanged their typical
clever banter before moving on to the next question, while Jasmine remained locked in the moment. What had that dream been trying to tell
her? Spencer entered the dream immediately after the party of strangers. Did that mean he was
the person she wasn't supposed to trust?

Somehow, that didn't feel right. She'd spent a great deal of time not trusting men. She'd changed the locks on her heart so many times that she'd simply stopped giving out the key. But there was something different about Spencer. Despite his slick hotshot facade, there was something very vulnerable about him. Even though he'd resisted her at first, he'd allowed her to see that side of him. Clearly, he trusted her. That made her want to trust him, too.

Spencer's cool, sexy baritone broke into her thoughts once again. "Now, I have a very special dedication for a young lady known to those close to her as Minnie. This song goes out to you from the man who wants to make your dreams come true."

Jasmine's heart jerked as she caught Spencer's eye. He winked just quickly enough for her to catch it before turning away.

He'd dedicated a song to her. And he'd managed to do it in such a way that only the two of them would know. It made her feel so special to know that the romantic Brian McKnight song was just for her.

She leaned against the wall, absorbing every lyric as though Spencer were speaking the words to her himself. Suddenly her body stilled as a revelation settled over her. Her skin tingled and her nerve endings hummed, but none of those reactions had anything to do with the song. She swallowed as she tried to comprehend what had just happened to her.

Jasmine White had just fallen in love with Spencer Powell.

Jasmine was still reeling with her newfound insight when Rudy came up beside her. "Nice song."

She nodded absently.

"One of your favorites?"

Jasmine shrugged. "Not really."

Rudy tried again. "So how long has this been going on?"

Her friend's not-so-subtle hints finally began to sink in. Slowly, Jasmine turned to face him. "How long has what been going on?"

He didn't have to answer. His meaning was clear in his expression.

Jasmine clutched her throat. "Oh, no. Is it that obvious? Does everyone know?"

Rudy put his arm around her and squeezed her shoulder. "No, it's not that obvious," he said kindly.

Jasmine released the breath she'd been holding. "How did you know?"

"I figured it out this afternoon when I got Spencer out of the shower to answer the phone. I'd looked for you before I went to get him, and you were nowhere to be found. Then, when I saw the way he acted, I put two and two together."

"What about Kirklin?"

Rudy shook his head. "Kirklin's too self-absorbed to notice things like that, but I thought I'd been picking up a vibe between you and Powell."

"You're not going to say anything, are you?" Jasmine asked, hoping.

"Nah, you're my girl. Besides, do you think this is the first time I've seen this kind of thing?"

"Thanks, Rudy. I owe you. My situation is complicated enough right now. If Pruitt found out . . ."

"Say no more. But can I give you some advice?"

Jasmine paused. "Okay."

"Be careful. I don't want to see you get in over your head. Cases like this can be hard enough without the distraction of a relationship. You've got to find a way to keep your emotions separate. Otherwise you could end up making a costly mistake."

Jasmine nodded soberly. "Are you speaking from personal experience?"

"Let's just say, I know what I'm talking about."

Tali walked up to Jasmine holding a frosty tropical drink. "These things are delicious."

"What is it?"

"It's called Island Paradise. I just sent a couple over to Gina and Spencer to celebrate our last night here."

Jasmine looked up and saw a waitress handing drinks identical to Tali's to Gina and Spencer.

"They're at the end of the set," Tali explained, "so they'll be long gone before the drink kicks in. You should try one—oh, you're on duty."

"That's right, but you can have one for me."

Tali smiled. "Sure thing."

A few minutes later, Gina and Spencer wrapped up their show and Jasmine met them on the other side of the room. Gina was pulling on a jacket over her bikini. "I can't wait to get out of this thing. After I change, do you guys want to hit a club or something? We may as well enjoy our last night here."

Spencer yawned. "I don't know about anyone else, but I'm going back to hit the sack. I think the week's activities are finally catching up with me."

"Me, too," Jasmine said, stifling her own yawn.

Gina looked disappointed. "See you back in D.C. then I'm going to hit some more outlet malls before I head home tomorrow."

Jasmine gave Gina a hug good-bye, then she and Spencer headed toward his room, Rudy and Kirklin trailing as usual.

Jasmine had moved Spencer into a condo not far from the hotel. It made her breathe a little easier to have him in a place no one outside the Core staff knew about, even if just for one night. They retuned to the condo without any surprises, threats, or excessive sand piles.

Part of her couldn't help wishing they'd changed accommodations a little sooner. The condo afforded them a lot more privacy than the hotel had. Spencer was in the master bedroom, and Jasmine was in the bigger of the two remaining bedrooms. Her room was connected to Spencer's through the bathroom. Kirklin had the third bedroom, and Rudy, who had night watch, would bunk on the sofa in the living room.

Everyone tromped around the condo getting settled, and Spencer gave her a seductive look that let her know that he wasn't finished with her yet.

It wasn't long after the lights went out that Jasmine heard movement in the bathroom. Seconds later, he pushed her door open. There was enough moonlight from the window for her to make out his silhouette. He pushed back the sheet on her bed and slipped in beside her.

"Alone at last," he whispered. She rolled against him and his arms enfolded her.

"Thanks for the song you dedicated to me. I've never had anyone do anything like that before."

"Mmm . . ." he murmured against her hair.

"I realized something important tonight, Spencer. I don't know if this is the right time to tell you, but I can't seem to help myself." Jasmine paused, realizing that Spencer wasn't reacting to her excitement. "Oh, no. Don't tell me . . ." She sat up, and the arm that had been around her shoulder fell limp at his side.

She was about to tell the man that she was in love with him, and he'd fallen asleep. She poked his chest. "Get up and go back to your own bed."

He didn't budge.

She shook him harder. "Spencer, wake up."

Suddenly her heart sped up. He wasn't moving.

She checked to see if he was breathing while reaching for his wrist to check his pulse. He was still breathing.

"Spencer, wake up."

Jasmine jumped off the bed and shook him with all her might.

No matter what she tried, Spencer wouldn't wake up.

14

As Spencer slowly came to consciousness, his first awareness was that his head felt as though it had been filled with lead. His eyes creaked open and his blurred vision took its time coming into focus.

Feeling disoriented and hung over, Spencer struggled to remember how he'd ended up back in his own bed, at home in Potomac.

He groaned quietly as bits of memory flashed in his head. Having his stomach pumped and waking up in a hospital room. The three-hour drive home in a stuffy, unventilated van. Then the indignity of being escorted to his bed on the arms of two burly bodyguards. So last night hadn't been a nightmare after all. It had really happened.

Gently, sitting up, Spencer scanned his bedroom and saw Jasmine's lithe body folded into an uncomfortable-looking half-reclined position in the chair across from his bed. He was surprised he hadn't noticed her sooner, since she was snoring so loudly.

"Jasmine," he called. "Come on, sweetie. Wake up."

Jasmine came awake with a start that propelled her to her feet. "What? I'm awake. What?" Rubbing her eyes, she moved close to the bed. "How are you feeling?"

"Like I really tied one on last night. This is looking like the worst hangover of my life."

She placed the back of her hand on his forehead, the way his mother might have if she'd ever been around when he'd been sick as a child.

"Well, the good news is a hangover isn't fatal," Jasmine said. "Do you remember anything about last night?"

"My memory's pretty sketchy."

"Well, apparently you're not the stud you always thought you were, Spencer. Do you know you passed out just before we were about to make love?"

Spencer could tell that Jasmine was forcing herself to sound light, but he could see her lip tremble slightly, betraying her real feelings. "That must have something to do with my waking up in the hospital?"

"Someone slipped you rohypnol, otherwise known as roofies."

Spencer was stunned by that information. "The date rape drug? I'm flattered that you wanted me so bad, honey, but I would have come willingly."

Jasmine turned her face away, and when she turned back he could see her blinking back tears.

"Sweetheart, I'm sorry I teased you. You know my sense of humor has no sense of appropriateness." Jasmine shook her head, waving off his comment. "It's not that. It's just—" She broke off to take a breath, and her voice shook when she spoke again. "You really scared me."

Spencer knew his situation had been serious, but he hadn't really felt the full weight of it until now. She'd spent the past several weeks convincing him that she was superwoman, and damn if he hadn't started to believe it. He didn't think anything could shake the steadfast Jasmine White.

"When I saw you like that . . . You weren't moving. I couldn't wake you up . . . I thought—"

Spencer held his hand out to her. He wanted to hold her. Comfort her. Let her know that he wasn't going anywhere.

She took his hand for a moment, squeezed it, then, before he could pull her close, she released his hand and moved across the room again.

When she turned to face him, Spencer could see that her vulnerable moment was over. The walls that kept her from really investing in their relationship were back in place.

"I put a pitcher of ice water by your bed," she

told him. "The doctor said you'd probably be dehydrated and you should drink lots of fluids."

Spencer poured himself a glass, more for something to do than anything else. He didn't know what to do when she shut down like that. He knew she'd been afraid of losing him. Not that he wanted to capitalize on a bad situation, but this was their chance to be closer than ever. Instead, he could feel the distance between them growing.

"So, are you going to hang around here and nurse me back to health?" he asked.

Jasmine paced back and forth in a space of carpet about two feet square. "I wanted to stay until you woke up. The doctor said you'd probably be disoriented. Now that you're awake . . ."

"You're leaving." He'd meant to ask a question, but his words came out an accusation instead.

"I haven't been home yet."

"Fine, Jasmine. Why don't you go home, grab a few things, and then come back here."

"I don't think that's a good idea."

Spencer felt his mouth going dry and it had nothing to do with dehydration. The hairs on his arms were practically standing at attention. He could feel in his gut that something was about to happen.

"Why not?" he asked, putting his guard up.

"Why don't we talk later? After you've gotten more rest."

"More rest? I've been sleeping for nearly twelve hours. Why don't we talk now?"

"Look, Spencer, this just isn't the right time."

With all the hedging she was doing, Spencer was pretty sure he knew what was coming. He felt his anger rising. "There's never a good time for this kind of thing, is there? Why don't you just spit it out?" he dared her.

"Spencer, you're getting yourself upset . . ."

He took a deep breath, making sure he appeared outwardly calm. "No," he said in a quiet even tone. "*You're* getting me upset. Don't coddle me. If you've got something to say, I want to hear it, and I want to hear it now."

"Fine." Jasmine sat on the edge of his bed. "I came here to do a job, Spencer. To protect you. To keep you safe. To keep you alive."

Spencer made a show of checking his pulse. "Yup, still beating. I guess that means you're doing a good job."

"Not good enough."

"You can't blame yourself for what happened with my drink—"

"Yes, I can. If I hadn't been . . . distracted, I might have noticed something. A detail, someone unusual, something."

"Jasmine, there were three of you there that night, and the others didn't notice anything, either."

"I don't care. You're my responsibility, first and foremost. I've let inappropriate feelings get in the way—"

"*Inappropriate?*" he exploded. "How can you say that?"

"They're inappropriate because they interfere with the job I came to do. An important job."

"So what does that mean? You and I are over? Just like that?"

"Spencer, things can't continue the way they are. I think you know that."

"I don't know shit. Why don't you tell me, Jasmine?"

"Look, I'm not saying it has to be this way forever, but for now I have to focus on one thing at a time."

Spencer shook his head. He was livid. The anger had built inside him and was ready to erupt. He was rarely truly angry. He'd often bickered with Jasmine just for sport, but his feelings were very different now.

"Let me get this straight. From now on, I'm just supposed to be your client? I'm supposed to go back to looking right through you? I'm supposed to forget what it feels like to make love to you? What you sound like screaming my name? I'm supposed to look at you every day without kissing or touching you?" He shook his head, throwing his hands up. "Yeah, that's cool. And you can go back to being invisible when I go out on dates. This is going to work really well."

Jasmine stared down at her hands. "It will be awkward at first, but think about what's at stake," she said softly, almost to herself.

"Awkward?" He choked on his laugh. After all they'd been through, she was still trying to shove him back to square one. Suddenly, he wished he'd never laid eyes on her. Bodyguards were supposed to be men. "I'll tell you one thing. All that crap about you doing your job just as well as a man is a load of bull."

Jasmine flinched as if he'd smacked her, but that didn't slow him down.

"Do you think I'd be in this predicament if they'd just sent a male bodyguard like they were supposed to? I doubt a man would have led me on, jerked me around, and then cut me loose because he suddenly discovered he wasn't as good at his job as he thought he was."

"Now you just stop right there, Spencer. That's not true."

"The hell it isn't true. The problem is that you're out of your league and you just didn't want to admit it. Now that you're finally realizing it, you can't face the fact that you blew it because you're a woman. Instead of committing to this relationship and this assignment, you decided to protect yourself and you ended up doing a half-assed job on both."

Spencer saw the struck-dumb look on Jasmine's face, and if he wasn't in such a state, he would have realized that he was going too far. But in the heat of the moment, he just didn't care.

Jasmine stood. "Okay. Anything else?" She paused half a second, then turned and walked out.

* * *

Jasmine stood outside, staring but not seeing anything. Her whole body felt numb. How had things gotten so out of control so quickly? She'd only been thinking of his best interests. Then, next thing she knew, he was incensed, yelling at the top of his lungs.

A dull ache pushed at the numbness in the general vicinity of her heart. Absently, she rubbed at the spot. She couldn't afford to give in to the pain just yet. Tali had called earlier that morning. She wanted Jasmine to come into the station to talk about Spencer. Jasmine hadn't been sure when he would wake up, but she'd assured Tali that she'd come as soon as she left him.

Grateful for something, anything, to do, Jasmine got into her car. Work was the only thing she had now. She had to focus. What if Tali *was* Spencer's stalker? She needed to start gathering tangible evidence, if there was any. Now that they were back in town, she'd have a better opportunity to keep an eye on the woman.

Before she knew it, Jasmine was pulling into the garage at the radio station. As soon as she started down the hall, she could feel eyes on her. She smiled and waved to the people she recognized, but she couldn't shake the feeling that they were all smirking at her.

Shake it off! You're just being self-conscious. Her internal pep talk wasn't working, and Jasmine found herself quickening her pace. She was relieved to finally make it to Tali's office. When she poked her head in the doorway, she saw that the other woman was speaking on the phone.

Tali motioned for her to wait. "No, let me investigate this further before you take any action. I'll be in touch." She hung up the phone. "Come in, Jasmine. Have a seat."

Jasmine sat down, watching Tali carefully. Was it her imagination, or was Tali being very formal with her? Did Tali suspect that she might be on to her?

"Tali, if you're worried about Spencer, I want you to know that he's recovering nicely. He's—" Jasmine swallowed past the catch in her throat. "He's back to his old self again."

"Well, that's certainly good news," Tali said curtly. "While, of course, I'm interested in Spencer making a speedy recovery, there's something else I'm anxious to discuss with you."

Jasmine blinked at the woman, puzzled. Tali had definitely grown a huge stick in her posterior region. There was no doubt about it now. She knew. Tali had to know that Jasmine suspected she was Nightmary. And if she did know that Jasmine knew, how was she planning to wiggle out of this mess?

"I'm all ears, Tali. What's on your mind?"

"There's no easy way to broach this subject, so forgive me for being blunt, Jasmine."

This should be good. "Don't worry about me. I prefer straight talk."

"Good, then you won't mind telling me if the rumors are true."

Jasmine was caught off guard. No one knew about her suspicions that Tali was Nightmary except Gina. She doubted Gina was broadcasting that fact. "Rumors?"

"The rumors that you're having an affair with Spencer."

Jasmine's body went cold. "What?" she asked stupidly. She could only hope that when Tali repeated herself, the question would be different.

It wasn't.

"Is . . . is that what people are saying?" Jasmine asked, trying to play it off.

"Yes, Jasmine. That's. What people. Are saying." Tali's smooth features were drawn tight with disgust. "That's all I've been hearing about since I got into the station this morning. It's the *hot* water cooler gossip."

Jasmine felt like the wind had been knocked out of her. A million things raced around in her head. Should she deny it? *Could* she deny it? How had they found out? She was so certain that she and Spencer had been careful.

"Well? Aren't you going to say anything?" The other woman was clearly angry.

That made *Jasmine* angry. "What can I say? I can't believe it," she said cryptically. Was Tali using this rumor business as a ploy to distract her from the real issue?

"You can't believe it because it's true or because it *isn't*?" Tali asked, staring at her.

Jasmine's temper, known for flaring at the worst moments, spiked. "I can't believe the people at this station don't have more interesting things to talk about. Especially in light of the fact that Spencer was just poisoned."

"Don't change the subject, Jasmine."

"Oh, I think that *is* the subject. I think the person who has the office buzzing about whether or not Spencer and I are having an affair doesn't want people buzzing about the *real* question. Who's doing these things to him?"

"Stop hedging, Jasmine. Are you and Spencer together or not?"

Well, there was a question she could answer. "*Not.*"

Tali's brows rose. "So you're saying that you and Spencer have never had a personal relationship."

Her face went hot. She drew the line at flat-out lying. "I . . . didn't say that."

"Ahh, so we finally get to the truth. You and Spencer were having an affair."

"That's not the point, Tali. You and I both know what this is really about."

Tali snorted. "Oh, we do? Please, tell me. What is this really about? Because I didn't know when I hired you as a bodyguard you'd interpret the term so literally."

The thin thread leashing Jasmine's temper snapped. She was instantly on her feet. "Oh, no you don't! Don't you dare judge me. At least I don't have to resort to stalking to get a man's attention."

Tali stared at her.

"What the hell—"

"That's right, Tali. I know all about your late-night trips to Spencer's room when you thought no one was looking. I've seen the way you look at him. It's not hard to add this up. You're Nightmary. That's why you hired me, then leaked the story to the *Washington Post*. Not only do you throw off suspicion but you get a little free publicity for the station."

"You. Are. Crazy!"

"No, *you're* crazy, Tali. You could have killed Spencer with that drug you put in his drink."

"I did not drug, Spencer, Jasmine. I'm not Nightmary."

"Really? Think about it. You had access to Spencer, his home, and his hotel. I saw you taking things from his room, and you were always close by when something major happened."

Tali looked livid. "This is insane. I'm not listening to any more of it. Get out. I don't think I have to tell you that you're off this case."

"That's fine. Just remember, I know your secret, and it's not going to be a secret for much longer."

Tali's fists were clenched. "Get out. So help me, if you don't get out right now—"

Jasmine spun on her heels, heading for the door. "Better get yourself a good lawyer."

Adrenaline was still pulsing through her as Jasmine marched out to the parking garage. She hadn't meant to lay all her cards on the table like that, but at least Tali knew her days were numbered.

Jasmine had just reached her car when her cell phone started ringing. "Hello."

"I want you in my office. Now."

Damn. "Nathan, before you—"

"Save it. Get in here!" He slammed the phone in her ear.

Jasmine wasted no time driving to the agency. She realized it would be a futile cause, but she mentally rehearsed her explanation on the off chance that Nathan gave her the opportunity.

Walking through the office, Jasmine had the feeling that every eye was trained on her for the second time that day. Trying fiercely to hold up her head, she marched forward, not allowing herself to make eye contact with anyone.

The only question was: How much did they know? Did *everyone* know about her relationship with Spencer? Did they know that she was most likely on her way to being fired?

Just her luck. Kirklin was in Nathan's office when she appeared in the doorway. For once, he was the one to duck his head and avoid her gaze. Clearly, he didn't want to embarrass her. Jasmine felt her anger returning.

"Look, Nathan, before you say anything, I deserve the right to explain my side of the story."

"Shut the door," he barked.

"You need to know that Tali—"

"I only want to hear one thing and one thing only. Did you just accuse our client of being a stalker?"

"I just said—"

"Yes or no."

"Yes, but—"

"You're fired. Pack your desk. Your final paycheck will be mailed to your home address."

"Wait a minute, Nathan. I think you should hear the evidence against her before you . . ." This time Jasmine trailed off on her own. The look on his face told her that she was wasting her breath. She left the office before she lost control completely.

Still trying not to meet anyone's gaze, Jasmine started collecting her things. Not wanting to hunt around for a box, she yanked a file drawer out of her desk, pulled out the folders, and began piling in her meager belongings.

She didn't care if he docked her for the missing drawer. There wasn't much she could afford to care about at that moment. The only thing that mattered was making it out of the room without all the other Core employees seeing her fall apart.

On her way to the door, Rudy stopped her. "What? You're not even going to say good-bye?"

"Good-bye," she said without turning her

head. If she did she was afraid the tears would come.

"Oh, so you're going to do me like that."

"Not now, okay, Rudy. I'll call you." With that, she quickened her pace and rushed out of the building.

Everything inside her was ice-cold and numb. She drove without seeing the road, punching dials on the radio without hearing any music.

It wasn't until she hit the highway doing eighty-five that feeling finally started to return with a pins-and-needles tingling in her chest. The pain spread quickly, forcing her to grip the steering wheel.

At once a deep, agonized sob wracked her body. The car swerved, and when she raised her eyes, she saw the lights, red and blue, flashing in her rearview mirror.

"Unbelievable," she whispered bitterly as she pulled over to the side of the road. She got her driver's license and registration ready, taking a second to dab at her eyes with a napkin she found in her glove compartment.

As the officer approached her window, she sniffled deeply, trying to compose herself. Blinking rapidly, she rolled down the window and handed out her driver's license and registration, careful not to make eye contact. *Please don't let it be someone I know,* she prayed silently.

"Oh, my God, Jasmine White?" the officer exclaimed.

Rolling her eyes, Jasmine turned to see which of her former co-workers had pulled her over. Involuntarily, her head fell back against the headrest. "You've got to be kidding me!"

A familiar face leaned down into the window, his pale lips stretched into the obnoxious grin she knew so well. Could this day possibly get any worse? Of course, she'd have to run into an officer she'd worked with who also happened to be a chauvinist jerk.

"White, well, well, well. I thought you'd fallen off the face of the earth after you ran away from the force."

Any other day, she'd give every bit as good as she was getting, but today, she was in no mood. "Look, Officer Colby, I was speeding. I admit it. Just give me the damn ticket and let me go."

He started to make a smart-ass remark. She could see it forming on his lips. Then suddenly he paused. Maybe something in her face told him not to mess with her right then.

"Hey, have you been crying?" he asked.

Jasmine pressed her lips tightly together. "Of course not; I never cry." Just to defy her, a hot fat tear streaked down her cheek.

"What's the matter with you?"

"Look, are you going to give me the ticket, or what? I'm going to be late for an appointment."

His eyes narrowed as he studied her face. "You're really upset."

Jasmine sniffed again. "You're very observant." She turned her head away to avoid his intense stare. She hadn't been lying when she said she never cried. With four huge older brothers, a girl learned quickly that tears weren't going to get her very far. It had been a long time since she'd shed any.

The officer was quiet for so long, Jasmine turned back to see what he was up to. His face had gone slightly ashen. "Hey, um, I'm sorry for those cracks I made. I didn't mean anything by it. Everyone knows you were a good cop."

Jasmine's jaw went slack. "Look, you don't have to—"

He waved off her statement, handing back her papers. "Why don't we just forget about this. Drive safe." He spun on his heel and marched back to his car.

Jasmine shook her head. Wow, she was so pathetic these days even one of the biggest jerks in the D.C. police department felt sorry for her.

15

When Jasmine was his bodyguard, Spencer had felt like a prisoner. Now that Kirklin was his full-time watchdog, he expected a certain measure of freedom. They were men. They could bond. He could lie around the house eating pizza and drinking beer without worrying about whether his hair was combed or he smelled like dirty sweat socks.

Spencer turned from the plate glass window that had recently come to remind him of prison bars. Kirklin was in his customary position since he'd take over the job three days ago—sitting by the door like a sentry.

Kirklin was always at attention, either pacing from window to window and door to door simply sitting there, watching him.

Spencer rolled his shoulders, trying to shake off that creepy feeling that Kirklin gave him. Jasmine might have been a colossal pain in the ass, but at least she knew how to blend. That's what she prided herself on most. In fact, having her around the house had been kind of nice.

He'd aggravated her just enough to keep the smell of muffins, brownies, or cookies emanating from his kitchen. He'd stocked up on baking supplies because he knew she liked to bake to relax. And she'd always been up for whatever challenge he placed in her path.

A smile came to his lips as he remembered the way she'd outdanced him at Sin City. She'd even managed to turn his date with a stripper around to her own advantage. She always matched him blow for blow.

Then he remembered her face when he'd told her she wasn't up for the job because she was a woman. No matter what he'd thrown at her in the past, she'd always given as good as she'd gotten. Except then. He'd been too angry to see it at the moment, but for the first time, Jasmine had been whipped.

The numbness he'd been forcing finally faded. He'd let his anger over the fact that she was willing to deny their feelings for each other yet again take over. He didn't lose control of himself often, but when he did, Spencer had a nasty temper. His fuse had burned hot for days, and it wasn't until today that he'd finally realized what he'd done.

He hadn't even questioned the fact that Kirklin had taken over guard duty. After he'd blasted Jasmine's ability to protect him, she'd obviously gone back to Tali and resigned from his case.

Spencer had actually believed he was relieved when Kirklin showed up instead of Jasmine the next day. Then he didn't have to experience the bittersweet pain of seeing Jasmine every day. He was sick of that routine of lusting after her from afar. That would be nearly impossible now that he knew what it was like to lust after her up close.

Spencer looked back over at Kirklin. He couldn't believe it. The guy was actually dozing off. This was ridiculous. No matter how complicated things were, he could work this out with Jasmine.

Spencer ran upstairs to his bedroom and dialed Tali at the station.

"Talibah Arkou speaking."

"Hey, Tali, it's Spencer."

"What's up? I hadn't expected to hear from you until next week. You really need the rest. Taking some time off is the smartest thing you've done in a while."

"Yeah, well, Tali, I'm not calling to come back to work early, trust me on that. Gina can carry the show just fine until I get back. I'm calling because this deal with Kirklin isn't working for me. I want Jasmine back."

"I'll just bet you do, but you know that's not going to happen."

"Why not?" Spencer asked. "I know she might catch a little bit of an attitude, but I'm sure she'll come back if you sweet-talk her."

"Sweet-talk her? Is this some kind of joke? Why would I sweet-talk the woman who accused me of stalking you?"

"What!"

"Spencer, why am I getting the impression that you're out of the loop?"

"Maybe because I am, Tali. What's going on?"

"Where have you been? I called Jasmine in to my office to discuss the rumors I'd been hearing about a personal relationship between the two of you—which, by the way, you and I are going to have to have a little talk about—and instead of owning up to it, she got angry and accused *me* of being Nightmary."

Spencer couldn't believe this. "Are you serious? That's crazy!"

"I know. Needless to say, I fired her."

"Shit."

"I'm sorry you don't like the new guy, but—"

"Okay, Tali, never mind. I'll take care of this myself."

Spencer hung up the phone and rushed out the door.

It wasn't until he was turning onto the highway ramp that he realized that Kirklin was probably still sitting in front of his door, snoring.

* * *

"What do you mean, you fired her!" Spencer shouted at Nathan Pruitt. He'd driven all the way to Core Group hoping to see Jasmine, or at least find out where she'd been reassigned. It hadn't occurred to him that they would have let her go.

Pruitt's face was a blustery red. "Of course I fired her. She blew the job."

"Oh, really, and you think Kirklin is a much better replacement for her."

"Ted Kirklin is one of our best close protection specialists. He's worked with—"

"He's supposed to be on the job now, right?"

Pruitt blinked at him. "Yes."

"Well, aren't you wondering what I'm doing here without him?"

Pruitt swallowed. "Isn't he waiting for you outside?"

"I'm sure you'll be interested to know that your best bodyguard is still back at my house keeping close watch over the inside of his eyelids."

"What are you saying?" Pruitt demanded, veins popping.

"He fell asleep and I walked out right under his nose. So, if Kirklin is, in fact, the best Core Group has to offer, especially now that you lost Jasmine, WLPS—and me, specifically—will not be needing your services any further."

Pruitt started sputtering and Spencer held up a hand to halt his jabber. "Why don't you call and rouse Kirklin from his nap, and let him know he can get all the rest he needs from his own bed, because he's been canned, too!"

Spencer stormed out of the office and got behind the wheel of his car. He drove around trying to figure out what to do next. After driving aimlessly, and still not coming up with any answers, he realized that it was beginning to get dark and that he should probably head home.

He was only a few blocks from his house when he saw a pair of headlights headed up the narrow residential street toward him.

"Slow down, buddy, this is going to be a tight squeeze."

The vehicle was still approaching, at an increasing rate of speed, when the alarm bells went off in Spencer's head. This white van had no plans of slowing down. It was coming right for him.

Throwing the car into reverse, Spencer crossed his fingers that Jasmine's fancy driving tricks would come back to him quickly. With his foot jammed on the gas pedal, the car shot backward up the road.

Spencer gritted his teeth and prayed there wouldn't be anyone behind him.

Jasmine stared down into her plate of cold pizza. She absently picked out the green peppers, wishing she could pluck out all the things she didn't like about her life just as easily. It was her own fault. She'd ordered the green peppers, and she created her own problems.

She studied the tidy pile of peppers. "This one is for blowing the best assignment of my miserable bodyguard career." As if to punish herself, she thrust it into her mouth, wincing at the taste.

"And this one is for failing my client." The tiny green square blurred between her fingers as her eyes welled with tears. She quickly dashed at her eyes.

She was sick of these girly tears she couldn't seem to get rid of lately. She'd learned early on that tears didn't solve a thing; they certainly weren't helping her now. She was unemployed and her savings were only going to carry her for so long. She was going to have to find a job and start putting these problems behind her.

Part of her wanted to just pick up and move away. She knew that would just be some weak attempt to run away from her troubles, but that didn't keep the idea from looking very appealing to her. She could move to the West Coast, where she wouldn't have to be afraid of her heart breaking every time she turned on the radio.

Before her tear ducts had time to catch up with her thought process, her doorbell rang. She quickly glanced at her watch. It was nine-thirty at night. Who would be stopping by at this hour?

When she pulled open the door and saw Spencer standing there, all she could do was gape stupidly. Finally, he darted a look over his shoulder and said, "Uh, can I come in?"

"What are you doing here?" she said, stepping aside to let him in.

"I didn't have anywhere else to go."

"Really? What's wrong with your house?"

"I don't think it's safe."

Jasmine finally noticed the cut on Spencer's left cheek. His eyes looked frantic.

Jasmine sucked in a breath. "What happened to you?"

"I was on my way home when someone in a white van started coming after me. Next thing I know, I was in a crazy, high-speed chase. My car was nearly totaled."

"Oh, my gosh! Where's your car now?"

"Out front."

Jasmine stepped onto the front porch. Sure enough, the hood of Spencer's gold special-edition Lexus was crumpled like an accordion.

"Oh, my Lord!" She stepped back inside. "I can't believe you drove it like that."

"I wasn't sure how far I was going to get. But I figured it was better to take my chances rather than stick around and let Nightmary catch up to me."

"That looks horrible. How did you crash it?"

Spencer rattled off the story, barely pausing for breaths. "I couldn't see the driver of the van, but it doesn't take a genius to figure out that Nightmary was behind the wheel."

"Wait a minute. Why were you out alone? I thought Ted Kirklin took over your case."

"He did, but after a couple of days, I fired him."

Jasmine raised an eyebrow. "Why? What happened?"

"He fell asleep on the job."

Jasmine allowed herself a moment's pleasure before she turned her attention back to the issue at hand. "Well, let's make a few phone calls and get this taken care of. We can get a tow truck over here, and call the police to file a report. Where are you going to stay tonight? Do you have a friend in the area you can stay with?"

"Uh, yeah . . ."

"Who is it?" she asked.

"You?"

"Me? You can't stay here. Frankly, I'm not even sure why you showed up here."

"I needed to be someplace safe, Jasmine. Near you was the safest place I could think of."

Oh, now he wanted to pour on the charm. It didn't matter. She wasn't buying it. "Well, that's very nice, but you can't stay here. Call Nathan Pruitt and tell him you need another body-guard."

Spencer shook his head. "I don't want any more guards from that place. Why would I patronize any agency that hasn't got the good sense to keep you on staff?"

"Aren't you just overflowing with flattery. How interesting since it wasn't too long ago that you implied that I had too much estrogen to be a good bodyguard."

Spencer chuckled sheepishly. "Oh, you're still mad about that?"

She merely glared at him.

"Look, I was angry. You know I didn't mean any of those things I said. The fact of the matter is, Nightmary is clearly still out to get me. And apparently she's decided that she wants me dead. I need protection and you're the only person I trust."

"Well, that's just too bad, considering that I happen to be out of the business now."

Spencer eyed her. "Didn't you used to work as a private agent?"

"Yes, but I'm not—"

"Fine. I'll pay double whatever your private fee was. I'm serious. Name your price. You may not think my life is worth much right now, but it's very valuable to me. If I wasn't serious about staying alive, I wouldn't be here. Look at my face," he said, pointing to his cut. "I can't afford to waste time on petty flattery."

"Okay, Spencer, you've got a deal. You've hired yourself a bodyguard. But things are going to be very different this time around."

"You got it, boss. I'll do whatever you say."

16

*S*pencer stood in Jasmine's kitchen wearing her powder blue robe, wondering where to begin. He wanted to prepare a gourmet breakfast-in-bed feast for her, but he was a little thrown off by her fancy setup.

All the kitchens he'd spent time in were fairly typical. Jasmine's was tweaked out with a bread machine; expensive pots and pans in every shape, size, and color; and a spice rack with ingredients even Martha Stewart never heard of.

Shaking off his stupor, Spencer gathered what he needed for an omelette and fried potatoes. He was thankful that he'd mastered breakfast foods when he and his sister were in high school. Once he got started he felt a little less intimidated.

He hadn't thought much about the home Jasmine would create for herself until he'd shown up on her doorstep yesterday, but now that he'd gotten a good look around, he had to admit it wasn't at all what he would have expected.

Jasmine was a no-nonsense kind of woman, and he'd expected her home to reflect that. Clean, neat, simple. Instead, her living room was lush with colorful throw pillows, glass figurines, and paintings of children holding flowers. She had a guest room devoted to her dollhouse collection, and her bedroom . . . well, her bedroom was replete with feminine pleasures.

There wasn't one moment during the time he'd known her that Spencer had forgotten that Jasmine was a woman. Yet, he still hadn't suspected that she was the kind of woman who indulged in satin linens, little soaps in the shape of roses, and baskets filled with potpourri sachets tied with ribbons.

It pleased him to see this ultrafeminine side of Jasmine. It reminded him that they had so much more to discover about each other. She'd been immersed in his lifestyle for several weeks, but he knew only one fraction of the person she was.

Suddenly, Spencer got a flash of Jasmine in the future, making lunches for the kids with juice boxes and homemade brownies shaped like stars. The house would smell like freshly baked bread, and her husband would be happy and satisfied, knowing she wasn't afraid to kick a little butt if he ever got out of line.

The image faded quickly. Spencer forced his thoughts back to preparing breakfast. He didn't want to think of Jasmine with a husband. He didn't dare entertain the notion of that man being him. His parents had a cold, sterile marriage, and they were cold, sterile parents. The only thing he'd learned from them was how to be indulgent and self-involved. Being a husband and father required putting other people's needs before his own. All his past relationships had proven he didn't know the first thing about that.

Arranging the omelette and potatoes on the platter as artfully as he could, Spencer found a tray-table atop the refrigerator and carried his offering to Jasmine's bedroom.

He pushed open the door to find Jasmine covered up to her shoulders with her back to the door. "Wake up, sleepyhead," he called from the doorway.

Jasmine's head lifted from the pillow slightly, but she didn't turn. "I'm awake. I heard you clanking around down there, so I decided to hide out up here rather than face whatever havoc you've been wreaking in my kitchen."

"Fear not, fair lady. I hath brought the havoc to you."

Jasmine sat up in bed, and the look on her face was priceless. Breakfast in bed was a simple and admittedly obvious ploy to score points, but Jasmine reacted as though he'd presented her with diamonds and gold. "How sweet! I've always wanted to have someone bring me breakfast in bed."

Spencer placed the tray over her lap and stretched out beside her. He picked up a fork and fed her the first bite of the omelette. "You mean to tell me no one's ever done this for you?"

Her smile was shy. "No one's done anything like this for me." Clearly, wanting to change the subject, she leaned forward for the next bite. "Where's your breakfast?"

Spencer danced the forkful of eggs in front of her mouth before taking the second bite for himself. "This is it. There's plenty here for both of us."

Jasmine picked up the second fork on the tray and began feeding herself. "This is delicious. You did a great job."

"Well, it's hard not to feel like a four-star chef in that kitchen of yours."

Jasmine smiled sheepishly. "If Williams-Sonoma gave frequent flyer miles, I'd have enough mileage to get to the moon and back."

"I knew you liked to bake, but apparently the addiction is a little more serious than that."

She smiled. "I've never told anyone this, but, for a brief period of time, I considered going to culinary school."

"Why wouldn't you tell anybody that? More importantly, why wouldn't you go ahead and do it?"

"I didn't want to hear the razzing from my brothers."

Spencer looked up from his forkful of omelette. "What? Why would they tease you about that?"

"You know . . . cooking. That's exactly the type of girly profession they would have expected of me."

Spencer shook his head to clear out the cobwebs. "Girly? Most of the finest chefs in the world are men."

"I know, but they wouldn't see it that way."

Spencer blew out an exasperated breath. "I don't get it. Even if they do think cooking is girly . . . News flash, Jasmine. You *are* a girl."

She waved him off. "Yeah, I know, but—"

"Wait a minute. You're not . . . ashamed of being a woman, are you? Growing up in a houseful of men, you don't think being a female was a, I don't know, disadvantage?"

Jasmine blanched. "I . . . no—why would you . . . of—of course not—"

Spencer wasn't surprised by her fluster. He picked up the empty tray and placed it on the floor, pulling her body against his.

"Sweetheart, just in case, I think this needs saying. You embody everything that's good in women. You're as strong and smart and capable as any man, and yet you're as beautiful and soft and sexy as a woman should be. Yes, you know your way around a kitchen, but you also know more about cars than most men I know. You don't have to prove your strength to me or deny your femininity to your brothers. Who you are speaks for itself."

Despite his words, it had never occurred to Spencer that Jasmine was capable of tears, but he saw them welling in her eyes now. Instead of speaking, she grabbed him around the neck and brought his mouth down to hers.

All the emotions she was feeling came through to him in that kiss. He wrapped his arms around her and kissed her back with everything he had.

Finally, when the kiss broke, Spencer felt the need to do what he always did when he felt emotions becoming too intense. No jokes came to mind to make her laugh, so he resorted to the next cheap trick. He tickled her.

They began rolling around on top of the covers until things turned passionate once again. He pulled the covers down so he could see the lavender lace of her bra. He dipped his head and buried his nose in her cleavage, planting kisses wherever his lips touched.

"Come here," Jasmine whispered. Pulling his face up to hers, she began pushing her robe off his shoulders. "This looks better on me anyway."

Spencer yanked off the robe with every intention of making love to Jasmine. He felt her soft tongue slide past his lips and responded instantly. And then he remembered—"Oh, my God, Maximilian!"

Jasmine pulled away, confused. "That's a new one. I must admit, I've never had a guy call out another man's name while he was making love to me."

Spencer flopped over on his back. "I'm sorry. Maximilian isn't a guy, it's my dog. I have to get home to walk him. When I left the house, I didn't know I'd be out all night."

"Since when do you have a dog?"

"I bought a retired police dog for protection."

On the drive over to Spencer's house, Jasmine flipped back into bodyguard mode. It felt good to be in total control. Now that she didn't have to answer to anyone, she planned to do a few things differently. Hopefully, Nightmary wouldn't find them until they were ready for her, but if she did, Jasmine had packed her gun, and she wasn't afraid to use it.

"Since we've got to stop by your house, make sure you pack enough clothes to last several days. Call the station and let them know you'll be taking an indeterminate amount of time off. Tell them you're going to Pennsylvania to visit your sister."

"Where am I really going to be?" he asked.

"We're going to play it by ear. Our biggest advantage right now is that Nightmary no longer has a definite place to find you. The problem is that she seems to have raised the stakes. Not being able to find you could cause her violent actions to escalate."

"Gee, that's a comforting thought."

"That's why we need to make sure she doesn't find you until after we prove that Tali's behind this. We'll just have to make sure we don't stay in one place long enough for her to locate you."

"Oh, geez, Jasmine. I heard you were fired because you accused Tali of being Nightmary. I thought you said that stuff because you didn't want to admit you and I had a thing going on. You can't possibly really believe she's Nightmary."

"Not only do I believe it, I intend to prove it. I just need to get you safely tucked away until then." She pulled into Spencer's driveway. "I'm giving you twenty minutes to get your stuff together. Then we have to get on the road."

Spencer pulled his keys out of his pocket and started for the front door. "I'm going to have the two best bodyguards money can buy on the job. You and Maximilian. Nightmary doesn't stand a chance."

Jasmine followed Spencer cautiously. "I can't believe you really bought a guard dog. Are you sure you know how to control it? Some of those dogs can be very aggressive. If you don't know which trigger words to avoid, you could turn the dog on attack inadvertently."

"Don't worry, the guy spent hours going over

the whole spiel with me. Now that Maximilian is retired, he'll mostly serve as a visual deterrent."

Spencer unlocked the door and disarmed the alarm, and Jasmine followed him into the house. "Well, this isn't the greatest timing. We're going to be a lot more conspicuous traveling with a dog."

"Maximilian," Spencer called inside the doorway. The dog loped out of the kitchen. "There you are, boy. Show Jasmine what a good guard dog you are. Go on, boy!"

Jasmine got down to Maximilian's level. The dog took one look at her and backed away with a distressed howl. She giggled, darting a look up at Spencer.

He frowned down at his new pet. "He's just a little shy."

"Yeah, just what you look for in a guard dog." Jasmine reached her hand out to Maximilian. "It's okay, boy. I won't hurt you."

The dog shrank back again, bowing his head as if to cover his eyes with his paws. Jasmine gently stroked his head, and Maximilian came to life, nuzzling up to her while she petted him. "Aw, good boy, Max!"

"Well, I told you he's retired. Obviously, old Max is smart enough to see there's no danger at the moment. I'm sure he was the most vicious German shepherd on the force when he was on the job."

"I hate to break this to you, Spencer, but Max

is a Belgian Malinois, not a German shepherd. And he's practically still a puppy. Much too young to be retired from the force. Did they tell you why they retired him from the program?"

Spencer shrugged. "They just said he was a retired police dog. I assumed it was because he'd served his time or whatever."

"If they retired a dog from the program early it was for one of two reasons. One, he was too aggressive and out of control." She scratched Maximilian behind the ears and received an affectionate licking. "And I hardly think that's the case here. Two, he was too playful or just a straight-up coward."

Spencer crouched beside Jasmine, giving Max a playful hug and covering his doggy ears. "Don't listen to her, Max. I know you aren't a coward."

Jasmine knew she'd have plenty of opportunities to tease Spencer about his choice of guard dogs, but she didn't want to linger. "Pack some things, Spencer. I'll take Maximilian out back to do his thing. We need to get moving."

Fifteen minutes later, Jasmine pulled out of Spencer's driveway with Spencer, his dog, and a giant bag of dog food.

"So, where are we headed?" Spencer asked.

Jasmine sighed, hoping she wouldn't need to have her backseat reupholstered. "My brother Coby owes me a favor."

* * *

In the lobby of Coby's apartment building, Jasmine dialed her brother's phone number on her cell phone. He picked up on the third ring.

"Hey, kiddo. What's up?"

"I need a huge favor. I was wondering if you'd mind if a couple of friends and I crashed at your place tonight. It's an emergency."

"It must be, for you to pull a Coby. Sure, you know you can hang out here. Lord knows I owe you." Then his voice turned wicked. "But I hope by 'a couple of friends' you mean cute girls."

"Not quite. Thanks. See you soon."

"Where are you?" Coby asked.

"On the elevator up to your apartment." They stepped off the elevator and Coby, still holding the receiver, poked his head out of an open door down the hall.

"Man, you could have given me some warning, Minnie. I didn't have time to clean the place up."

"Like it would have mattered," Jasmine said before disconnecting the line.

Coby started up the hallway toward them. "Spencer! My man. Welcome to my humble abode. Is that your dog?"

Spencer greeted Coby like they were long-lost pals. "You know it. That's Maximilian, my guard dog."

Jasmine snorted.

Spencer shot her a scolding look. "Shhh, you'll hurt his feelings."

"Exactly my point."

They all crowded into Coby's small apartment. Jasmine remained in the doorway, taking in his new digs.

Spencer set his bags down in front of Coby's leather couch. "Hey man, I like your place. Where'd you get this?" he asked, pointing to the disco ball hanging from the ceiling.

"You like that? A deejay in New York hooked me up when Club Neon went out of business."

"Big surprise." Jasmine laughed. "You ever notice, no matter how broke a brother says he is, he always finds the cash for a big-screen television and a stereo system that could blow off the walls."

"Hey, when times are hard you have to make do with just the essentials," Spencer said.

"You know what I'm saying!" Coby reached across the sofa to slap hands with Spencer.

Jasmine rolled her eyes, realizing that she was in for a whole lot more of that kind of annoying bonding. Spencer and her brother had way too much in common for her own good.

"Ooh, you've got a Playstation 2," Spencer exclaimed. "What games do you have?"

"Here we go," Jasmine said to no one in particular as Coby leaped over the couch to pull out his vast game collection. She looked down at Maximilian. "Looks like we're on our own, Max."

Just then the dog stood up and loped around

the couch to join the boys. "Fine, guess I'm on my own."

Jasmine's head kept nodding forward as she tried to stay awake while the boys played yet another rematch of whatever racing game they were playing. "I'm going to bed, guys."

"Wait, wait," Spencer said, not taking his eyes off the screen. "Just let us finish this round and then you can go to bed."

"No, you don't get it. I'm going to bed right now. And since you're sleeping on my so-called bed, I'm taking *your* bed, Coby. Looks like the two of you are bunking together tonight. If you ever stop playing with your joysticks and go to bed."

Spencer looked Coby up and down. "Looks like I got the short end of that stick."

Coby looked back. "Hey, just as long as you're clear that, while you're in my apartment, no part of your stick is going anywhere near my sister."

17

*T*hursday afternoon, Spencer and Jasmine arrived at Tinman's house just in time for brunch. Tinman and his wife, Sandy, and their three kids had just gotten back from grocery shopping.

Everyone was home because Tinman had the day off from the firehouse and Sandy ran an Internet store out of their basement.

Between the half-eaten package of Oreo cookies and the fact that they had company, Tinman's twin five-year-old girls were ready to bounce off the walls. They kept popping out of their chairs, circling Jasmine and Spencer with jam-sticky fingers, and regaling them with elementary school woes.

Sandy was busy feeding the baby in the bedroom, and no sooner did Tinman pick up one girl and set her back in her chair than the other one would pop up. Finally, he gave up and declared brunch officially over.

Afterward, he called Jasmine into the living room so they could talk alone. "The kids are just a little wound up right now because they're so excited to see you two."

Jasmine nodded, knowing there was more coming.

"By the time the sun sets, they'll be exhausted and go right to sleep. They won't be any trouble at all."

She raised a brow. "That's . . . nice . . ."

Tinman grinned, clearly abandoning the subtle approach. "You know Sandy and I are happy to put you guys up for the night. It's not an imposition at all—"

Jasmine smiled, knowing what was coming next. "But . . ."

"Since you two are going to be here, I was wondering if you guys would do us a favor."

"You want us to baby-sit tonight, don't you?"

"Sandy and I haven't had a night away from the kids since Justin Junior was born. I thought I'd surprise her with dinner in a restaurant that has candles instead of crayons on the table."

Jasmine laughed. When he'd been on the market, her big brother Justin had been the biggest ladies' man alive, but Sandy tamed him, and he adapted to family life as though he'd been born for it. He was an attentive husband and father, and he and Sandy deserved a night to themselves.

"No problem. I'd love to watch the kids for you tonight. It will be fun."

Justin and Sandy hadn't been gone thirty minutes before Jasmine began to regret those words.

"Erica, come here so I can dry you off!"

Max barked loudly as the little girl chased him down the hall. She'd jumped out of her bath to play with him. Max, valiant guard dog that he was, streaked away from the child, scrambling under the dining room to hide.

"Gotcha!" Spencer scooped the little girl up as she flew by him, wet and naked, trailing suds. He deposited her into the towel Jasmine held spread wide.

While Jasmine wrestled with Erica, Angela, already clad in her pajamas, went docilely into Spencer's arms. Hoisting her onto his back, he skipped her off to bed.

"Erica, hold still." Pulling on the child's nightgown was like trying to remove a thorn from a lion's paw. She jiggled and wriggled as though they were engaged in some elaborate game. "What's gotten into you?"

Jasmine knew the girls were just showing off for Spencer's sake. Usually, when Jasmine came to visit, the girls acted like she was royalty, climbing all over her and begging for her to help them brush their teeth and read stories. Now, suddenly, she was old Aunt Jasmine and Spencer was the new king in town.

Spencer came out of the girls' bedroom. "Need some help?"

Resisting the urge to pout outright, Jasmine knew when she was beat. "Something tells me you're going to have better luck." She passed Erica over to Spencer, the little girl's Pokèmon nightgown on backward and twisted around her waist.

Jasmine rolled her eyes as Erica held perfectly still for Spencer to right her nightgown. "That's better," he said, "Time for bed, kiddo."

Jasmine glared at him. "Well, we know if your career in radio fizzles out, you can always run a day care."

Spencer winked at her. "You forget I have a kid sister. I've had many years of practice getting a woman to do what I want."

Jasmine ignored the lascivious grin he gave her behind Erica's back. Grudgingly, she waited in the doorway as Spencer plunked Erica down in the bed across from Angela's. She was sure the girls were going to ask Spencer to read them their bedtime story.

Just as she'd expected, Angela directed Spencer to retrieve their *Princess Marmalade* storybook from their bookshelf.

Little Justin Junior was sleeping peacefully. Jasmine was just about to leave to go peek in on him when an eruption of squealing turned her back.

"We want Aunt Jasmine to read to us."

Spencer held their favorite book in her direction. "You just said you wanted me to read to you. Which is it?"

Jasmine started to turn around again.

"Both of you," the girls squealed.

Spencer shrugged in her direction. "Come hither, Princess Jasmine, we have a tale of castles and dragons to tell."

Not sure how they were going to make this work, Jasmine joined Spencer at the child-size yellow table between the girls' beds. "Very well, Lord Spencer, you go first."

Spencer read the first page of the storybook, exaggerating his inflections with each word, then slid the book across to Jasmine. Not to be outdone, Jasmine gave an animated display, contorting her expression, which sent the girls into a fit of giggles.

The two of them took turns passing the book, getting sillier with each page they turned. By the time they reached the end of the story, the girls were exhausted from laughing so much and went right to sleep.

Jasmine's brother Rome, the eldest of the White clan, kept his house immaculate, as though he were expecting a naval inspection of his barracks.

When Jasmine and Spencer crossed his threshold with Max in tow, she could see his nose turn up right away.

"You didn't mention a dog."

Jasmine tried to sound upbeat. "Oh, you mean Max? He's such a good dog." As long as Tinman didn't tell him about the potted plant Max turned over while he was running from Erica, she just might convince Rome to let Max stay.

"A dog is a dog. He stays outside."

"Thanks for letting us crash here, Rome," Jasmine said. "We're trying to stay mobile until we can get a handle on Spencer's stalker situation."

Rome nodded. "Staying mobile is fine for the short term, but you can't keep that up forever. What's your next plan of action?"

Jasmine shrugged. "We haven't had a lot of time to formulate plans; we've been playing it by ear. Right now, my top suspect is his station manager. That's why I feel we need to keep a low profile."

Rome scratched the goatee on his chin. "That's not going to work. You're going to need a better plan. After dinner we'll have a strategy meeting."

Rome had always taken his role as the big brother very seriously. Whenever he saw a problem, he always felt it was his personal duty to step in and make sure things stayed on track. Many times over the years, Jasmine had resented that interference, but this was one time she was actually grateful for the help.

There was too much at stake for her not to let him help her.

Order and routine were the standard in Rome's household. Jasmine and Spencer were not fitting in at all. Rome ran a tight ship, and his wife and two kids toed the line per his instruction. With two extra people in the house and a dog in the backyard, Rome's orderly household had been thrown off balance.

Jasmine tried to make herself useful by helping Marla in the kitchen, but they ended up tripping over each other awkwardly, which resulted in tonight's chicken jambalaya's landing overturned in the sink.

Spencer offered to make up for the ruined dinner by ordering takeout for everyone. Unfortunately, Rome's finicky children, twelve and nine, refused to eat the barbecue because it wasn't aesthetically pleasing.

By the time dinner was over, everyone was feeling cranky and bickering over every minor issue.

Jasmine and Spencer joined Rome in his study. They traded looks as they shyly seated themselves on the leather sofa. Rome had a way of intimidating even the most confident of men. She could tell Spencer was feeling a little like a kid sitting in the principal's office.

Rome spun in an arc behind his desk as he scratched his goatee. "I've been thinking about your problem very carefully, and I think I have a solution that will benefit us all."

"I'm all ears," Jasmine said.

"Well, have you considered taking Spencer up to the property in Richmond? No one Spencer has come in contact with would know anything about it, so you all can set up camp there while you investigate this stalker situation."

Jasmine nodded. "That's not a bad idea. It's far enough away that Nightmary won't find him, but it's still close enough for us to keep tabs on what's going on around here."

"I think the two of you should leave tonight," Rome said. "Marla will be happy to pack some rations for you just to get you started."

Jasmine laughed. "I guess you two would give us your fine china if it meant we didn't have to spend another minute under your roof. We didn't mean to be such a nuisance."

"Not at all, but I'm sure the dog will appreciate having the big yard to roam around in."

"Well, that sounds like a plan," Jasmine said. "We'll get on the road as soon as we can get our things together."

They all turned as a furious cry came from upstairs. "Jerome! That dog is digging up my flower beds!"

Spencer ducked his head. "Don't worry, we're leaving."

* * *

Spencer dozed during most of the drive to Richmond. It was almost midnight when they finally reached the property. Jasmine ran through the house opening windows to air the place out, while Spencer unpacked the car.

Max bounded out of the car and immediately began to explore. A few minutes later she heard a frightened yelp, and Max nearly knocked her over rushing up to her. She knelt down, soothing the jittery dog with a scratch on the head.

"What's wrong, boy?"

Spencer rolled his eyes as he dumped his duffel bag in the hallway entrance. "It was a chipmunk on the porch. Max took one look at him and took off."

"Aw, that's okay, baby. Mama's not going to let anyone hurt you."

Spencer raised a brow at the baby voice Jasmine had suddenly affected. "Oh, now he's your baby? Just a couple of days ago you were making fun of Max for being such a coward."

"I wasn't making fun of Max. He can't help the fact that he has self-esteem issues. I was making fun of you for buying a guard dog that flunked out of the police academy."

Spencer sighed, dragging the rest of their bags into the house. "What did Marla pack for us to eat? I'm famished."

"How can you be famished? You ate all the food from dinner that the kids wouldn't touch.

Plus, you slept all the way up here. You haven't expended enough energy to have worked up an appetite again."

Spencer patted his stomach. "I'm a growing boy." He grabbed one of the grocery bags of food.

"Don't make a pig of yourself. The nearest grocery store is thirty minutes away."

"Ooh," he said, pulling a bottle of wine out of the paper sack. "Seems to me, your brother and sister-in-law wanted us to have a romantic evening."

Jasmine tried to look over. "What's in there?"

He closed the bag and blocked her view with his back. "Never mind that right now. All you talked about on the drive up was taking a long soak in your grandmother's old-fashioned tub. Why don't you get started on that while I take care of this."

Jasmine started to protest, but she realized that she just didn't have the energy. "Okay, but don't let me come back and find you've devoured all the food without me."

He winked at her. "Now, would I do that?" He held a finger to her lips when she started to open her mouth. "Don't answer that."

Kicking off her shoes on the way upstairs, Jasmine smiled to herself. It might actually be nice to have this place to themselves for a few days. Maybe for this brief period of time they could forget what had brought them there in the first place and just relax.

* * *

Spencer chuckled under his breath as he un-packed the bag. Next time he saw Jasmine's brother Rome, he had to make a point to thank him for the setup. Wine, grapes, cheese spread, a loaf of French bread, two steaks, and chocolate pudding. That was all he needed to get the mood started.

Pouring two glasses of red wine, Spencer tip-toed up the stairs to the bathroom where Jasmine was bathing. Her head was tilted back against the wall, and her eyes were closed. The tops of her pink-painted toenails peeked out of the bub-bles near the faucet.

He smiled at the pink polish on her toes. The more he learned about Jasmine the more he en-joyed her contradictions. On the surface, she was bold talk and all the fire she needed to back it up. But under the surface, she was soft and achingly vulnerable. She delighted in the most simple feminine pleasures, like frosty pink polish for her toes hidden under her practical, ass-kicking shoes.

She kept the nails of her slender fingers short and polish free because, Spencer knew, she couldn't have anyone mistaking her for the kind of girly female who would bother to paint them. But her toes gave her secret away: Jasmine was the most feminine of women.

Suddenly, he felt a heavy heat in his groin. In-voluntarily, he released a low groan.

Jasmine's eyes fluttered open. "Spencer?"

"It's me, honey. I brought you some wine."

She reached out her hand for the glass. "Mmm, wine and hot bubbles. I'll sleep like a rock tonight."

"I know something else that will help you sleep." He walked over and knelt by the edge of the tub. Picking up a washcloth, he began scrubbing her back.

"I see right through you, you know."

He leaned back. "Do you want me to stop?"

"Not on your life!"

The next morning, Jasmine opened her eyes to find herself curled against Spencer's back. She was used to the momentary disorientation that came with waking up in a new location every day, but each time she woke up next to Spencer was like rising from a beautiful dream and finding it had become a reality.

She ran her hand over his smoothly muscled arm, and he made a sound very close to purring in his sleep. She was considering the best and most pleasurable way to wake him when she became aware of an eerie sensation at the back of her neck.

Turning toward the sun streaming in through the large curtainless windows, she saw a male figure, hands cupped around his eyes, peering in through the glass.

Instinctively releasing a startled scream, Jasmine jumped up, stark naked, and grabbed her gun.

"What the hell's going on!" Spencer came awake behind her. "Jasmine, wait, that's—"

Feet planted, Jasmine raised her SIG-Sauer at the intruder. He immediately backed away from the window, starting to raise his arms in surrender but doubling over instead.

Shocked, Jasmine realized he was laughing. Her panicked haze cleared, and she realized the figure was her brother Coby. For a split second her hand tightened on the gun as she considered pulling the trigger anyway.

Lowering her weapon, she turned as Spencer wrapped a blanket around her from behind. "What are your brothers doing up here?"

"Brothers?" Turning back to the window, she saw that Sonny had come up behind Coby, who was obviously filling him in on his brush with death.

She waved them around to the front door so Spencer, who had already pulled on a pair of jeans, could let them in the house. By the time her brothers followed Spencer into the living room, Jasmine had jerked on a pair of shorts and a T-shirt.

Coby took one look at her and started laughing again. "Uh, Minnie, your shirt's on backwards."

That's when Jasmine lost it. "What's wrong with you two anyway? You can't wait at the front door like normal people? Do you have to go skulking around the house, peering in windows, and scaring people half to death? And what are you doing here anyway?"

Sonny, always the diplomat, immediately tried to soothe her. "We didn't mean to scare you, Jasmine. We did knock on the front door, but you obviously didn't hear us. I sent Jacob around to the back to make sure the two of you were all right."

"Oh, okay. I'm sorry I yelled at you. It was just, you know, not the best way to wake up."

"You should be sorry. You almost shot me!" Coby smirked, clearly more amused than upset over the idea.

Now that all the confusion had been sorted out, Max took the opportunity to slink out of the corner where he'd been cowering.

Coby immediately dropped to his knees to greet the dog. "Hey, buddy! Smart idea staying out of Jasmine's line of fire."

"So, what brought you two up here?" Spencer asked.

Sonny glanced around the room, observing the evidence of their romantic evening, before politely looking away. "Why don't Jacob and I wait in the kitchen while the two of you get yourselves together? Then we'll tell you why we came." He walked out of the room, dragging Coby with him.

Jasmine took a look around herself and felt an embarrassed heat sting her cheeks. In the center of the room were rumbled covers and pillows beside an empty wine bottle and two glasses. Strewn clothing, including her bra and panties and Spencer's boxer briefs, were in plain sight. No wonder Sonny was uncomfortable.

She looked up at Spencer, who was standing across the room, taking in the scene himself. "Well," she said, pasting on a fake smile. "Good morning! We're off to a great start, wouldn't you say?"

For once, Spencer didn't pick up on her playful tone. He shook his head. "I don't like this. Something must be wrong for your brothers to drive all the way up here. It's a two-hour drive and it's only late morning. They must have gotten an early start to get here."

Jasmine flitted around the living room, trying to straighten up. Her gut feelings told her he was right, but she didn't want him to worry, so she said, "Don't get ahead of the game. If it were Tinman or Rome, I'd say trouble for sure. But it's Sonny and Coby. With those two it could be anything. I told you about the little family dispute over the house. Coby probably heard we were up here and mentioned to Sonny that he was going to come out to measure the bedrooms or something. Sonny probably decided to tag along."

Spencer just shook his head and finished dressing. "I don't know about that."

Several minutes later, they joined Sonny and

Coby in the kitchen. Coby was already helping himself to the leftover cheese and crackers.

"Okay, guys, what's up?" Jasmine asked.

"Why don't you let me explain," Sonny said when Coby tried talking with his mouth full. "I got a call from Rome early this morning. Jasmine, your alarm went off around five A.M."

"Oh, no!" Jasmine slapped her forehead.

"The police were dispatched, and since you listed Rome as your emergency contact, they let him know that your place had been trashed. They couldn't tell if anything was stolen."

Jasmine sighed. "This is the last thing I need right now."

"He knew the phones up here had been disconnected, and your cell phone is out of range, so Rome called around looking for someone to drive up and let you know what happened. He wanted to come himself, but he had to stay with the kids. Do you think this has something to do with Spencer's stalker?"

Jasmine chewed on her lower lip. "It's a definite possibility. I have to get back there. What do the two of you have planned? Can you stay up here with Spencer until I return?"

"Wait a minute," Spencer protested. "If you're going back, I'm going with you."

Jasmine was in no mood for Spencer's resistance right now. "I'm not going to argue with you. You're staying here." She turned to her brothers.

"I'm going to shower and change. Keep an eye on him."

As Jasmine got out of the shower, she heard the front door open and close and some additional voices followed by commotion. Dressing quickly, she bounded down the stairs to discover that Rome had shown up with his wife and two kids.

"What's going on?" she asked.

"I had to make sure you guys were okay," Rome said. "If you need some extra protection, I have my rifle in the trunk."

Jasmine could see the kids playing with Max in the living room while Marla watched over them. "Why did you bring Marla and the kids?"

Rome sighed sheepishly. "I had no choice. Marla threatened to leave me if I left them behind. I promised them a family weekend. She said whatever I was doing, they were doing it, too. Anyway, there's safety in numbers."

Jasmine put her hand on her hip. "Did you all show up because you thought I couldn't handle this situation?"

Rome looked at her in surprise. "Why would you say that? I came to back you up, not to take over. That's what family is for."

Jasmine felt her heart soften. "Oh. Well, in that case, thanks. The more the merrier, I guess. You all can keep Spencer company while I check out the damage back home."

An hour later, Jasmine was ready to leave, confident that Spencer was in good hands with her three brothers, a dental hygienist, two kids, and a cowardly dog to protect him.

She had just climbed into her car and was about to start the ignition when a blue Toyota pickup truck pulled up behind her, blocking her in.

Tinman jumped out of the driver's side, grabbing a fireman's ax from the back. Jasmine got out of the car. "You too?" she yelled.

Just then the passenger door opened and her mother stepped out. "And me. I caught him just before he left the house. When I found out everybody was up here, there was no way I was going to let him leave me behind!"

Jasmine opened and closed her mouth. She had to have the craziest family on earth.

Spencer loved being surrounded by Jasmine's family. They were such a loving, tight-knit unit, he could almost forget the unfortunate circumstances that had brought them all together.

The only downside of being cooped up with the White clan was that Jasmine's four, big, older brothers were very protective of their baby sister. Each one had taken him aside to inquire about his intentions toward Jasmine. He'd wanted Jasmine to be the first one to hear him confess his feelings aloud, but since they were out in the country where no one could hear him scream, he decided to go ahead and let them in on his little secret.

Since the house had been empty, there weren't enough provisions to maintain nine people and a dog, so Coby took their mother into town to stock up on supplies. They came back an hour later with lawn chairs, sleeping bags, games, and enough food to feed an army.

"Look what I brought!" Coby said, holding up a boom box. "Party over here. Deejay Coby's in the house!"

It wasn't long before funky tunes filled the house. Rome started grilling hamburgers, and the kids got a heated game of Monopoly started right away. Spencer looked around, realizing that this was exactly the atmosphere he'd missed out on growing up. He only wished Jasmine was there enjoying her family with him.

He knew she was good at her job, but he couldn't help worrying about what she would find when she got back home. If it hadn't been for him and his troubles, her place probably wouldn't have been broken into.

He heard the doorbell ring, and since everyone else was occupied watching the Monopoly game or cooking, Spencer opened the door, expecting to see another of Jasmine's relatives.

"Gina, what are you doing here?"

"Spencer, thank God you're all right."

"I'm fine. What's going on?"

"Jasmine called and told me to get over here

right away. She thinks Nightmary is on her way here, and she told me to take you someplace safe."

"Is she okay?" Spencer asked.

Gina looked very concerned. "I think so, but, we'll find out soon enough. She wants us to meet her in town."

"Okay, just let me tell everyone what's going on."

"Make it quick. I don't know how much time we have."

*S*pencer got into Gina's car and pulled on his seat belt. "How did Jasmine sound when she called you? Was she in trouble?"

"I don't know, Spencer. We'll just have to hope for the best," Gina answered, backing down the driveway. "The two of you have been scarce for the last week. Where have you been all this time?"

"All over. Hey, do you have your cell phone on you? I want to try to call Jasmine. I'm really worried about her."

Gina pulled over to the side of the road. "Here, let me get it for you." She dug in the backseat for her purse. When she finally sat forward, she didn't have a phone in her hand.

Spencer's mouth dropped open. "What are you doing?"

She held up a bottle of pills. "We can do this the easy way or the hard way," she said, holding up the gun in her other hand.

Jasmine walked into the WLPS station like a woman on a mission. Clearly, Nightmary didn't know who she was dealing with. Both her town house and Spencer's house had been broken into. None of the big-ticket items had been stolen, so Jasmine was certain Nightmary was the culprit. She was obviously tired of being ignored.

Jasmine suspected that the woman had been looking for some clue to Spencer's location. Fortunately, Jasmine couldn't think of anything she'd left in plain sight that might identify her grandmother's property as a possible hideout for Spencer.

She headed down the hall and burst into Tali's office. No one had been able to substantiate Jasmine's theory that Tali was Nightmary, but she was still Jasmine's best source of information.

Unfortunately, the woman Jasmine found sitting in Tali's office was not Tali. It was a young woman she'd never seen before.

"Who are you?" Jasmine asked, hoping her rudeness would distract the girl from the fact that she didn't belong there herself.

The girl stood, revealing a Howard University sweatshirt. "Hi, I'm Tali's new intern, Mandy. I just started this week, so I haven't met everyone yet."

Jasmine extended her hand. "Hi, I'm Jasmine. Spencer Powell's personal assistant. I dropped by to pick up some papers for him and decided to stop in and speak with Tali. Is she around?"

"No, but she'll be in tomorrow. Do you want to leave her a message?"

"No, I'll catch up with her later."

The girl started to turn away, then spun around suddenly. "Oh! Did Dr. Hill find you? If you're the Sandman's assistant, then you must know where he is."

"Uh, yes. Did Gina have a message for Spencer?"

"Yes, she's been urgently looking for him for the past few days. She told me if anyone called or mentioned Spencer's name to let her know. If she hasn't gotten in contact with you, maybe you should call her. She said she had something very important to talk to him about."

"Thanks for your help," Jasmine said, dashing out of the office. She'd been meaning to call Gina and check in, so her friend would know that everything was okay. The woman was probably frantic wondering what was going on.

Perhaps Nightmary had contacted her as well. If she'd trashed Jasmine's and Spencer's homes, maybe she'd go after Gina next. Jasmine decided against calling ahead, opting to drive straight over to Gina's house.

Jasmine pulled into Gina's driveway, noting immediately that her friend's car was missing. Deciding to leave a note for Gina to call her, Jasmine started searching her car for scrap paper.

When she got out of the car to post the note on Gina's front door, a white van parked down the street caught her attention. The van had a broken headlight and a huge dent on the front bumper.

Instinct drove Jasmine away from Gina's door, toward the van parked in the street. Something told her that it was too much of a coincidence that many of Spencer's run-ins with Nightmary involved a white van.

After inspecting the damage, Jasmine tried to peer inside the van windows. Unable to get a good enough view, she pulled out her pocketknife and tinkered with the locks.

She was in. What she found made her blood run cold. There were cameras and photos of Spencer spread throughout the van. Suddenly, it all made sense: the treats, the attempts on his life, the suspicion that Nightmary was someone he knew very well . . .

As cold realization washed over Jasmine, she closed up the van and ran back to her car.

She had to warn Spencer.

Jasmine dialed Coby's cell phone, praying that he had enough battery life and signal to receive her call.

"Coby here."

"Coby! It's Jasmine. Can you put Spencer on the line?"

"Spencer? Isn't he with you?"

"With me? What are you talking about? I left him in Virginia with the rest of you to look out for him."

"Didn't you send Gina up here to bring him to you? She just left with him about twenty minutes ago."

"Gina?" Jasmine's heart fell into her stomach. "Coby, I just found out that Gina *is* Nightmary. You let Spencer leave with her?"

"Damn! I'm so sorry, Jasmine. I thought she was your friend. Spencer didn't act like anything was wrong, so—"

"Never mind. I've got to find him. If either one of them calls, you let me know immediately."

"Sure thing, Sis. Let me know if we can help."

"You've helped enough already."

Spencer came into consciousness with a searing, white-hot pain behind his eyes. His scrambled thought processes tried to reconnect as he struggled to open his eyes and see where he was.

He felt like he'd been locked in a dreamless sleep for eons and he couldn't make sense of the random images that were starting to form before his eyes.

Candlelight? Where was he? His last memory

was of Jasmine. They'd made love after a romantic bath and massage at her family property. Is
that where he was now?

His eyes searched the room. Hotel. He smelled
fresh flowers. There was a room service cart with
covered plates and a bottle of wine across the
room.

Wine. Is that why he had this splitting
headache? Had he drunk too much and spoiled
Jasmine's romantic plans for the evening? He
couldn't let all her preparations go to waste.

Spencer struggled to lift himself upright.
Whoa! He clutched his head as the room started
spinning. He must have really—

Jasmine walked out of the bathroom. "Ahh,
sleeping beauty is awake," she said.

That wasn't Jasmine's voice. He squinted to
refocus his gaze. Gina. What was Gina doing in
his and Jasmine's hotel room?

"Oh, shit." He couldn't stop the words from
tumbling out as his memory came crashing back.

"I'll take that as a compliment," she said,
smoothing the sides of her ice-blue silk bathrobe.
Gina walked over to the dinner cart. "You must
be hungry."

Spencer rubbed his temples. "How did you
get me here? I was unconscious, right?" He had
no idea what she'd given him. If she'd drugged
him with roofies again, he could have walked in
on his own.

Gina smiled, clearly proud of herself. "The bellboy helped carry you up. It seems you partied a little too hard tonight, my dear husband, and you passed out."

Spencer blinked rapidly, trying to come to terms with his situation. How could Gina Hill, one of his closest friends, be Nightmary? She was a psychologist, for heaven's sake. Who would have guessed she was the one who needed a shrink?

What did he do now? Should he confront her or play along? Not sure exactly what she had in mind for him, Spencer decided he'd better play along. She'd tried to hurt him many times already, and he needed to stay alive long enough to get himself out of there.

He was grateful that his quick-witted tongue never failed him.

"Gina, sweetheart, if you wanted to be alone with me, all you had to do was ask."

She smiled coolly. "Not so fast, playboy. I know Jasmine is the one you really want. But after tonight you won't be able to remember her name."

Spencer swallowed, trying to remember if Gina had mentioned Jasmine's being in danger before she made him take those pills. Was she lying in the street unconscious somewhere?

"Well, that's . . . flattering. I . . . I didn't know you felt that way about me, Gina."

She picked up a fruit platter and carried it over to the bed. "Of course you did. What about that weekend we spent at Wisp?"

Spencer's eyes went wide as he tried to remember what, if anything, could have happened with Gina at a ski lodge in the mountains. The station had sponsored a ski weekend there almost two years ago. As far as he could remember, they'd done a few live shows, and he'd spent most of the rest of the weekend on the slopes.

"Don't tell me you've forgotten, Spencer. It was such a romantic night."

Spencer chewed on his lower lip. The closest they'd come to a romantic night was the time he'd found her in the ski lodge bar really knocking them back with a couple of young interns from the station. He'd been afraid she'd find herself in a compromising situation, so he'd taken her back to her room and tucked her into bed.

Nothing had happ— Wait, she'd tried to kiss him. She'd wrapped her arms around his neck and tried to pull him into bed with her. But he'd chalked that up to all the alcohol she'd been imbibing. He'd gently disentangled her arms from around his neck and left. The next day he was sure she hadn't even remembered doing it.

Not exactly sure what Gina wanted him to remember, he tried to placate her. "Gina, you know I remember every moment we've shared together vividly."

"I knew you hadn't forgotten. I wasn't sure,

though, because the next morning you acted like it never happened. That hurt my feelings, you know."

Oh, God, she believed that they'd slept together that night. She must have had some drunken dream after he left and didn't know that it wasn't real. Or was she just straight-up crazy?

Either way, he had to stay on her good side. "I didn't mean to hurt your feelings, Gina. I want you to know I'd never do that intentionally."

She reached out and held a strawberry to his lips. "Well, none of that matters because we're finally together now."

Spencer bit the fruit she offered him, chewing slowly. "Can I ask you a question?"

She smiled at him. "That depends. What is it that you want to know?"

"Why didn't you just tell me how you were feeling? Why did you use Nightmary to get to me instead?"

"That was clever, wasn't it? I thought when you believed someone was stalking you, you'd turn to me. I am a psychologist, after all. Surely, you'd want to talk things over with me. I could have given you advice. We would talk, and eventually, you'd realize that our one night together meant as much to you as it did to me."

Spencer swallowed. Could he throw her off guard by letting her know that they'd never spent any night together, or would that just send her off the deep end completely? He couldn't take any chances, so he tried to keep her talking.

"I'm so sorry, Gina. You never let on that you were upset with me over that weekend."

"Well, I'm no fool, Spencer. I'm a grown woman. I know how these things go. We do work together, after all. I followed your lead as soon as you walked into breakfast the next morning and started acting like nothing ever happened. I knew you wanted me to do the same thing."

"So instead of telling me how you felt, you decided to get my attention another way?"

"It was working, too. You didn't want anyone to know just how much those letters and calls bothered you, except for me. You always confided in me. Until Tali decided you needed a bodyguard. Jasmine ruined everything." The woman suddenly dropped her plate. "Do you love her?"

Spencer held his breath. He'd already told her as much on several occasions "Yes. But I only fell in love with her because I didn't know that I had a chance with you, Gina." His plan seemed to be working. Gina was clearly mentally disturbed, going from lucid to a dreamy state minute by minute. He had to be careful not to enrage her, to keep her swept into a fantasy.

"No!" she shouted. "You're just like the others."

"What others?" Spencer asked, trying to look very concerned.

"Men. You all leave. My father left my mother, and so has every other man that's ever come into our lives. After our night together, I thought you'd be different, but you've proven that you aren't. You've never looked at me as a lover even once since that night."

"Is it too late for me to make that up to you?" he asked gently.

"How? How are you going to make it up to me?"

"We could have another romantic evening, right here. Isn't that why you brought me here?"

"Yes, Spencer, but I didn't expect you to give in so easily."

"Why wouldn't I, Gina? You're one of the most beautiful women I know. Of course, I'm happy to be here with you. In fact, you know what I want to do?"

"What?"

"I'd love to take a bubble bath with you. Wouldn't that be romantic?"

"That would be nice, Spencer."

"Great." He reached out and picked up a slice of honeydew melon from the plate sitting in front of her. "I'm going to eat a little something to get my strength up, and you can run the bath."

"Okay, I'll be right back."

As soon as Gina disappeared into the bathroom, Spencer lunged for the purse he'd spotted sitting on the windowsill. He dug through it, hoping to find her gun or the pills she'd given him earlier. The only thing of use he could get his hands on was her cellular phone.

He took it back to the bed with him and stashed it under his pillow just before she came out of the bathroom again.

"That fruit isn't going to be enough for you, Spencer. Look what other goodies I brought for us." She tugged the dinner cart over to the bed. "There's cheese, crackers, bruschetta, salmon spread, and honey-roasted cashews."

"Isn't the bathtub going to overflow?" he asked.

"It's a huge tub made for two."

He smiled seductively. "Don't you think you should check on it? Make sure the water doesn't get too hot?"

"I'll be right back."

Spencer grabbed the phone under his pillow. His first thought was to call 911 for the police, but he knew as soon as he started talking Gina would hear him and most likely shut him up permanently with her gun. His best bet was to leave the line open and hope that he could say enough to tip someone off to his whereabouts.

The 911 operators would most likely cut him off before they figured out what was going on, so he dialed Jasmine's number and prayed she would be able to find him.

Jasmine tore through the city, not sure where she was going but certain she had to get there fast.

She'd never felt so panicked in her entire life.
Where was Gina's head? Would she hurt Spencer
or did she just want to get him alone somewhere?

Her first thought was to drive to the police department and try to enlist some help. She wished
she had some clues as to where Gina might have
taken Spencer.

She had just pulled into the driveway when
her cell phone started ringing. "Hello?"

Silence.

"Hello? Is anyone there? Spencer?" She started
to hang up when her gut told her to hang on a little longer.

Finally, her patience was rewarded. "Our bath
is almost ready, Spencer. Are you done eating?"
It was faint, but the voice was unmistakably
Gina's.

"Uh, not yet. This is really good food. Maybe
we'd better call room service and order more."

Spencer! Room service? Gina had him in a hotel. He was trying to let her know where he was.

"There will be plenty of time for room service
later, Spencer. We've got all night."

Gina plucked the room service menu out of
Spencer's hands, but not before he had the
chance to read the name of the hotel.

"Wow, the Wyndham-Price is pretty fancy,
Gina. This room must be costing you a fortune.
Maybe you'd better let me chip in for part of it."

"Don't be silly. It's my treat."

Spencer held his breath, hoping that Jasmine hadn't hung up and had heard him say the name of the hotel. Now, all he had to do was find some way to stall Gina until Jasmine brought the police.

He had total faith that Jasmine would rescue him. And it didn't even bother his pride in the slightest that he needed her to. Suddenly, having a girlfriend who knew how to kick a little ass was an extreme comfort.

Jasmine pulled in front of the Wyndham-Price hotel at the same time as the police she'd called for. She jumped out of the car and started to follow the officers into the hotel.

One of the men she didn't recognize stepped in front of her, blocking her way. "I'm sorry, ma'am. This is police business. Please wait here."

She pulled out her identification. "My name is Jasmine White. I'm the one who called you guys. That's my client in there. I need to be—"

"I'm sorry, ma'am. Please step back."

Suddenly, Officer Feldmeyer appeared at the young officer's side. The last time she'd seen him was six weeks before she'd resigned from the force, when she'd been holding a gun to his genitals.

She immediately started to back away.

"Officer, this woman is formerly a D.C. cop. Trust me, you don't want to mess with her. Let her pass."

Jasmine was stunned speechless. Finally, she managed to squeeze out a "Thanks" hastily flung over her shoulder as she rushed into the hotel with the other officer.

Gina pushed the room service cart away from the bed and started for him. "Let me help you get out of those things."

Spencer leaned back on the bed. "You know, I'm not feeling so well. Maybe I should lay down for a minute. What were those pills you gave me anyway?"

Gina's eyes narrowed. "I knew it. You're stalling. You think you can play me, don't you?"

Spencer scrambled backward on the bed. "I don't know what you're talking about."

"What are you hiding over there?"

Spencer tried to grab the cell phone but Gina got to it first.

"What the hell do you think you're doing? You think if you talk long enough someone will come and save you? Well, it's not going to happen." She disconnected the phone and threw it across the room.

Reaching into the folds of her robe, she pulled out her gun. "I knew you weren't any different than the others."

Spencer gulped, sure he was about to suck in his last breath, when the hotel door burst open.

Jasmine was the first one in. "Gina, girlfriend. Anyone ever tell you that you need to work on your phone manners? It's impolite to hang up without saying good-bye."

Gina spun around with her gun poised to find herself face-to-face with a very pissed off Jasmine backed up by three police officers with weapons trained on her.

"Drop your weapon. Do it now!" one of the officers shouted.

Wisely realizing she couldn't beat those odds, Gina dropped her weapon.

Gina was arrested, and Spencer and Jasmine spent some time answering questions for the police. Just when she'd thought she'd finally be able to get out of there, Officer Feldmeyer walked over.

"So you're a private investigator now," he commented.

"Yeah, although I think I'm officially out of work as of right now." She wanted to bite her tongue, but Jasmine knew what had to be said. "Thanks for your help outside earlier."

Feldmeyer's face turned bright red as he waved her off with his hand. "Oh, no. Forget it. Besides, I guess you could say I owed you one."

Jasmine laughed. Probably for the first time in a while, she could look back on that time in her life and not feel anger. "Yes, you did."

"So anyway, I'm glad everything worked out. Um, if you're between jobs you should think of coming back to the force. We could always use good cops." With that unexpected comment and a casual wave, he walked away.

Jasmine just stood there with her mouth hanging open. This day had just been one surprise after another. The biggest surprise to Jasmine was that the idea of being a cop wasn't so strange. In fact, even though she enjoyed close protection, what she really wanted was to be able to take a more aggressive role in crime investigation and prevention.

Maybe it was time for her to consider rejoining the ranks of those sworn to protect *and* serve.

Spencer walked up behind her and put an arm around her waist. "Before you say anything, I just want to tell you that I've never been so happy to see anyone in my life as I was when you came busting into that hotel room. I love you so much."

Jasmine's body went still as she slowly turned to face him. "What?"

"I've told you that before . . . no, whoops, that was the first time, wasn't it?" Then he pulled her into his embrace and kissed her deeply.

*J*asmine entered her house Friday night tired, but content for the first time in a long while. Unable to resist another peek, she pulled one of her five copies of the *Washington Post* from under her arm. This time it was *her* picture on the front page of the Style section.

She still couldn't believe that Gina had turned out to be Nightmary. Jasmine had been so caught up in having a new friend she'd missed the signs. Worse yet, she'd accused Tali of stalking Spencer.

Jasmine shuddered thinking of the way she'd spoken to the other woman. Eventually, Tali accepted her profuse apologies. The fact that her groveling had been immortalized in all the local papers hadn't hurt. Tali was a sucker for good publicity, so that, plus having her star radio celebrity back, had put her in a forgiving mood.

Ever since Gina's arrest, both she and Spencer had been receiving plenty of media attention. Jasmine had joined Tali and Spencer for drinks one night, and they'd talked about Gina for hours. It was difficult to come to terms with the fact that their former friend had been so mentally disturbed.

They finally agreed not to blame themselves for being taken in by Gina's lies. The woman had gone to great lengths to avoid suspicion. The police had found thousands of dollars worth of surveillance equipment in Gina's basement. The sophisticated technology had given her an airtight alibi. Nightmary could call while Gina was on the air or even standing in the room, and no one would have suspected her.

Jasmine walked past her answering machine, noticing that her messages were in the double digits. Kicking off her shoes, she decided to listen to them in the morning.

She'd just spent the evening at her brother Rome's house where they'd been having a family meeting.

While she had been driving around town trying to find Spencer and Gina, her family had been spending quality time at Grandma's home. Jasmine had been a little miffed that they'd been able to have such a good time while she'd been confronting a psycho—until she realized that they hadn't come charging after her because they had full confidence in her ability to handle the situation on her own. Now she understood that they'd believed in her all along, and she'd been her own worst enemy.

Best of all, her family had finally been able to agree on what to do with the property. Having everyone in one place that weekend had served two purposes. It had given them a chance to catch up and spend time together as a family, but it also gave them the opportunity to really appreciate the family home they'd inherited.

There wasn't any way any of them could vote to sell or dismember the house now. For a while, Coby had tried to hold out for a bed-and-breakfast, but finally even he concurred that it was more fun as a family retreat. They agreed to contribute money and furniture so they could gather the family there for holidays and summer reunions.

Jasmine was relieved that they'd finally resolved that matter. She was tired of being caught in the middle when one of her brothers wanted her to persuade another sibling of his point of view.

As she undressed in her bedroom, she noticed that it was just after ten o'clock. Was Spencer back on the air now that his "stalker" was safely in jail? She hadn't spoken to him since yesterday, when they'd both been answering questions about Gina down at the police station.

Unable to contain her curiosity, Jasmine reached out and flipped on WLPS. Pulling an oversized T-shirt over her head, she paced the bedroom floor while a commercial for a cellular phone carrier faded out. Seconds later, that familiar baritone floated into the room.

"You're listening to WLPS Washington ninety-nine point three, and this is the Sandman bringing you nineteen continuous slow jams." Spencer introduced the next song, and the slow strains of a Maxwell ballad started playing.

Jasmine wondered how they planned to handle the hole Gina's absence from the show had created. Would they hire a new sidekick for Spencer?

Before her deliberations got too far, she heard her doorbell ring. Again she glanced at the clock, wondering who would show up at her front door so late on a weeknight. She'd just left her brothers, so it shouldn't be one of them.

Looking out the window, she saw Spencer's gold Lexus parked in the driveway. Running down the stairs, she tugged open the front door before remembering her attire.

Spencer grinned at her from the doorway, eyebrows raised in his favorite leer. "Nice outfit," he said, his eyes lingering on her long bare legs under her pink T-shirt.

"What are you doing here? I just heard you on the radio."

He grinned. "It's a pretaped show. Didn't you get my messages? I called you at least three times. Finally, when you weren't picking up, I started calling your brothers. Rome told me that you'd left a little while ago and should be home by now. So here I am."

"You decided to just drop by? It's almost eleven o'clock at night."

"Don't get your hopes up, this isn't a booty call."

Jasmine rolled her eyes and shut the door behind him. "Why are you here? Don't tell me you're in the market for a bodyguard again so soon."

"No." Then he grinned. "At least, not the way *you* mean. I'm here because you obviously weren't planning to come to me."

"Well, I've seen you. I've seen you on the five o'clock news, the ten o'clock news, and the—"

"I'm here to find out what's going on between you and me."

Jasmine swallowed hard. She'd been wondering if what they'd started would be strong enough to last now that the danger was over. They were so different. If it weren't for the fact that they'd been dealing with such intense highs and lows over the past few months, would their relationship have existed at all?

"What *about* you and me?" she asked, eyebrows raised.

He made a face at her question. "I know you love me. I've already told you how much I love you."

She bowed her head. "I wasn't going to hold you to that one. True love confessions don't count in the heat of passion and moments of life or death."

"Well, my life isn't in danger now, and I'm saving the heated passion for later, so . . . I'm telling you that I love you."

Jasmine felt both overwhelming elation and intense trepidation when she heard his words. Feeling her knees weaken, she lowered herself onto the living room sofa. "Spencer, we have such different lifestyles. We're such different people. Now that the threat to your life is gone, we don't even know if we'd have enough in common to keep a relationship going."

He shrugged, shaking his head as though he didn't see the problem. "There's only one way to find out."

"It's not that simple, Spencer. We have the potential to really make each other miserable. We'd fight all the time."

"Who wants one of those boring relationships where people get along all the time? I like a challenge. I need a woman who will give as good as she gets."

"I don't think we should rush into this. Maybe we should take some time to think about what

we really want. A lot has been going on. I think
we should take things slow—"

"Okay, that's it." Spencer turned away and
pulled the coffee table into the middle of the
room. "Come on, let's go."

Jasmine just sat there dumbfounded. "What?"

"We're going to settle this in the proper White
family tradition. We'll arm wrestle. If you win,
we do this your way. We'll take things slow,
think things through, and see where this relationship goes."

"And if you win?"

"We'll do this thing my way. We'll jump into
this relationship with both feet and hold nothing back. We'll spend every minute we can together, loving each other, talking, laughing,
fighting, making up and making love . . . over
and over again." He slapped the coffee table top
and got down on his knees in front of it. "Let's
go."

Jasmine got down on her knees and clasped
hands with Spencer. "You know I beat you last
time. What makes you think you have any hope
of winning this time?"

Spencer just winked at her, and the struggle of
power began. After a few minutes during which
neither one of them made any significant
progress, he said, "You already know why I'm
going to win this time. It doesn't matter how
strong you are."

Jasmine gripped the table with her left arm.

Had he been working out? Maybe he'd been secretly lifting weights in preparation for this rematch he hoped to wage for the sake of his pride. That was probably why he thought he couldn't lose this time. "Why not?"

"Because this time love is on *my* side. Nothing's stronger than that."

Before she even knew what had hit her, her hand went straight down to the table. "Wait . . . how? That's cheating!"

"How did I cheat?" Spencer stood, brushing off his jeans. He reached down to pull her to her feet, repeating his question. "How did I cheat?"

"You . . . you distracted me."

"That never mattered before, Jasmine. Last time, the more I tried to distract you the harder it was for me to beat you. What? Are you saying you want to go again?"

"No! Uh, no. You won, fair and square."

"Does that mean you're going to admit that you love me?"

Jasmine stepped forward and looked up into Spencer's eyes. "I do love you. With all my heart," she said sincerely, then added, "So there. You've done it now. You're stuck with me."

Spencer lowered his head and kissed her. "Good. Now I plan to collect my prize." He picked her up, and she wrapped her legs around his waist.

Together they started up the stairs to her bedroom.

* * *

A couple of hours later, they lay in bed, cuddling.

"Hey, Tali told me that Nathan Pruitt offered you your job back at Core. Are you going to take it?" Spencer asked.

Jasmine's eyes went wide. "Do I look crazy to you?"

"So what are you going to do? Start up a private practice again?"

"Actually, I'm thinking of going back to the police force. I had a very interesting talk with the recruiter at the Montgomery County Police Department."

Spencer slapped his forehead. "Oh, no, I thought you were dangerous before. Now you'll actually have some authority."

"That's right. I'd have many more toys to help me keep you in line."

"Ooh, I bet you'd look sexy in that uniform. I've always been a sucker for a girl in a uniform. Will you let me play with your handcuffs?"

"Only if you're a very bad boy."

"Hey," Spencer said, grinning broadly. "You know that's my specialty. Let me demonstrate." He pulled her into his arms and covered her mouth with his.

Epilogue

"*T*his is certainly a pleasant change from the last time I saw this place. Happier circumstances, too," Spencer said as they walked into the newly furnished White family home on Thanksgiving.

"Looks like everyone beat us here. Even Dina and Tim got here before us." Jasmine peeled off her coat and waved into the living room, where everyone had gathered.

Spencer bent down to whisper in her ear, "Hey, I told you I could get the job done in fifteen minutes, but you told me not to rush it. We might have been a little late getting on the road, but I think it was worth it."

"Shhh." She elbowed him as her mother came out of the kitchen to greet them.

"Better late than never," her mother said, giving them each a hug. Then she turned to the crowd in the living room. "They're here. We can eat now."

Everyone moved into the dining room and took a seat at the new table. Jasmine's mother told them to bow their heads while she said grace.

"We all have so much to be thankful for this year. This is the first Thanksgiving in many years we've all been able to get together in one place." She named all the accomplishments each of her children had had over the year, starting with the eldest and working her way down. "And Lord, I'm so thankful that my youngest son, Jacob, finally has a steady job."

Jasmine smiled at Spencer. His radio show had moved to the six-to-ten morning slot that he'd been coveting. When he was asked to put together a team for his new morning show, Spencer asked Coby if he'd like to do the traffic and weather reports, with the opportunity to spin some records from time to time. Of course, Coby had jumped at the chance.

"Finally, Lord, I want to thank you for the blessings you've brought to my only daughter, Jasmine. I pray that you will keep her safe as she pursues her career in law enforcement. I'm so thankful that she has finally fallen in love with someone special." Mrs. White turned to Spencer and smiled. "You're just like family to us,

Spencer, and we feel the same way about your sister and her husband. So, since you already fit into the family so well, feel free to make it official. Will we be hearing wedding bells one of these days?"

Jasmine covered her face in embarrassment. "Mom!"

"Don't worry, Mrs. White," Spencer said, putting an arm around Jasmine's shoulder. "I don't plan on letting her get away. In fact, now's as good a time as any . . ."

Jasmine froze as Spencer stood up at the table and reached into his pocket, then placed a small box on the table. There were surprised gasps from around the table. Across from them, Coby called out, "You go, boy!"

Spencer took Jasmine's hands in his and pulled her to her feet. Then, as her eyes blurred with tears, he knelt at her feet and slipped an engagement ring on her finger.

"Jasmine, I love you with all my heart. We've been through so much together. You've saved my life more than once, and you've even threatened it a few times."

A few giggles broke out, and Spencer paused to smile at their family members looking on.

"But the only thing that matters is that my life wouldn't be worth a damn without you in it. Will you be my wife?"

Jasmine's heart was filled with overwhelming

joy. A year ago she never would have imagined that she could feel this much love and happiness from one person.

"Yes, Spencer. Yes, I'll marry you!"

He stood, and she went into his arms in a crushing embrace as the rest of their families cheered and clapped. Jasmine whispered in his ear, "Did everyone know about this?"

"No, just me and your mother. She agreed to give me a cue."

Jasmine took his face between her hands and brought his lips down to meet hers. Finally, after several seconds, someone cleared his throat.

"Hey, when you two are through, can we eat?"

Spencer smiled at Coby before turning back to Jasmine. "You all can start without us. I have everything I need right here."

Coming Next

SAY YOU NEED ME

by Kayla Perrin

February 2002

♡

The following is a sneak peek...

Darrell should have known it was too good to be true. Five minutes of sanity, but then she reverted right back to being insane.

"What did you say you do?" he asked in a sardonic tone, staring down at the crazy woman. She couldn't be more than five foot five.

"I'm a librarian."

"Right." Darrell stretched the word into three syllables. "Maybe you went into the wrong profession. Ever consider wrestling?"

Serena made a face. "What, I don't have a right to be angry?"

This wasn't about her not having a right to be angry. It was about Darrell trying to reconcile the fact that the cute, seemingly demure woman who'd caught his eye at the restaurant yesterday wasn't actually demure. Then again, maybe she was normally sweet as pie, but his brother had brought out the worst in her. Lord knew his twin brother, Cecil, had brought out the worst in so many people, including their father.

"Yeah, you have a right to be angry. You just . . . surprise me, that's all."

"I'm normally mild-mannered—until you cross me." Serena punctuated her words with a sardonic smile.

Darrell gave her a slow once-over. Other than appearing demure, she wasn't the typical woman Cecil got involved with. She dressed simply, not flashy, and Cecil always went for flashy. Darrell guessed her to be in her late twenties, a little young compared to the women Cecil usually conned. Cecil tended to date older women, often married, women who easily spoke of money and class and appreciated the attention of a smooth-talking playboy.

But Cecil was a man, and when he wasn't pulling a scam on a woman, he'd date a drop-dead gorgeous woman until he was bored, then move on to another one.

Not that Serena wasn't attractive, because she definitely was, but not in the sleazy way his brother appreciated. So, how the hell had they ended up getting involved?

"Darrell?"

His eyes flew to hers. "Yeah?"

She gave him an odd look, clearly wondering

what had been on his mind. Then she shrugged. "What do you say? Can we work together? I know Miami, so I can help you look for him here. Besides, two heads are better than one."

Darrell didn't respond, contemplating the thought.

"No offense, but I'm really the one who ought to be wary," Serena added. "Considering you *are* Cecil's brother."

"I'm nothing like my brother," Darrell retorted.

Darrell's quick answer made Serena think he'd been spouting that line his whole life, almost like a knee-jerk reaction. That, added to the way his jaw hardened and his body tensed, and Serena realized that she'd pushed one of his buttons. Which made her wonder what Darrell's and Cecil's relationship had been like growing up and how different they truly were. Judging by Darrell's tense demeanor, Serena guessed they were quite different and that Darrell had often taken flack for his brother's actions.

"I didn't mean to offend you," she told him.

"Maybe not, but your comment makes me think your suggestion is a bad idea. Why would you want to spend any time with me?"

"Because I'm desperate."

"Oh, thanks," Darrell replied wryly.

"I don't mean . . ." She exhaled sharply. "Look, this isn't the best situation for either of us. We don't know each other. But we both want the same thing: to find Cecil. And I'm willing to work with you if you're willing to work with me."

"Is that so, Slugger?" Darrell raised an eyebrow, but a grin lifted his lips.

"I guess you'll never let me live that down."

"Hey, I like a woman who can protect me from the bad guys."

"Oh, stop." Serena felt embarrassed enough.

"I'm just playing with you."

Darrell smiled down at her, a genuine smile, and Serena's heart suddenly pounded so hard, it was like getting punched from the inside. She didn't expect that reaction just from looking at him, but she couldn't help it. Darrell Montford really was attractive. He had a lady-killer smile that lit up his bright brown eyes, coupled with an athletic body that had well-sculpted muscles in all the right places.

But it wasn't only the physical qualities that were attractive. There was something about him, something she inherently trusted.

Why hadn't she met *him* instead of Cecil?

Check these sizzlers from sisters who deliver!

SHOE'S ON THE OTHA' FOOT
BY HUNTER HAYES   0-06-101466-4/$6.50 US/$8.99 CAN

WISHIN' ON A STAR
BY EBONI SNOE   0-380-81395-5/$5.99 US/$7.99 CAN

A CHANCE ON LOVIN' YOU
BY EBONI SNOE   0-380-79563-9/$5.99 US/$7.99 CAN

TELL ME I'M DREAMIN'
BY EBONI SNOE   0-380-79562-0/$5.99 US/$7.99 CAN

AIN'T NOBODY'S BUSINESS IF I DO
BY VALERIE WILSON WESLEY

      0-380-80304-6/$6.99 US/$9.99 CAN

IF YOU WANT ME
BY KAYLA PERRIN   0-380-81378-5/$5.99 US/$7.99 CAN

CRAZY THING CALLED LOVE
BY CINDI LOUIS   0-380-81978-3/$6.50 US/$8.99 CAN

BRING ME A DREAM
BY ROBYN AMOS   0-380-81542-7/$6.50 US/$8.99 CAN